HONORABLE INTENTIONS

HONORABLE INTENTIONS

DONNA MACQUIGG

FIVE STAR
A part of Gale, Cengage Learning

GALE
CENGAGE Learning™

Detroit • New York • San Francisco • New Haven, Conn • Waterville, Maine • London

Copyright © 2008 by Donna MacQuigg.
Sequel to *The Doctor's Daughter* (Five Star, 2007)
Five Star Publishing, a part of Gale, Cengage Learning.

Set in 11 pt. Plantin
Printed on permanent paper.

LIBRARY OF CONGRESS CATALOGING-IN-PUBLICATION DATA

MacQuigg, Donna.
    Honorable intentions / Donna MacQuigg. — 1st ed.
      p. cm.
    Sequel to: Doctor's daughter.
    ISBN-13: 978-1-59414-696-1 (hardcover : alk. paper)
    ISBN-10: 1-59414-696-9 (hardcover : alk. paper)
    I. Title.
  PS3613.A283H66 2008
  813'.6—dc22   2007047951

First Edition. First Printing: May 2008.

Published in 2008 in conjunction with Tekno Books.

Printed in the United States of America
1 2 3 4 5 6 7 12 11 10 09 08

To my husband Jim. Thanks for always being there.
And to my family. Thanks for cheering me on.
I'm truly blessed.

CHAPTER ONE

Territory of New Mexico, 1881

Don Miguel Dominguez Mendoza Estrada turned his horse
down Main Street in search of Pedro's Cantina. Though he
didn't often travel to Santa Fe, Pedro's reputation for having
the coldest beer in the territory was well known even in Mexico.
In fact, several cantinas had copied Pedro's secret, storing their
beer in a deep hole in the ground. There the chunks of ice
brought down from the mountains would not melt so easily.
Miguel had no sooner passed the Santa Fe Livery than he spotted Pedro's.

Although several couples seemed in a hurry to get out of his
way, he never expected he was the cause of their distress. Only
when a number of men ducked behind a wagon did he think to
turn to see what they were staring at. A young man stood in the
door of the livery, pointing a rifle. Before Miguel could react,
the boy fired.

Lydia Randolph glanced at the clock on the mantle, wondering
who could be calling when she had barely arrived home and
hadn't even had time to unhitch the buggy.

"Josh. Josh Barns, what's the matter?" The boy's expression
caused her heart to leap into her throat. "Is it Papa?"

Josh jerked off his hat. "No, Miss Lydia, it ain't your pa. I
shot a man, and the sheriff sent me to fetch you to patch him
up."

7

"The sheriff?" Lydia asked as she grabbed her bonnet and shawl.

"Yes, ma'am," Josh said, his excitement almost tangible. "I shot the bank robber, Antonio Garcia. I'm going to be rich as soon as I get the reward."

Lydia accepted his help into the buggy. "You're going to be rich?" She released the brake and picked up the reins. "Could you explain?"

"Yup. There's a reward. A five-thousand-dollar reward, dead or alive, and I caught him."

"If my services are needed, I presume he's still alive?"

"I ain't that good a shot, Miss Lydia"

"You sound disappointed," she chided as she turned the buggy toward Santa Fe's jail.

Josh climbed back on his horse. "Oh, no ma'am, it's just that I was only trying to knock his hat off, but I got him in the arm instead."

"Thanks for coming, Miss Lydia. He's back here." While she studied several wanted posters pinned on the wall, the sheriff took a big ring of keys from a hook.

"I was hoping we wouldn't have to bother you, but I've changed the bandage twice, and I'll be darned, the damn thing won't stop bleeding."

He led the way to the last cell of three in his jail. A man rested on the cot, his back braced by the stone wall, his wrists shackled together, connected by a long chain to the shackles on his ankles. A bloody, makeshift bandage drew her attention to his upper left arm.

But it wasn't the fact that the bandage looked soaked with blood, nor the fact that the man appeared to be very well dressed; it was the way he stared at her—the steel-blue color of his eyes—his gaze dark and brooding with a spark of defiance that made her suddenly apprehensive. Just like his poster, he was sinfully handsome, but his hair didn't seem as long and unkempt, his moustache not as bushy.

"This lady is a nurse," the sheriff began as he unlocked the cell door. "She's going to check your arm, *comprende, hombre?* One false move and I'll finish what Josh started."

The sarcastic edge to the sheriff's tone seemed to have no effect on the man as his gaze lingered on Lydia. Still, he refused to speak as she and the sheriff stepped inside the cell. The sheriff tossed the prisoner the ring of keys, hoisting his rifle upward and pointing it at the outlaw's chest. "Undo your cuffs, but move real slow like."

A muscle jumped above the tight set of the prisoner's jaw, a sign to Lydia that moving his arm caused him a great deal of pain. After only a few moments, the cuffs fell onto his lap and his gaze flicked back to the sheriff's.

The sheriff pressed the barrel of his rifle against the man's chest as he grabbed the keys. "I'll be watching," he muttered as he stepped aside and leaned against the bars.

Lydia swallowed down her apprehension. The texture and cut of the man's garments made it difficult to believe him a common criminal, but after another glance at his powerfully handsome features, the dark, glittering eyes, the neatly trimmed jet-black moustache, she decided he was anything but common.

She reached for the knot, and as soon as she removed the bandage, fresh blood oozed from the wound and wet his sleeve.

"Oh, dear," she murmured, grabbing a clean cloth to press against the wound. "Will you please remove your jacket and shirt?"

He clenched his jaw, but without a sound, he did as she asked.

Nervous butterflies fluttered in the pit of Lydia's stomach as she glanced at his bronze, muscular torso, noting in the center of his bare chest, nestled in a few curly hairs, a small, gold and silver crucifix at the end of a beautifully woven chain.

She had seen men half-dressed before—often assisting her father with his male patients—but never in her life had any of them been as bold or as powerful as the one whose body she gazed upon now, nor had other gazes been like the gaze that explored her features. She sensed he understood that she felt embarrassed by the way his eyes softened and he gave a very slight arrogant smile.

"This will need stitches," she said, horrified at the husky sound of her voice as she grabbed another clean cloth and asked him to hold it to the wound. He trapped her hand for a moment, and she felt certain he had done it on purpose. She searched his face, wondering if he also felt the undeniable attraction she did.

"I'll need some water," she said breathlessly, dragging her gaze from her patient's at the same time she slipped her hand out from under his hand. She cleared her throat before turning to the sheriff. "I'll need some hot water and a stool or chair."

"Heck, the bullet just grazed his arm. Can't you just wrap it up good and tight?" the sheriff asked with a disgusted smirk.

Lydia took a calming breath, relieved to have someone else to look at for a few moments. "No. The wound is too deep. That's why it's still bleeding. It won't heal properly unless it's sewn."

The sheriff shook his head, picked up the cuffs and none-too-gently fastened one end to the prisoner's right wrist, the other end to the metal frame of the cot. "Remember what I said, *hombre*. If I hear this lady call out, I'll blow your head off, and ask questions after."

Lydia dug around in her medical bag, appalled by the way her heart hammered against her breast. What had gotten into her? She was a professional, for heaven's sake.

"The sheriff has made a mistake," the outlaw said in heavily accented English. His voice sounded deep, sensual, drawing her gaze back to his. "My name is Don Miguel Dominguez Mendoza Estrada. I am the son of—"

"Don't let him go filling your head with that foolishness." The sheriff carried in a small stool and a chair, breaking the spell that had come over her. "Here, the chair is for you. I'll be back with the water in a minute and you can put it on the stool."

"The sheriff is a, how do you say . . . a mule-headed jackass," the prisoner growled, leaning his head back wearily against the wall. "If he would do as I asked him to do, he would soon realize his mistake, and after he does, maybe you will allow me to thank you properly . . . perhaps to buy you supper?"

Lydia gave a doubtful laugh. "I don't think he believes he's made a mistake. There's a poster on his wall that has your face on it, and I'm not in the habit of dining with wanted criminals."

She sat in the chair and placed her supplies on her lap. She had wanted to avoid any conversation, and certainly didn't want to know anything about a man who had such a hefty price on his head for murder and robbery. If the circuit judge were in town, she knew the man would be hanged within the week.

Yet that knowledge only increased her nervousness, making it even more difficult to be so close to the man. She swiped at a loose strand of hair, feeling the wetness of perspiration on her temple. What was wrong with her? Usually she felt so confident—unaffected by her patients.

"I am who I say I am, no matter what the sheriff says."

"You'd best shut your trap." The sheriff placed a bowl of steaming water and some more bandages on the stool, unaware that he had caused Lydia to jump ever so slightly.

"Thank you," she managed to say as the sheriff leaned back against the wall to watch. She took a small bottle from her bag and opened it. "This will sting a bit."

She removed the cloth and poured the liquid over the wound. Again a muscle jumped sporadically above the prisoner's jaw

11

and his once relaxed fingers curled into fists. Without preamble, she carefully threaded a needle, aware that both men watched her every move.

"You must hold very still," she ordered, but somehow sensed he wouldn't move. Occasionally she caught sight of his jaw clench when she probed very near the deepest part of the wound, but he never bemoaned his discomfort. Only when she finished with the bandage did she chance a quick look at his face. He appeared pale, with tiny beads of sweat dotting his smooth brow.

"You must rest, and try not to move your arm if possible until the swelling goes down." She tied a triangular scarf around his neck and helped him place his arm inside before she packed her things and stood with medical bag in hand. "Don't change his bandage for two days, and if it doesn't look good, please send for me at once."

"*Muchas gracias, señorita. Tu es muy bonita,*" she heard the prisoner say.

"What did he say?" Lydia asked the sheriff as he escorted her to the door.

"He said thanks and that you're very beautiful."

Lydia felt heat warm her cheeks. "I-I see. As I said before, if you need me, just send Josh."

"I'm sorry we inconvenienced you, Mr. Estrada, but it was an easy mistake to make. Just look here, for yourself." The sheriff grabbed the wanted poster off his desk and held it out to the Mexican nobleman. "This here fella looks just like you."

Miguel took the poster and glanced at it only to appease the annoying little man. *Inconvenience?* He had another word for the two days he'd spent in jail, eating watered-down stew and sleeping on a flea-invested cot.

In this day and age, one would think it safe to travel as long as one had the documents to confirm one's identity. But had that sufficed?

No. Americans were too suspicious of each other. They much preferred to believe an ambiguous sketch on a piece of paper to the official seal of the Estrada family's noble name.

Miguel folded the paper and tucked it inside his ruined brown bolero. "I am free to go?"

"Yes, sir, Mr. Estrada, you're free, and again, I'm sorry about the little mix-up. We can't be too careful, you know. If I were you, I'd keep that telegram from your Pa on you at all times. You wouldn't want someone else making the same mistake I made."

The sheriff gave a half-smile, and Miguel knew he wanted him to reply, but he preferred to watch him squirm.

"Ah, well, your horse is stabled down at the livery. He's a fine animal too. Josh Barns is taking real good care of him."

Miguel nodded, wincing as he took his arm out of the sling to strap on his gun-belt. He lifted his black sombrero from the hook by the door and put it on. *"Adiós,"* was all he could bring himself to say and remain a gentleman.

The sun was just barely rising and somewhere in the sleepy town a cock crowed. Even with this unfortunate delay he still had several days before his appointment with Sayer MacLaren. He thought to find the beautiful nurse who had tended his arm, but assumed she would still be sleeping. He smiled, remembering how she had blushed when he had just looked at her, and he remembered how difficult it had been to look away. She looked *muy bonita*, he admitted again.

He found the livery and after waking the young man, asked for his saddlebags. "Where can I find a place to bathe and to get some food?"

"Welp," Josh said as he rubbed the sleep from his eyes. "You can try Molly's Bath House if you want. She usually has clean towels. And as far as grub, Bonnie's Eatery has the best in town."

Miguel paid the barber for the haircut and shave. Smoothing his black moustache, he went in search of Molly's Bath House. He had hoped to be on the road before now, but since he was Molly's first customer of the day, he had to wait for the water to heat. Afterwards, it felt good to be clean, even though he had to wear clothes not designed for traveling, but for meeting the colonel and his young wife.

Later, after he finished his morning meal, he decided that the food tasted just as the young man had said—excellent. Miguel stepped off the boardwalk pressing the heel of his hand against his wound to help ease the ache in his arm and headed toward the stable to pick up his horse. Speaking in Spanish, he led his prized stallion out of the stall, tossed his black Mexican saddle onto Diablo's back and pulled the cinch tight. After he attached his saddlebags and bedroll, he slipped a silver bridle over the animal's sleek head and led it over to where the young man raked out stalls.

"*Señor,*" Miguel said to get the boy's attention. "Next time, be sure of your target before you shoot." Miguel tossed him a silver coin before he swung up and into the saddle, and with his arm tucked into his bolero for support, he trotted his horse down the road in the direction of the mountains named by his ancestors. Miles later, he stopped in the shade of several ancient cottonwoods to rest.

Raul Martinez took off his hat and dragged his arm over his sweaty face before he picked something out from between his teeth. Two days ago he and his men had robbed the Wells Fargo stage outside the mining town of Cerrillos. Although they came away with over five hundred dollars in cash, one of his men had been injured in the arm and another, an hour ago, fell from his horse, dead from a gunshot wound to the back. Now, in the shade of a large rock formation, they rested their skinny, sweat-caked horses.

Raul glanced up at the vultures circling above before he spat on the ground. "If I had a shovel, I would bury poor Carlos, but . . ." He shook his head and gave a resigned sigh. ". . . I do not have a shovel. Besides—even vultures must eat."

CHAPTER TWO

Lydia smiled to herself, thinking that her sister, Rebeccah, would be surprised to see her so soon. Although she had checked at the clinic twice, it seemed no one in Santa Fe needed her services. The thought of work wasn't unpleasant; she'd always enjoyed nursing, but it was beginning to be the same every day. Sore throats, minor cuts and bruises. Never anything exciting, at least not until she tended Antonio Garcia.

The moment she thought about him, she shook her head as if to erase his memory from her mind. Had she seen something in his dark blue eyes, or had she just imagined it? Even when she got home after tending to him, she couldn't sleep—kept seeing his face, kept feeling his gaze on her body like the sensual touch of a lover.

"I should be glad I don't have to see him again," she muttered. But even as she scolded herself, a little voice deep down inside her denounced the thought, and reminded her that she had been disappointed when no one from the jail had come for her to check the outlaw's bandage.

To keep from dwelling on something that could never be, she looked at the package by her side. The tiny dresses she had purchased for the baby were just adorable. Sayer was due home any day now, and she wanted to see his face when he first laid eyes on his new daughter.

She sighed and began to daydream of a man just as wonderful as Sayer, but for herself. Deep in thought, something caught her attention and when she gazed out over the vast horizon, she spotted several large birds circling high in the cloudless sky a short distance away.

"Vultures," she murmured, remembering what Sayer had told her about the birds. She swallowed down her revulsion, unable to draw her eyes away. Then she remembered how Sayer had gone on to explain that it was safe to assume that, as long as the birds remained in flight, whatever lay on the ground still lived. She shaded her eyes with her hand to get a better look.

Hesitant at first, she decided that whoever or whatever was out there might need help. Checking to make sure her father's rifle was still under the seat, she pulled the buggy off to the side of the road near a large formation of rocks.

The sun was hot and high and even though she wore a wide brimmed straw hat, she still shaded her eyes as she glanced once more at the sky. She searched the area, but didn't see anything out of the ordinary except a few tracks leading to the other side of the rocks several yards away. Lydia took a clean handkerchief from her pocket and patted the beads of perspiration that moistened her brow before she reached for the rifle.

A meaty hand clamped down on her arm at the same time the rifle was wrestled from her grasp by another man. By their large-brimmed hats and serapes, she knew they were Mexican. Her fear subsided. She had many Mexican friends, and even those she didn't know in the area were polite and respectful. Yet when these men leered at her, her mouth grew dry and her heart began a rapid dance against her ribs.

Panic wrenched her from her bout of docility. She stomped down on the first man's arch and tugged her arm free. The man howled in pain, but the second man caught her, and none too gently hauled her back against his chest. His breath felt hot near her ear as he said something in Spanish before he flung her to the ground. The other one reached down and dragged her to her feet, preparing to hit her. She squeezed her eyes tight waiting for the blow.

"I would not do that if I were you, *amigo,*" came a man's voice. Though the words were spoken softly, they were edged with cool authority—the thick accent proclaiming him to be Mexican also. Lydia opened her eyes. He wore a wide-brimmed black sombrero that obscured his features, but it wasn't necessary to see his face. The way he sat astride the huge horse and the arrogant set of his broad shoulders told her who he was.

This time her outlaw wore black, and he was riding the biggest black horse she had ever seen. Where he had come from she couldn't fathom, and by the others' expressions, they were as surprised as she. The hot sun glinted off a large ruby on the man's finger as well as the silver-colored barrel of his elegantly carved, ivory-handled revolver.

"I will not tell you again, *señor.* Let the *señorita* go." The moment he cocked the monstrous gun, the bandits released her and nearly fell over themselves as they scooted away.

"*Venga aquí* . . . come here," the outlaw said in a commanding tone. When he motioned for her to come to him, she raised her chin, too proud and too stubborn to let this new threat glimpse even a hint of her fear.

Aware for the first time that her hair had come down from its neat chignon, she brushed it back behind her ear, snatched up her hat and put it on. She took a step his direction—but to whom did she trust her welfare? The black-hatted man was a known criminal and looked as ominous as the two who had grabbed her. As before, his clothing appeared to be perfectly tailored, lightly dusted from traveling, but elegant and accented with silver. She took a step, but three more assailants stepped out from behind the rocks with their guns drawn

"The *señorita* was trying to tell you something, *hombre,*" the leader said. The sound of a rifle cocking ricocheted off the rocks.

18

"I think you should have listened to her. Now, do as I say and put down your weapon."

Lydia felt her mouth go dry. Carefully, her would-be rescuer uncurled his long fingers from his pistol and held the gun up for the others to see.

"*Excelente,*" the leader said. The short man's belly hung over his wide belt. Another belt loaded with bullets crisscrossed his chest. "Climb down from your horse and turn around," the bandit ordered. "I never shoot a man in the back. I always like to see his face before I kill him."

Lydia tried to swallow past the tightness in her throat, but she couldn't. The black-clad man slowly stepped down from his horse and turned to face the bandit's leader, his pistol pointed down, his hand well away from his hip. She stared at his broad back, the way it tapered down to narrow hips and muscled thighs that strained against the material of his black, concho-decorated trousers.

Dear Lord, she inwardly moaned. It was one thing to treat gunshot wounds, and entirely another to watch a man gunned down where he stood. She felt sick, but she willed herself to be strong as the man raised his head and squared his shoulders in an unspoken challenge.

"*Dios mio,*" the bandit gasped when he looked at her champion.

Lydia took a breath, only now aware that she had held it. By the amazed look on the bandit's face, she wondered if he had just seen someone he recognized. The leader spoke again, only this time in Spanish, and she couldn't understand a word.

Her champion answered in Spanish, but she sensed some of the danger had passed when he holstered his gun. He pushed his hat back on his forehead and relaxed his stance, holding his left arm as if all the movement caused him pain. The two men conversed for several minutes. Her champion motioned in her direction and they all laughed, igniting her fury.

"Excuse me," she said with a rebellious lift of her chin.

Her champion turned, his strange steel-blue eyes locking with her icy green ones. "If you want to leave here alive, *bonita mia*, I suggest you keep quiet."

She started to protest, but when she noticed the tiny sporadic muscle above his jaw tense, she sensed the danger was far from over. Again the men conversed, and she wondered what they said. It annoyed her beyond reason, but she stayed rooted to the spot, trying to be as inconspicuous as possible. When finally he came and gently grasped her arm, she allowed him to escort her across the mesa toward the rocks, his horse in tow.

"Whatever happens," he began, keeping his voice soft and low as they followed the bandits, "you must trust me. These men are very bad, and if you do not do as you are told, they will not hesitate to kill you, after they take their pleasure with you."

"Really," she countered, matching his tone, pleased her voice sounded stronger than her shaky knees felt. "And if they are so bad, why are you still alive?" She cast him a quick sideways glance, surprised to see a very slight, very arrogant smile under his coal-black moustache. Her heart did a strange little flutter, but she immediately contributed it to her apprehension and the fact that she was surrounded by outlaws.

"I am alive because they, as your sheriff before them, believe me to be someone else." He guided her around a large patch of prickly-pear cactus, covered with large yellow flowers. Not only did her mouth feel dry from fear, the heat seemed to be taking its toll. One of the bandits spoke rapidly in Spanish and her escort froze.

"What's happening?" Lydia whispered, when he motioned for her to walk around the rocks. A man crouched over a body. Flies crawled over the matted blood on the man's brown shirt.

"Let me through," she said in a voice she barely recognized as her own.

"He is dead." One of the Mexicans leered at her—his teeth especially white under his thick moustache.

"I am a nurse. Are you sure?" she said calmly, even though her heart had begun to pound again. Had her attention not been focused on the man on the ground, she would have seen the others exchange hooded glances.

Miguel stood back and watched as the young English woman knelt by the dead man's side and placed her fingertips on his neck. He instantly admired her courage. He had seen others check the heartbeat of the unconscious in the same manner, but they had not been surrounded by a band of desperate men.

He tied his horse to a scrubby cedar tree before he went over and gently grasped her arm, lifting her to her feet. "It is apparent that he is dead. Come away. There is nothing left to be done for him."

She looked at him again with those defiant green eyes. The sun glinted off her coppery-red hair, her smooth features a little pale, most likely from viewing the dead man's grisly wound. The sight of her made Miguel's heart beat a little faster, fueling his desire to protect her.

"Stay here," he ordered when he had guided her a little way from the others. When he returned to her, he said, "I did not make the connection when first we met, but now I believe you to be *Señorita* Randolph, Doctor Randolph's daughter?"

Her shock was evident by the subtle change in her expression. Although she still glared at him, her features softened, but only slightly and only for a moment. "Yes, you are correct. Do you know my father?" One red brow raised in challenge. He liked that trait, knew if they were to survive she would need to be strong.

"No. We have never met, but my uncle knows him well." He

drew her a little farther away, placing his finger before his lips to remind her that they must be discreet. "You must not tell these men who you are. You must let me do all of the talking, *tu comprendes* . . . do you understand?"

"How do I know I can trust you? 'Tis apparent these men know who you are."

"I like a woman who is not afraid, but now is not the time to be courageous. There are only two of us, and five of them. For now, I think it is better that you keep wondering." He smiled, but it didn't show in his eyes.

She thought it odd, but he left, briefly knelt by the dead man, and while the others weren't paying attention, seemed to search him before returning to her side. "What were you doing?" she asked.

"I thought I knew him, but I did not," he said is a low voice, glancing cautiously around.

"But you know some of the others, correct?"

He shrugged, wincing just a little. "The fat *hombre* is Raul Martinez. The tall, skinny *hombre* is Placido Lovato. I do not know the young one's name, or the names of those two over there, but you must believe me when I say they are all very dangerous banditos, wanted even in Mexico."

"And you? Are you also wanted even in Mexico?" Her heart thumped painfully against her breast when his gaze fused with hers. When at last he looked away, she became aware that the leader had turned from his men and walked toward them.

"You are a nurse, no?" Raul questioned.

She cast a quick glance at her rescuer before answering, but nevertheless spoke the truth. "Yes." She sensed her champion's annoyance at her blatant disobedience of his order, but who was he to tell her what to say or how to behave?

Raul seemed to digest this information for a moment before he grabbed her arm and half led and half dragged her toward his men. "That one may be dead, but I have another still living and I'd like to keep him that way. Placido is wounded and needs your help."

"Unhand me," she ordered firmly, planting her feet as best she could in the gravely dirt. The leader's scowl sent sparks of fear straight to the center of her belly, but her false bravado worked. He released her. She stepped past him, toward the man sitting on the rock. Her fingers shook ever so slightly as she worked at the bloodstained knot around the man's knee.

"My father keeps extra bandages and supplies in the box behind the seat of his buggy," she said, and before she could ask, Raul hollered to a man to fetch them. She didn't turn around to see if her rescuer had followed her to the injured man, but sensed he was close on her heels.

"What are you going to do to me after I help him?" she asked Raul, ignoring the way the injured man stared at her with a lecherous smile.

Raul laughed. "What do you think, Antonio? What should we do with this beautiful cactus flower?"

The two men shared another conversation in Spanish, but this time she couldn't glean anything reassuring. "I must warn you," she began, ignoring the fact that the man Raul called Antonio was subtly trying to get her attention. When she cast him a quick glance, he shook his head in a silent warning.

She frowned. How dare he caution her? Wasn't he just another, better-dressed bandit? "My name is Lydia Randolph. My sister's ranch is only a few miles away. If you allow me to leave, I shan't press charges with the local authorities, I shall—"

Raul's eyes widened for a moment and he laughed. "So, my little flower, if we let you go . . ." He glanced at the others and drew several more guffaws. ". . . you promise not to tell the sheriff?"

"Yes, that is correct." Out of the corner of her eye she caught a glimpse of the fellow known as Antonio. He rolled his eyes and shook his head in exasperation. "I will simply continue on my way and pretend that none of this ever happened." She finished tying a clean bandage neatly on the wounded man's leg before she turned and met Raul's bemused glare.

"I do not know," Raul said, as if he were contemplating her offer. "What do you think *amigo?*"

Lydia turned her full attention to the man who had acted as her champion, a man who frightened her almost as much as the others. A thousand thoughts raced through her head, but only one lingered—his poster hanging on the sheriff's wall. These men knew him, yet he had said his uncle knew her father. Surely she would remember the man, especially if he looked anything like his nephew.

The face of one man came to mind—the handsome features of Don Fernando Gutierrez, the charming Mexican rancher who had taught her how to dance the Mexican two-step. Impossible. Don Fernando was dead—killed after it was discovered that he had been the mastermind behind the many robberies that had plagued the area last year.

"This man is not my keeper," she replied tersely. Once more male laughter resounded off the rocks, but she refused to drop her gaze from the handsome bandit's, even though the tight set of his mouth softened with a slight smile.

"You and your men should leave," her champion stated with cool authority. "I will see to the *señorita.*"

"You?" Raul asked, shaking his head. "I think that is like leaving the fox to guard the chickens, no?"

"*Sí,*" several of his men agreed in humorous unison.

The leader grabbed Lydia's arm and pulled her a little closer. "Antonio is a very bad *hombre.* He has killed many men. But he likes you. Perhaps I should leave you with him—"

"No," she said, cringing at the breathy sound of her voice.

Raul's smile caused her stomach to lurch. "Perhaps I should keep you for myself." She shivered at the same time he gave a loud bark of laughter, catching her chin roughly between his thumb and forefinger. "Either way, I cannot let you leave. You see, my little dove, I have an *amigo* who needs a nurse."

"Your *amigo* is fine," she stated, matching Raul's glare. "It's only a flesh wound." Raul's features grew soft, and at the same time his eyes fell to her mouth and he dragged one dirty finger down her cheek.

She shuddered and turned her face away until she heard the frightening sound of a gun being cocked. When she looked, somehow Antonio's gun had appeared in his hand, the barrel pressing against Raul's temple.

"Let her go, or I will have to kill you, *comprende?*"

Two of the bandits drew their guns, but Antonio spoke to them in Spanish, pressing his gun even harder against their leader's skull. Raul swallowed very loudly, heaving a sigh of relief when his men holstered their weapons and backed down.

"Easy, *amigo*," Raul said, raising his hands in surrender. "Is this how you treat family?"

Her champion's frowned deepened and for a moment she sensed he didn't understand, but he quickly recovered and gave a sinister grin. "*Sí*, when they behave like pigs."

Raul looked hurt. "I just wanted a little kiss. Here, you take her. I have no desire to die for the *chica*. She is yours . . . a gift from me."

The man called Antonio didn't immediately withdraw the gun. Instead he motioned for her to go and get his horse. And she did, as fast as she could. The stallion snorted and she jumped, but she never let go of the reins even though her hands shook.

"Get on," she heard him order, but she couldn't—didn't know how or where to begin to mount the beast.

"I cannot," she replied, searching for a way to do as he wanted. "The stirrup is covered, and . . . and I don't know how. I've never been astride a horse in my life."

She heard him swear under his breath as he dragged Raul closer. He let go of the bandit, but kept the muzzle of his gun pressed against his back.

"Here," he said in a frightening whisper, "put your foot in there."

She tried, but the horse was too tall.

"*Pronto*," he nearly shouted, and this time she grasped the strap, and with his left hand shoving against her bottom, she managed to pull herself up. Once on the animal's back, she clung to the large, flat saddle horn while the stallion nervously danced around. Antonio and Raul argued in Spanish until Antonio carefully un-cocked his gun before he slipped it into his holster. Instead of swinging up behind her as she expected, he stood, holding his arm, while the others went through her father's box, collecting most of his supplies and stuffing them in a burlap sack.

"In the name of God," she cried in a hoarse whisper. "What are you doing?" She glared at Antonio when he only gave her the briefest of looks. "We could have escaped. We could have—"

"*Silencio, bonita mia,* my arm hurts, and you are giving me headache."

She stared at him in utter disbelief. "I'm giving you a headache?" she repeated in a furious whisper, unable to see his face, as it was hidden by his black sombrero. For the first time she noticed the carved silver hatband. It was more beautiful than some of her grandmother's jewelry.

"*Sí*," he confirmed as he continued to watch the others.

"I can pay you a handsome reward," she hissed.

"I have no need of your fortune."

"Then out of decency, for heaven's sake," she said, furious

when he ignored her. "You . . . you—" She tried to think of something to call him that he would understand, remembering what Santos had called the hens in the henhouse. You . . . you *gallina!*"

He raised his head and looked at her. *"Gallina?"* he repeated with an offended expression. Inwardly she rejoiced. Her insult had gotten the reaction she wanted. Now if only she could convince him it would be brave and honorable to help her escape. He scoffed, drawing her attention.

"First you sew my arm with a very dull needle, and then ignore my warnings, which I made only to protect you, and now . . ." He shook his head as if trying to understand. "Now you call me a chicken?"

"Sí," she shot back. "Why aren't we escaping? Are you afraid?"

He heaved a long, impatient sigh. "Because, *bonita mia,* I do not wish to die this day."

"But . . . but . . . I don't understand," she sputtered, so angry she could barely keep from kicking him. "You obviously had the advantage. You could have got on this . . . this monster with me and we could have ridden away. You could have left me at my sister's ranch and none would have been the wiser."

"You think?" he asked, mounting the horse and settling in behind her. She gasped when he wrapped his arm snugly around her waist and pulled her back against his chest, nearly upsetting her hat.

"Do you really think it would have been that easy?" He muttered something in Spanish, and she knew if she could understand, it wouldn't have been complementary.

"You had the advantage," she hissed, trying to keep her voice down as the others came closer. Desperation pushed her on, breathed new life into the panic she had fought to control.

"It may have looked like I did, but it was only for the moment." He motioned to where the youngest man climbed down from the rocks. "Do you see that *hombre?*"

"Yes," she said indignantly, staring at the man. "How did he get up there without us seeing him?"

"I saw him. Do you see the rifle he holds, too?" his tone sounded thick with sarcasm.

"Yes," she snapped again, feeling wretched. "I'm not blind."

"I had wondered for a *momento*," he muttered under his breath.

"Well, what of it?" she demanded, using anger to hide her fear.

"The rifle was pointed at you the entire time. Had we tried to escape, you wouldn't be so angry with me." He gave an indifferent shrug. "You'd be dead."

She gasped at the same time he pulled her a little tighter and whispered near her ear. "And that, my beauty, would have been a tragedy."

Much to her dismay, her champion . . . *no, her outlaw,* she silently amended . . . gathered the reins and urged the big horse into motion.

CHAPTER THREE

"Those men seemed afraid of you," Lydia stated an hour later when they had slowed their pace and she'd finally let go of the saddle horn. At the moment she wasn't sure who frightened her most, the outlaws or the huge black horse she rode. When she looked over her shoulder, her outlaw gave her a grin.

"That is true. They think I am the notorious bandito, Antonio Garcia."

She frowned even more, wondering why he said it the way he did. "I see. So does that mean you've killed more innocent victims than they have?"

His smile appeared arrogant, his eyes full of humor. "Perhaps . . . perhaps not."

"Where did you come from? When I got out of the buggy, I didn't see anyone."

"You did not look very hard. The men who came from behind were lying in the dirt behind some sage, and I, I rested in the shade of the trees. You never saw them, and they were too preoccupied with you to see me."

"So why didn't you just ride away?"

"And leave one so beautiful alone with these men?" He feigned a shiver. "That too, would have been a tragedy."

"I see. So you're a noble outlaw?" She ignored his soft laugh. "Then why are you staying with these men?" When he didn't speak, she turned slightly and looked at him. Once more she was stunned by his appearance—the color of his eyes, the ebony brows that made them even more striking. "Why won't you answer?"

He looked past her for a moment before he gave her a very slight smile. Had she known that her life was still very much in danger, she wouldn't have cared about his answer. "Raul is . . . how should I say . . . not a smart man. Apparently his eyesight isn't very good either. His friend is in need of medical care, and because of that, he has insisted we go along. To refuse would raise suspicion—and we have enough of that already. We cannot afford more at the moment."

"Do you know where we are going?" she asked, resigned to the fact that she depended on him for protection from the others until she could escape or be rescued.

"I do not know. I have heard that there is a village used by all the banditos hidden in the mountains near Magdalena. It was once used by ancient Indian tribes, but is now a Spanish colony on the Rio Salado. Only a chosen few know the way and it is heavily guarded. It is a place where no law-abiding man goes."

"And that is how you know of it, I assume. You've been there?" Again his smile made her heart do a little dance, but she quickly chided herself, remembering what Raul had said—that Antonio Garcia was a very bad man.

"Perhaps, perhaps not," he said, annoying her further.

"How far is it?" she asked.

"Two, maybe three days. I do not know for certain."

"Good heavens. Are we to ride astride this . . . this beast the entire time?" she cried, unaware that her expression had gone from calm and controlled to frantic.

He glanced down at her with a concerned frown. "It is the only way."

She started to protest, but thought better of it. Taking a deep breath, she added, "What will happen once we get there?"

"I think it is better, for now, that you do not have all your answers. I made it clear that you are mine. No one will touch you as long as I am alive."

"And what if something happens to you?" The moment she voiced the thought, she regretted it. A bandit he might be, but he still had saved her life. To think of him murdered because of her caused her to shiver.

"You are *fria* . . . cold?" he amended.

"No, I was just thinking about . . . about the man we left. We should have buried him."

Her riding partner pulled her a little closer. "Do not think of such things, *bonita mia*. Our paths have crossed for a reason. We may not know to what extent yet, but each, in our own way, is dependant on the other. Of this I am sure. Consider something more pleasant. By now your family has missed you at the ranch, *si?*"

"Why do you ask?" She brushed a loose strand of hair from her face, meeting his gaze.

"So they can rescue us." He gave her an encouraging smile. "Now, is it possible that they will be following soon?"

Her shoulders sagged ever so slightly. "M-my sister didn't know I was coming."

"Your father will miss you when you do not return to Santa Fe, no?"

"He's fishing with his friend Fergus Carmichael. Sayer, my brother-in-law, won't be there either. He has been in Durango since the beginning of last week where he hoped to buy some more horses." She inwardly winced when the man's dark brows snapped together.

"Sayer? *Señor* MacLaren?"

"Yes."

"*Dios mio,*" he murmured.

"What . . . what did you say," she demanded.

"*Nada* . . . nothing."

"Yes you did. Every time you have something bad to say you say it in Spanish.

"I do not," he countered.

"*Dios,*" she repeated, thinking back. "Santos said it meant . . . God! *Dios* means God. I'm sure of it."

"*Bien,*" he stated flatly.

"Why were you praying?" she asked urgently.

"I was not praying, *señorita,* I was—"

"Swearing?" she asked, blinking up at him.

"No, I was . . . complaining."

She gave him a skeptical look. "Because?"

"Because," he said gruffly, "if what you say is true, no one is going to miss you."

"Precisely." She gave a superior nod. "And, what exactly did you mean, we are dependant on each other?" she asked tersely.

"I spoke too soon," he muttered, still frowning.

"I have a right to know," she charged.

"Very well. Without me you would be . . . how should I say it?" he murmured as if asking himself. "Perhaps violated is a good word. *Si,* without my help you would have been violated or worse, dead. Without you, I would . . ." He paused for several moments. "I will think of something, I'm sure."

"What do you mean by that?"

"I mean, that I had hoped someone would come for you, and I could . . . never mind. Now that they know you are a nurse, it is of no importance. Back at the rocks, you mentioned your sister's ranch, but I do not think Raul is smart enough to make the connection. Do you remember when I bent over the dead man?"

Memories of the man's wound and of her outlaw flashed through her mind. "I don't think I could ever forget that poor man," she murmured.

He leaned a little closer, his breath warm against her ear. "I must have your word that you will tell no one."

Again she glared at him. "Who would I tell?"

"I asked you not to speak before, but it didn't stop you," he chided, glancing at the others to make sure no one paid them any attention. "I put a telegram in his pocket."

"A what?" she asked in a hoarse whisper.

"A telegram—from my father. Hopefully someone will see the buggy by the side of the road and stop to search for you. They will find the body and when they search it, they will know that you are with me. I have met Sayer MacLaren, he is *muy inteligente*. What is important is that you do not, under any circumstances, tell these men anything more, especially that you are family to Sayer MacLaren."

"Why not? Are they afraid of him?"

"*Silencio*," he whispered when one of the men glanced their way. They were quiet for another mile as the sun slowly settled on the horizon. Just when she thought he'd forgotten their conversation, he spoke so only she could hear. "It is known by many that Señor MacLaren made a very good marriage and is now very wealthy. If these men learn that you are his sister-in-law, well, it is something I do not wish them to know. It is bad enough you told them your name."

"Why?" she repeated. "I assure you, I am not as well known as you've been led to believe."

"Nevertheless, if they think you are important, they will never let you go. They will hold you for ransom."

"Ransom?" she cried incredulously. "This isn't medieval England, for heaven sakes."

"You think that only the English kidnap wealthy nobles?" He laughed, then muttered something in Spanish and shook his head.

"You did that on purpose," she accused.

"Did what?" he asked in feigned innocence.

33

"Said something in Spanish."

"It is my native tongue. Why wouldn't I use it?"

"Because, it isn't polite." She raised her chin defiantly.

"How can using one's own language be considered impolite?"

"When one uses it deliberately to confuse another."

His smile grew arrogant. "Listen and you will learn."

"*Tu me causes un mal de tête,*" she said, thankful that she had studied French. Only after she leaned back against his chest and gave a satisfied sigh did he respond.

"Then close your eyes and rest, *mon petit beauté* and perhaps your headache will go away."

"I told you, Fergus," James Randolph began. "We should have taken the trail to the left instead of the right, just like I said. We'd have been back at the ranch hours ago. I'm so damned hungry I could eat a horse."

James rode down the trail with Fergus Carmichael as the sun began to sink behind them. A week's growth of grey speckled beard gave the kindly doctor's tanned face a rugged look. His thinning hair appeared to be even blonder than usual, bleached by the summer sun. In short, he looked like a man who had enjoyed his trip—enjoyed getting dirty and not having to shave every day. Dressed in a red-plaid shirt, he looked more like a rancher than Santa Fe's only doctor.

"Well, don't go layin' the blame on me," Fergus warned in his thick Scottish burr.

"Yeah, well . . . hey, look there. Isn't that my buggy up ahead?" James squinted through his spectacles. "I'll be. I wonder if Lydia's come out to meet us."

Fergus slowly scanned the area. "How would she know we were comin' this way? We've been lost for the last three hours," he said with a skeptical edge to his accent as his reddish, hawk-like brows snapped together.

The doctor lifted up in his saddle. "Lydia? Lydia, are you out there?" he hollered. Both men waited for an answer that never came.

"I don't see any sign of her," Fergus stated with a worried frown. "Come on James, I don't like the looks of this. Maybe she's at the ranch."

"*Hola,*" Santos said as he stepped aside to let James and Fergus in. James put a small package on the table, took off his hat and hung it on the hook by the door. "Welcome, *Doctor, Señor* Carmichael, *Señora* MacLaren will be so happy to see you."

"Is Lydia here?" James asked. "We found my buggy on the side of the road. That package was in it."

The Mexican's face creased with worry. "No."

James' heart skipped a beat. "What do you mean, no. I thought . . . I assumed Lydia was here." He exchanged glances with Fergus.

"No, *señor,* she came here a week ago, but she went home."

"Is there a possibility you just missed her—that she came while you were doing something else?" the doctor asked, his worried frown growing more intense.

"*Sí,*" Santos nodded. "That is possible."

Fergus had already headed for the door where he paused, lifted his hat from the hook and jammed it on his head. "I'm goin' back to where we found the buggy."

"I'm going with—"

"Father, is that you?" Rebeccah came into the room with her newborn daughter.

"Well I'll be damned!" James exclaimed with a smile. "You've had the baby. Let me see. Oh my, she's in pink." He smiled at his youngest daughter. "A girl. A darling little girl." He took the infant into his arms and gazed down at her. "I was just asking Santos about Lydia."

"What about Lydia?" Rebeccah asked.

"My buggy's down the road a bit." He nodded to the package on the table in the foyer. "That was on the seat. It worried me there for a minute, but now that I see this little angel, it all makes sense. Where's Lydia? I want to tell her how proud I am that she handled this all by herself."

"She's not here," Rebeccah said.

"Then where could she be? She wasn't on the road or Fergus and I would have seen her." James met his younger daughter's worried gaze. "Santos, take some men and go back with Fergus—see if perhaps she's returned to the buggy." James handed the baby back to his daughter, catching Santos by the arm. "And hurry, please."

An hour later, James pushed his spectacles back on his nose and heaved a long sigh as he tried to reassure his youngest daughter. Santos had brought the buggy back to the ranch, but reported that he had found no sign of Lydia, and that Fergus had stayed to search the surrounding area.

"It is too dark to look for tracks, *señora*, but I will go out at first light *mañana*."

"I'm sure there's a logical explanation." James put his arm around Rebeccah.

"How can we be certain? What if she's hurt or—"

"Now, now, don't go getting yourself all worked up. We mustn't jump to conclusions. Fergus has gone back to see if she's home. If she's not there, he's going to check my office." He gave her a fatherly smile even though his heart twisted with worry. "Sayer'll be home soon, and won't he be surprised? Why, just look at this little darling."

James took the infant from his daughter and held her up against his chest, patting her back. Slowly he stood and strode to the window so Becky couldn't see how worried he felt. All the while he cooed to the baby, he inwardly prayed for the safety of his own child.

Morning came, and when James heard the baby cry, he rose and dressed. He had no sooner had his first cup of coffee when Santos came inside. "*Doctor,* you must come with me."

James put down his cup. "What is it?" he asked, following the old man to the door. Two horses were saddled and ready.

"Come, I will show you." Once in the vicinity where they'd found his buggy, Santos stopped and pointed a short distance away, toward a large rock formation. "There is a dead man over there. *Señor* Fergus is with him." Santos retrieved a paper from inside his shirt. "We searched him and found this. His name is Don Miguel Estrada. This paper says he was coming to meet with *Señor* MacLaren."

"Let me see that," James muttered. He quickly scanned the paper, pausing on a smear of blood. "What's this?" he asked more to himself than Santos.

"Blood. There were vultures . . . the man's clothes are covered in blood."

James pushed his spectacles up on his nose. "Could be, but it almost looks like a mark of some kind." He turned the paper, but couldn't make anything out.

Santos peered over his shoulder. "I see nothing, *Doctor.*"

Disgruntled, James folded the paper and put it in the inside pocket of his coat. "Yeah, I guess I'm just desperate to find a clue," he muttered.

Lydia heaved a tired sigh and tried to get more comfortable. Although the terrain looked rugged and rocky, trees were scarce. Gone were the tall pines and native grasses that surrounded her sister's ranch, replaced with scrub cedar, cholla cactus and lots of sand and gravel. The lack of anything green made the landscape appear desolate.

With no trees, there was no shade, and the heat radiating from the flat stones nearly became unbearable. Little puffs of dust rose from the sandy soil each time the horses' hooves hit the ground. Bees buzzed in and out of the tiny yellow flowers on the rabbit bushes and the yellowish flowers of the prickly pear, but other than a few lizards and insects, nothing stirred. As the trail wound toward some rocky, yet barren, mountains, the riders were forced to go single-file, and she realized they were avoiding the hustle and bustle of the booming town of Albuquerque.

After another hour, they followed a muddy river when they could, weaving in and out of the dense trees and brush, shaded by the cottonwoods and willows. She shifted her weight, wincing at the knot that had formed between her shoulders. "How much farther?" she asked.

Raul turned and even though his smile looked friendly, it made her shiver. "Be patient, *señorita*. We will make camp in about an hour once we are far away from the city. There will be water there for the horses, and you and Antonio can have some fun together."

"You, sir, are a swine," she countered before her guardian could answer. Raul's laughter did nothing to cool her anger. Her insult had no effect as he turned his attention back to the trail.

"That man is . . . is disgusting," she said scornfully.

"Shush, *bonita mia*, it is not wise to taunt him. It is too hot to worry yourself so much about the future. We must focus on the present, for what we do now can change the future."

"What do you mean?" she asked, venting her anger and humiliation on her guardian.

"*Ay caramba*," he ground out impatiently. "Must you question everything I say?"

"Perhaps if you would speak more explicitly, I wouldn't have to."

"Very well," he countered and returned her glare. "I am not a man to take what I want from a woman, especially if she is as disagreeable as you!"

She gave an audible gasp. "Disagreeable? You think I'm disagreeable?" She gave a haughty laugh. "You and your . . . your *amigos* kidnap me, force me to ride this . . . this monster mile after mile without so much as a moment's rest. I have been insulted and humiliated, yet when I refuse to be intimidated any further, I'm accused of being disagreeable?"

She raised her chin and turned away from him—the ribbon on the back of her hat tickling his nose. "I am not the one who is disagreeable, Mr. Garcia."

"I would prefer you not call me by that name," he countered, his breath warm by her ear, his arm a little tighter around her waist.

"Really? How about I call you rude, or perhaps insolent?" She nearly yelped when he gave her a gentle squeeze.

"No, I do not like those either."

"Well that leaves, obnoxious, or possibly insufferable."

"Are you finished?" he asked.

"By which name shall I address you, Mr. Garcia?" She turned, and the moment she looked at him her heart gave a little shudder. She forgot what she was going to say as his eyes raked boldly over her, pausing on her mouth. The anticipation became almost unbearable, and as if he could read her mind, he bent his head and captured her mouth in a short but thorough kiss. When he pulled away, his eyes twinkled with devilish delight.

"Miguel," he murmured so only she could hear. "I would prefer that you call me Miguel."

CHAPTER FOUR

"Mi-Miguel?" Lydia finally managed to say, feeling the heat of a blush creep up her neck and into her cheeks when her outlaw grinned and warned her to speak softly by touching his forefinger to his lips—the same lips that had just turned her inside out. She quickly twisted away, rendered speechless by what had happened. She'd been kissed before, but never, never like this. She shivered and once more his arm tightened around her waist in response. Did he think somehow holding her and kissing her offered some comfort? For God's sake he was a killer, and now he knew she felt attracted to him.

Was she insane?

Is this what she had wanted when she'd hoped for some adventure?

"I need to get down," she murmured, disturbed by her own reaction.

"*Amigos,*" he called, "The *señorita* needs to stretch her legs."

She wondered if the others had heard when finally they rounded the bend and there was water trickling down from what looked like a pile of rocks. Odd, she surmised. If she'd been by herself, she would never have noticed the little spring. A moment later her captor stopped his horse and dismounted.

"Thank you, Mr. Garcia," she replied tersely when he helped her down, ignoring his whispered Miguel. When she glanced at him, he smiled, cradling his injured arm, and she knew his wound still hurt. As a nurse, she should ask if she could help him, but she couldn't, especially not after what just happened.

"Are you all right?" he asked.

She inwardly groaned, wishing she had asked. "Yes," she lied as she moved farther away. "I just need a few moments to myself." She glanced around for a place that would offer some privacy, relieved when the others ignored her as they tended to their horses while she picked her way through the scruffy bushes.

The spring formed a small pool under the shade of several sturdy trees. She found a rock to sit upon while she bathed her face and tried to tidy her hair. The moment she closed her eyes, he appeared there, in her thoughts, his vibrant gaze fusing with hers, his long fingers sinking into her hair as he deepened his kiss.

Angry and mortified, she splashed more of the cool water over her face. She dried it with her skirt, noticing a tear in her petticoat. Cautiously, she glanced around before she tore a strip off, tying it on an overhanging limb that wasn't too obvious. When she finished, she went back to the men and the horses. Her outlaw, as she decided to call him, helped her back on his horse and their journey began again.

By the time they made camp, Lydia was too exhausted to care how she looked or what would happen next. She practically fell into her outlaw's arms when he reached up to help her down from the horse. When he carried her over to a fallen log, away from the others, propriety dictated that she should protest, but she couldn't find the strength, even when he removed her hat and laid it aside.

As she watched from under heavy lids, he unsaddled his horse and carried the saddle over to where she sat. He tipped it over and laid it upon the sand, then gently pushed her back against it. The wool lining smelled like his horse, but it felt soft and comfortable, and helped to ease the ache in her back with its support. While a couple of the men went in search of wood, another stacked rocks in a circle. The last thing she noticed, before she dozed off, a man used a stick and string to try and make a fire in a pile of dry leaves placed in the center of the rock circle.

"Wake up, *bonita mia*," came Miguel's soft voice. "You should eat something. It might be a long time before our next meal. I was not prepared to travel so far, and did not bring supplies."

Lydia slowly opened her eyes. It was dark, but the smell of food made her stomach growl. The men sat around a crackling fire, laughing and eating. Her hopes plummeted. If they were worried about being followed, they sure didn't show it. Staring at them, seeing how relaxed they were, she began to wonder if she'd ever be rescued. Still brooding, she looked up at the handsome man standing above her. Miguel or Antonio? she asked herself, deciding under the circumstances it didn't matter. He held two sticks with roasted meat skewered on them.

"What is it?" she asked, as she accepted a stick. He sat down beside her.

"*Conejo*—rabbit," he said, smiling when she made a face.

He tore some off. "Try it. It is very good."

She pulled off a little of the meat with her fingers. He was right. It tasted delicious. At first she felt self-conscious to be eating in such a primitive manner, but before long she finished and even licked the juice off her fingers. She tossed the stick aside and stood, dusting off her skirt with her hands. Thirsty, she went to the river to get a drink. One of the men called and she heard the name Antonio, but she didn't pay much attention, only vaguely aware that her outlaw answered to the name, stopping to converse with Raul.

Alone, she lifted her skirt slightly and tore some lace from her pantaloons, tying it on a nearby branch. After she offered a silent prayer that someone would miss her soon, she drank from the creek, washed her hands, and hurried toward the camp to see if she could learn anything that might tell her where they were. As she got closer, her self-proclaimed guardian spoke again, only this time he used Spanish the entire time. Her temper flared. Her situation had become precarious at best, and with the language barrier, it seemed even more desperate.

Obviously by his dark expression, her outlaw wasn't happy with the Raul's comments. As he approached, he warned, "Do not ask me any questions." She wondered how he knew that was exactly what she had planned to do. He grabbed her wrist and none too gently pulled her along. "I am in no mood to explain at the moment."

He took his saddle blanket from a limb where he had let it dry, spread it on the ground and motioned for her to sit. His expression appeared so grave, she immediately obeyed. Much to her surprise, he also sat, bracing his back against the fallen log. He removed his sombrero and raked his long fingers through his shiny black hair.

Odd, she thought. Unlike the others, his hair looked clean and neatly trimmed like his moustache, but even though he appeared pale and pressed the heel of his hand over the wound on his arm, she couldn't let herself forget that he was probably exactly like them. If only she knew for sure she could trust him.

"How did you get out of jail?" she asked, raising her chin in defiance. "Did you hurt anyone? Those men are my friends."

He looked at her, and she thought for a moment she saw anger flash in the depths of his vivid eyes. "No," he replied sarcastically. "I did not." He leaned a little closer and whispered. "Your sheriff released me once he realized his mistake. I am who I say I am."

She heaved a long, impatient sigh. "Very well. To them . . ." She nodded toward Raul and the others. ". . . you are Antonio, but . . . for now," she said with emphasis, "I will think of you as Miguel."

"That is good, but you must call me Antonio," he corrected. "To use my real name is too dangerous."

She stared at him. "If it pleases you," she replied caustically. "Now I'd like to know what you and Raul were talking about." she asked. When she felt she'd waited long enough, she added, "Well?"

He looked at her, quiet for a long moment, and she silently scorned her impatient nature. Nevertheless, she matched his stare, raising one brow to emphasize her determination to have an answer.

"You are a very stubborn woman."

"Answer my question," she demanded.

"Nothing," he finally replied, dragging his hands down his face. He hid his anger and fatigue well, but by the tiny muscle that jumped above his jaw, she knew something had happened to bother him.

"Are you ignoring me on purpose?" she snapped. "I asked you a simple little question."

"*Si,* and as I said, in due time, I will answer it," he replied gruffly.

"If it concerns me, I have a right to know," she continued stubbornly. He faced her, and that's when she saw anger glinting in his eyes. She raised a determined brow, but inwardly cowered. Up until now, he had tried to offer some type of reassurance, but she sensed something was dangerously different.

"There are some things better left alone."

"If you spoke about me, I should be the judge of that, not you," she retorted. He turned, his expression so grim, she instantly regretted her impatience.

"Very well," he began tersely. "Raul told me there is a man at Rio Salado who needs your help, and that is why you cannot leave." Miguel forced a stiff smile. "I, on the other hand, may leave at any time."

His confession startled her. "Am I to understand that you are free—"

"To go as long as you remain," he finished. "The fool thinks I am Antonio Garcia."

"What else?" Lydia asked, growing more and more worried. "You conversed for a very long time."

"Is that not enough?" he asked in that way that infuriated her.

Fear made her bold. "No, it is not."

"Very well, Raul asked if I still wanted you." Miguel's tone sounded harsh, but she knew his anger was not directed at her.

She dropped her gaze from his. Why couldn't she just let him handle things? Why did she have to constantly push for answers? He put his knuckle under her chin, forcing her to look at him. The anger had left, replaced with a heart-rending tenderness so intense that she couldn't pull away. Slowly and seductively his gaze slid from her eyes to linger on her mouth.

"When you look at me like that," he murmured, drawing closer. "Only a saint could refrain."

His lips were cool when he kissed her, his fingers warm and strangely sensual as they sank into her hair. A soft groan tore from his chest at the same he deepened the kiss. Lost in these new and intoxicating sensations, she innocently leaned into him. Only when she felt him lift her did she realize that her arms were around his neck. She gasped and tried to pull away, but he held her tight.

"Trust me," he whispered near her ear a moment before he kissed her neck.

"Why should I?" she gasped again, intensifying her struggles.

Several of the men called to them in Spanish, laughing, and she knew without being able to understand that what they said was most likely crude and indecent. She tried harder to push away, momentarily confused that he wouldn't let her down, frightened that if he carried her to the place where she'd washed, he would find the cloth she had tied to the tree.

"Trust me," he repeated, kissing her again in front of the others.

"No," she said in a strangled whisper, trying to avoid his mouth. Fear replaced the passion that only moments ago he had stirred to life.

"No, please." She shoved against his chest with all her strength, but to no avail. Left with no other recourse, she drew back and slapped him. The moment her palm left his cheek something flashed in his eyes.

"Trust me," he whispered again and at the same time he tried to nuzzle her ear. Growing more and more frantic, she continued her futile effort to fight him off, but he only continued to walk, taking her away from the others to the privacy of the trees.

"Put me down or I'll scream," she warned with every ounce of scorn she could muster. She continued to struggle against his hold, but he was much stronger—a primal strength that she couldn't overcome until she grabbed his injured arm. Only then did he put her down, but he pressed her back against the rough bark of a tree.

"Scream," he urged, and she did as his hand closed over her breast and he kissed her again. But this time his kiss was ravenous.

The moment it ended, another, more outraged scream tore from her throat. She tried to push him away, dragging her nails down his cheek. He stopped instantly, his hair tousled—his chest rising and falling with each ragged breath. Slowly he touched his fingers to his cheek, glancing at the slight smear of blood. Without preamble, he turned away, but when she tried to run back to the camp, he caught her wrist.

"No. No, not yet."

Something sounded different in his voice, something she couldn't discern. She felt base, dirty with the knowledge that at first, deep down inside, she'd wanted what his kiss had promised. When he turned to face her, she inwardly swore that she wouldn't surrender without a fight.

"I-I am not one of your little whores that . . . that you can—"

"Shush," he said, catching her hands when she went to strike him again. "I know, I know," he confirmed as he tried to pull her closer. *"Lo siento,"* he whispered. "I am sorry, but you must believe me, when I say I had no choice."

"No choice?" she repeated contemptuously. She shoved him back, surprised when he released her. "You are despicable," she cried as hot, angry tears flooded her eyes. "I was just beginning to trust you—to believe that you would protect me, but—"

"Shush, *bonita mia, por favor.*"

"Speak English," she ordered, blinking back her tears, wondering if she were angrier at him or herself. Dear God, she thought, aware that in spite of what had just happened, a part of her still wanted to trust him.

"Those men back there are the kind of men who take without asking, everything and anything they want. When I threatened Raul back at the rocks, I told them that I would have you for my woman. Tonight . . ." He paused as if searching for the right words. In the moonlight she could see his jaw clench and unclench as he raked his hair back off his forehead. "Tonight, I had to show them that what I said was true."

"Why didn't you tell me? I . . . I could have played along. I could have pretended—"

"Do you think those men are fools?" he asked incredulously. "Do you think that you are so good an actress that you could have contrived that scream or done this to me?"

He pointed at the raw welts on his cheek. "No, *bonita mia.* To convince them, they had to hear your fear, and when we return, these marks on my face will show them that I am also a man who will take what I want when I want it."

She pressed her fingers against her mouth, trying not to cry. He came to her, would have taken her into his arms, but she refused. "Leave me alone," she said in a suffocated whisper.

"You are trembling," he replied a little desperately. He quickly took off his jacket and held it out to her. "Forgive me, but I had no time to think of another way."

Feeling sick, she accepted his bolero and shrugged into it, grateful for its warmth. After she regained her composure, she tossed her tangled hair over her shoulder and ignored the others when Miguel led her back to camp. At his bidding she sank down on the blanket and scooted to the edge when he retrieved his bedroll and joined her. He covered her with his blanket before he stretched out beside her on his back, his right hand resting on the butt of his gun.

"Sleep," he urged softly. "Nothing more will happen tonight."

Raul exchanged glances with Placido. "See, *amigo,* it is as I said," he began in Spanish. "No matter that he is wearing fancy clothes and riding that fancy horse, he is Antonio." Raul gave a surly laugh and shrugged down under his serape. "Only Antonio can get that kind of a response out of a woman."

Placido's frown grew more intense. "Maybe what you say is so, but there is something different. Something I cannot put my finger on, but . . ." Placido poked himself in the belly. ". . . something here that tells me he is an impostor."

Raul rested his chin on his chest, using his sombrero to shield his eyes from the fire's light. "You worry too much," he continued in their native tongue. "If there is something wrong with your gut, you probably ate something bad. Now, shut up and let me get some sleep. We have a long way to go before we reach Rio Salado."

Chapter Five

Sayer MacLaren barely had time to get off his horse before Rebeccah ran out the door. Her face looked pale, her eyes were wide. One look at his frightened wife made his mouth go dry and his heart skip a beat. He caught her in his arms, completely aware that she no longer carried their child.

"Oh, honey," he murmured, kissing her hair as she wept. "It's all right," he whispered over and over again until she looked up at him.

"Lydia is missing," she sobbed. "Fergus found some tracks, yesterday, and . . . and the sheriff is forming a search party. Oh, Sayer, it's terrible. Papa found a body, and there were vultures, and poor Lydia. Something dreadful has happened to her, I'm sure of it."

"Slow down, Becky. Take a deep breath and start from the beginning." A moment later, James came out of the house and hurried up to them.

"I'm sure glad to see you," the doctor said, his brow crinkled with worry. "I need your help, son. Lydia's missing and by the tracks we found, I think she's been kidnapped."

Sayer looked at his father-in-law, and then back at his wife. "I hear you, James, and I'm going to help, but I gotta know something first." He took a calming breath. "Becky, tell me, honey, what happened to our baby?"

Rebeccah blinked up at him as if he'd lost his mind. "Nothing, sweetheart, she's fine. Didn't you hear me?" she cried.

"Lydia is the one in trouble."

Sayer's knees nearly buckled with relief. He wanted to pick up his pretty little wife in his arms and swing her around, but under the circumstances, he knew she'd never understand. Her sister was missing, and even though he had only, this second, found out he had a baby girl, he couldn't show either his wife or his father-in-law how happy he felt. He walked with them back to the house, asking questions that might shed some light on how Lydia had disappeared.

"It'll be dark soon," Sayer commented. "I'll leave at first light and see what I can find out from the sheriff and Fergus. Now, where's my daughter? I'd like to introduce myself."

Sayer sat in the rocker by the fire, cradling his daughter in the crook of his left arm. In his right hand he held a telegram. "It's from Don Estrada's father, all right. And, I wish I could see something in that blood smear, but I can't." Sayer shook his head and put down the paper. "Don Estrada seemed like a nice enough fella. He and I were thinking of doing some business together."

"I reckon he rode up on some trouble and that's why they killed him," James stated.

"Didn't you say he'd been shot in the back?"

"Yes, that's what I learned after I collected the body. At first I thought he was shot in the face. Some vultures got there before I could determine exactly where he'd been wounded and made a mess of things. Why's that so important? Maybe he was riding away from whoever shot him. Who knows? Maybe he tried to get to the ranch for help?"

Sayer shook his head. "The man I met didn't seem the type who would leave a fight, especially if a woman was in trouble."

"Well, we'll never know." James stood, heaving a tired sigh. "I've got to get back to my office tomorrow. I'll stop by and send a telegram to his family."

"Good, that will save us some time. Fergus and I plan on leaving early in the morning."

"Promise me that you'll find her and bring her home safely," Rebeccah said, kissing Sayer goodbye as they stood by his horse. The big chestnut stallion nudged her hand, looking for a treat.

"I promise," Sayer said with more conviction than he felt. He hugged her longer than usual. "And you promise me that you won't overdo it—that you'll take it easy for awhile." When she nodded, he kissed the tip of her nose before he turned to tie his saddlebags on the back of his saddle, attaching his bedroll.

"I expect I'll be gone a while, but I'll send word every chance I get." He accepted his rifle from Fergus and slipped it in the saddle socket. "Now, while I'm gone, you tell Katie—"

"Katherine Louise," Rebeccah corrected with an unyielding smile.

Sayer raised one brow. "That's an awful big name for such a little girl." He swung up on his horse and gathered up his reins. "Anyway, you tell Katie that her daddy loves her every day I'm gone, promise?"

He gave his wife one last look, then almost as an afterthought, took off his hat, bent down, and gave her a long, intoxicating kiss. When he let her go, she appeared flushed and breathless. "That should hold you till I get back."

With a satisfied grin, he put on his hat and rode down the dusty drive.

"Don't worry, lass," Fergus called out as he followed Sayer. "I'll take gude care of him, and we'll bring your sister back safe and sound. You'll see."

Fergus urged his big roan gelding into a gallop until he rode along side of Sayer then pulled his horse's pace down to match Sayer's. "Looks like we might be in for some more rain."

Sayer nodded, his smile replaced with a dark frown. "Yeah, I noticed. The trail's going to be cold by now anyway. Let's hope we can make up for lost time before it hits or it'll be next to impossible to follow their tracks."

By the time they arrived at the spot where Fergus and James had found the abandoned buggy, the wind nearly blew their hats off. Sayer swung down from his horse and examined the tracks. By the looks of it, there had been several shod horses, but there was no way of telling how many. The tracks had been ridden over, but he managed to find one clue. One of the horses had a right-rear shoe missing. Leading his horse, Sayer followed a single set of hoof prints toward a ravine filled with cottonwoods. There he determined that the lone horse had shoes, and had eaten some leaves off a low hanging branch.

"From what Santos told us about Don Estrada gettin' shot in the back," Fergus grumbled. "I'd assume we're lookin' for a pretty rough bunch. If they're all Mexicans, I'm thinkin' that they'd be headin' south, back to Mexico."

"I suppose," Sayer stated, jamming his hat more tightly on his head before he stepped up into the saddle.

"What did you see?"

Sayer gathered up his reins, glancing at the ground once more. "One of them is riding a horse with only three shoes, and someone was here in these trees alone, but rode up to the others."

"I don't get it," Fergus said as they took off toward the Ortiz Mountains. "Why would a bunch of outlaws want tae drag a woman along, especially one who's afraid of horses?"

"What did you find out from the sheriff?"

"He's thinkin' the men that took her are the same ones who robbed the stage as it was leavin' Cerrillos. There was six of 'em, all Mexicans, all pretty desperate men, although not very lucky. There's reports that two of them were wounded."

Sayer nodded. "That could be why they took Lydia—they needed some doctoring."

"You'd think, if'n that was the case, that after she patched them up, they'd let her go. She'd only slow 'em down."

"Yeah, but, maybe somehow they found out who she is. It was only a few months ago that the newspaper printed that story on Doc and his daughters, and I'm sure it mentioned that Lydia, along with Rebeccah, is heir to her grandmother's fortune. Come on." Sayer urged his stallion out of a walk into a ground-covering canter. "If they've got her, they won't be able to travel very fast. If I know Lydia. She'll fight every inch of the way."

The sun struggled to shine through the heavy storm clouds, and a cool wind kicked up the sand when Miguel helped Lydia into his saddle before he swung up behind her. He waited until she adjusted her skirts, but when she tried to give him back his jacket, he refused.

In the daylight, his white shirt appeared to be of the finest material, comparable only to those she had seen in the better shops in London. She glanced at the others, clad in their homespun clothes and tattered serapes, thinking that Miguel's clothing better suited a nobleman than a bandit. She was given a strip of salt-dried meat and a flat tortilla, and ate, as the others did, while they traveled farther and farther away from the Rio Grande. Hour after hour they rode, ever southward, the wind whipping up the sand in contrast to the smell of rain heavy in the air. Miguel barely spoke to her, and it was just as well, for she had nothing to say.

The weather held until the outlaws made their evening camp. This time Miguel cut sticks and fashioned a crude shelter, ignoring the taunts of the other men. When she asked him about it, he explained that they said he spoiled her. He had just tied his slicker on the top of the shelter when it began to rain, but instead of joining her, he tended to his stallion when the thunder and lightning of the storm spooked the horses. Too tired to care, Lydia soon fell into a troubled sleep.

When she awoke, she was alone, and it was dark and strangely quiet. The storm had waned, leaving in its wake a freshness that she knew existed only in this rugged land. She rose up on her elbows with the fleeting thought that perhaps she could steal a horse and try to escape, but she dashed the thought as quickly as it came, deciding to tie another piece of lace torn from her clothing to a branch near some flat rocks where one might sit to rest or eat.

Most of the men sat on the ground leaning against the trees, their heads bowed in sleep, protected by their serapes and wide-brimmed sombreros. It was easy to pick Miguel out from the others. As if he sensed her watching, he slowly lifted his head, his eyes locking with hers. How dangerous he looked in the pre-dawn light, in his dark clothing and with the big gun strapped to his hip. Suddenly cold, she pulled the blanket closer, rolled on to her side and tried to go back to sleep.

"*Bonita*," Miguel said, keeping his voice low so as not to startle her. Even asleep, with her hair tangled, she was a sight to behold. As he gazed down at her, curled up like a child in his bolero and blanket, his heart twisted with an ever stronger need to protect her. She wasn't like any other woman he had ever met. Like the fiery color of her hair, so too was her spirit.

He knelt, wondering what had come over him when he had kissed her as he brushed a strand of silky hair away from her flawless cheek. When he had made advances to her, he had only wanted what he got, a scream and a fight, but when he held her for that briefest of moments—when she had yielded—something snapped inside him.

Behind those innocent green eyes smoldered a woman who had awakened a hunger inside him so intense that had she not scratched him, he wasn't sure he would have stopped. This knowledge unsettled him and made him feel vulnerable—something he couldn't afford to be in the presence of the outlaws who held her captive. So far his deception had worked, but he feared that before too long, someone would notice—someone who knew Antonio well.

Miguel put his hand on Lydia's shoulder and gave her a little shake. "*Bonita mia,* wake up. It is time to leave."

She awoke with a start.

"Don't touch me," she warned as she pushed away, standing without his help.

She tried to tidy her appearance, frowning the whole time, and he made a silent promise that as soon as they arrived in Torreon, he would buy her a new dress and some shoes more suitable for the rough country. While she sought a few moments of privacy, he saddled his horse, wondering if she would leave more cloth. If she did, he'd have to buy a new petticoat too.

"That is a fine *caballo,*" Placido stated as he ran his hand down the animal's sleek neck. "Where did you say you got him?"

"I told you. I stole him."

"From who?" Placido inquired. "Is he the one who shot you in the arm?"

Miguel narrowed his eyes, matching the man's stare. Apparently Placido had noticed that Miguel favored his injured arm. An alarm sounded in his head, but he had no choice but to ignore it. "That is of no importance. What is important is that you remember this horse, like the woman, belongs to me, and as I said before, I will kill to protect what is mine. *Comprende?*"

Miguel stared at the disgusting man for several moments before he led the horse away to await Lydia in the shade of a large piñon tree. When he was far enough away, he lifted his revolver out of the holster and spun the cylinder to make sure the rain had not harmed it. For a fleeting moment he glanced at the men. Five of them—he had six bullets before he would have to reload.

He snapped the chamber shut and shoved it back in his holster. Perhaps if he were more like the real Antonio, he could gun them down. But not today. His arm ached, and the thought of killing five men—one of them only a boy—turned his stomach.

"Are you planning to shoot someone?" came Lydia's voice.

Miguel spun. "Are you ready to leave?" he asked, forcing a smile. By the way her eyes shot daggers his direction; he could tell she still felt angry. He thought to reinforce his declaration—that he was not an outlaw—but decided that for now, it would be better if she believed him to be Antonio Garcia.

All too soon they were back on the trail, leaving the Ortiz Mountains as they wound their way ever southward, past the San Pedros, across the arid mesas on their way to the small village of Torreon. Although Lydia had never been there, she had heard that Torreon appeared to be a sleepy little place, housing a small mercantile and a cantina, but every dusty little town she could think of had a cantina.

It had become painfully obvious that no one searched for her. If she got the chance to slip away, she'd have to know how to get back home. Still too angry to converse at any length with her guardian, she kept a diligent eye on the sun and the ever-present mountains, memorizing certain things to follow on the way back, after she escaped.

"Though they are not as large as the Sangre de Cristos, they are beautiful in their own way, are they not?"

Lydia inwardly scolded herself for jumping when Miguel spoke. She wasn't afraid of him, was she? After last night, she wondered.

"It depends," she replied. "If I were looking at them from my home, or in the company of someone I cared for, I believe they would be beautiful. But I am not home, nor am I in the company of anyone I could ever care about, so they are simply huge mounds of dirt and rock sprinkled with stunted trees and crawling with thirsty lizards, venomous snakes, and stinging insects."

"*Ay caramba,*" he murmured, so close to her ear he made the tiny little hairs on her arm stand up. "Stinging insects?" he repeated, his voice filled with feigned disgust.

He gave an exaggerated shudder, and hesitated just long enough for her to wonder what he was about. When she cast him an indifferent glance over her shoulder, he opened his eyes wide and looked afraid. It was then that she really noticed the scratches on his cheek.

"I hate bugs," he whispered. "Had I known they were crawling all over the ground, I would have slept in a tree."

She turned away quickly—refusing to forgive him so easily, regardless of his amusing excuses. Perhaps he thought because he felt justified in his actions, she should let bygones be bygones. Part of her wanted to, but she couldn't. She had always thought of herself as strong—able to sew up wounds, deliver babies and clean up blood, lots of blood, after one of her father's surgeries.

But today, she didn't feel very strong. She had felt real panic, and had reacted to the threat. What frightened her more was how he had made her painfully aware of her helplessness—that if he had really wanted her, he could have had her and she could have done nothing to prevent it.

She glanced down at her wrists, remembering how he had held her arms pinned back against the tree. She closed her eyes and saw again the lust in his eyes, felt again his hands on her body. Yet that wasn't where her dilemma ended. She had responded to him—grown wildly excited in a strange and primal way.

"The miles will go faster if you speak with me." Miguel's soft voice drew her away from her despair. He was an outlaw, a criminal no better than the others, she reminded herself. He gave her a gentle squeeze, causing her to look down at his hand—the long tanned fingers splayed across her waist. Before she could push it aside, another memory reappeared. *For now, I am the notorious bandito, Antonio Garcia.*

She saw herself in his arms, recalled the passion that flickered deep in his enchanting eyes a heartbeat before he captured her mouth in the most intoxicating kiss she had ever experienced. She saw his satisfied expression—heard him tell her his name was Miguel.

"Very well," she replied rebelliously. "I want to know who you really are, and why you were in jail."

She was sure he gave a muffled groan. "I want to know how you know my brother-in-law. Then and only then will I trust you enough to speak to you, *comprende?*" She emphasized the last word with a haughty toss of her head.

He dodged the wilted ribbon as it brushed against his nose. "I really do not like your *sombrero*," he murmured.

"What does my hat have to do with anything?" she said a little desperately as she turned to face him. "And why must you always change the subject?"

He shrugged his shoulders and tried, in her opinion, to look contrite. "I do not wish to complain, but now, I must."

"Complain?" she repeated, so astonished that it rendered her momentarily speechless.

"*Sí.* I have tried to be polite because of the . . . how do you say it in English?"

His frown would have been comical had she been in a better mood.

"You know, because of the . . ." He motioned with his hand for her to continue.

"Circumstances?"

"*Si, si,*" he agreed, giving her one of his devilishly handsome grins. "Circumstances. But, now I must protest."

"Oh for heaven's sake, I've forgotten what it is you're talking about."

"Your *sombrero.*"

"My hat? Really," she said, rolling her eyes. Her condescending attitude seemed to go unnoticed.

"Someday, when I teach you how to speak my language, you will know that you should roll your Rs, not your eyes," he countered. "However, that does not change the fact that your hat is most annoying."

She glared at him. "I'm dreadfully sorry."

He nodded, pointing at the wilted bow on the back. She took off her hat to see what he meant. She flicked the sagging ribbon with her fingers, trying to stand it back up.

"Oh, dear," she said sarcastically. "Under the circumstances, I'm afraid there's simply nothing I can do about it." She blinked up at him, completely unaware how feminine she looked. "I forgot my sewing basket, and I certainly cannot traipse about the countryside without protection of my hat. Don't you agree?"

"Of course," he concurred. "A lady must wear a hat in the hot sun . . . to protect her delicate skin."

She knew he agreed on purpose, sensed he was up to something. A small knife suddenly appeared in his hand. A second later the offending ribbon had been neatly severed and dropped onto the ground.

"There, the problem is solved."

"Where . . . how—?" she gasped.

"Here," he said matter-of-factly. "There is a sheath sewn into my boot."

"How convenient," she replied indignantly, irritated that he had once again totally surprised her. "I really must learn to be more observant," she muttered under her breath, yet she sensed he had purposely shown her where he kept the weapon.

"What did you say?" he asked, sheathing the blade.

"Nothing I wanted you to hear."

As he had done before, he covered his heart with his hand—a gesture she found quite irresistible. "You wound me. I solve the problem and instead of your thanks, I receive your disdain. Perhaps if I buy you a new hat you will smile for me again, *sí?*"

"I assure you, Mr. Garcia, it will take much more than a new hat to make that happen."

CHAPTER SIX

Sayer touched the rocks around the long-dead fire. "These could have been here a long time," he muttered as he glanced around the abandoned camp. "There's no way to tell for sure."

"By the tracks over there by the trees, several horses were tethered there, but like you said, the rain makes it hard tae know how many." Fergus walked with Sayer as they led the horses toward the spring. "We'd best fill our canteens while we're restin'."

As the horses drank, Sayer glanced at the ground, ever searching for a clue. "Look here," he said, kneeling down on one knee. He traced the shape of a footprint preserved from the rain by the thick foliage on the trees. "This is too small for a man's," he said, scouting the surrounding area. "And, what's this?"

He stood, reached out and plucked a small piece of lace from a small, low branch. "If this is what I think it is, Lydia was here." Sayer quickly tied his canteen to his saddle before he swung up on his horse's back. "Let's go. My guess is that they're only a day or two ahead at best."

They had no sooner started down a rocky slope than eight men wearing badges came around the bend on the same trail. "Howdy," the leader said, pulling his horse up. "You fellas see anyone matching this description?" The marshal turned and pulled out a poster from his saddlebags and held it out. The paper flapped in the breeze, upsetting Sayer's young stallion.

"I'll get it," Fergus grumbled. He glanced at it, waiting for

Sayer to get Rounder settled down and close enough to reach it. "You'd think that horse would stop that by now."

"Yeah, you'd think," Sayer replied matter-of-factly. He grabbed the paper, staring at it for several minutes. "Antonio Garcia," he muttered uneasily. "Who is he and why are you looking?" Sayer asked.

"Aren't you Colonel MacLaren?" the marshal queried.

"Yes, but I'm out of the army now, Marshal . . . ?"

"Quade. Marshal Bill Quade from Las Cruces. The man on that poster broke outta my jail a week ago. Gunned down my kid brother and wounded two of my men. It says there's a five thousand dollar reward on his head, but I'll toss in another thousand if you catch him. Either way will do—dead or alive."

Sayer looked at the poster again. "Do you know anyone by the name of Don Miguel Estrada?"

The marshal shook his head. "No, don't reckon I do. Why are you asking?"

"He looks a lot like this man on your poster." Sayer glanced at the paper again. "Says here this Antonio fella has brown eyes and a small scar on his cheek."

"Yeah, so what? Maybe the guy you know and that man on the poster are the same man. Maybe he's using two names."

Sayer shook his head. "No, the man I met didn't have a scar."

"Well, if you see either one of them or hear about their whereabouts, I'd be much obliged."

Sayer folded the poster and tucked it inside his shirt. "There's no chance in running into Don Miguel. He's dead. We think the men we're looking for killed him and kidnapped my sister-in-law. Her name is Lydia Randolph. She's got long red hair, isn't too tall, and is pretty as a picture. If the men who took her are the ones who killed Don Miguel, one of them might be riding a big black stallion and using Don Miguel's name."

"I'll keep that in mind." The marshal turned to several of his men, but they all shook their heads. "We came up here to water the horses. Haven't seen a soul except you two fellas."

Sayer nodded and gathered up his reins. "Well, I'll ask you the same favor, marshal. If you see these men, they're wanted for robbery and now for kidnapping. We're on our way south to Torreon, but we'll be checking the telegraph offices wherever and whenever we can. If you hear anything, wire Doctor James Randolph in Santa Fe. He'll forward any news on to me."

The marshal swung down off his horse and stretched. "I reckon we're gonna head over to Albuquerque when we're done here. We'll ask around. There might be someone there who's seen them, but my priority is Garcia. I won't rest 'til he's dead."

Albuquerque appeared to be full of people, both gringo and Mexican. If Antonio draped his serape over his gun and pushed his sombrero down to obscure his features, he felt sure he could enter without drawing any attention to himself. Keeping to the side streets, he hoped to buy a few supplies and maybe have a drink of tequila at a little Mexican cantina he frequented close to the banks of the Rio Grande.

He swung off his horse and tied him to the hitching post. Hunkering down a little so he wouldn't appear too tall, he chose a table near the back of the saloon in a place where he could observe without being seen. He drew his pistol and held it in his lap under the serape, placing a silver coin on the table, fully aware that the proprietor would serve him and not ask any questions.

He took a sip of his tequila, watching as two men came in and sat at a nearby table. Odd, he thought, for gringos to patronize this part of town. His curiosity was appeased when they stopped the proprietor and handed him a wanted poster.

"Have you seen anyone who looks like this man?" one man asked. Antonio's hand tightened on the butt of his Colt .45, but the wise old Mexican only shrugged his shoulders and shook his head.

"*No hablo ingles*," the old man said, serving the men their beers. The men tossed the proprietor his money and took long drinks before putting their glasses down.

"You'd think if they're gonna live in these parts, they'd learn the language," the first man muttered. "How are we supposed to find this guy if no one understands English?"

"I'm thinking Colonel MacLaren was right. No man in his right mind would come into a town this size with a price on his head, especially if he hooks up with those others and that white woman."

Antonio's dark brows snapped together. Who were they talking about? The picture on the poster was clearly his.

"I reckon if they've got her, they ain't gonna parade around with her. I overheard the colonel telling Marshal Quade she's a looker."

"My wife's sister lives in Santa Fe. She says that the Randolph girls are two of the richest women in the territory. If I were those men, I'd be asking for a pretty hefty ransom." The man raised his glass and drained it. "Those damned fools probably don't even know who they got."

"Yeah, I reckon. But, maybe they're hightailing it to the badlands as fast as they can. After all, I wouldn't want to be the man who killed that Mexican nobleman . . . what was his name?"

"Estrada? Don Miguel Estrada, I think."

"Yeah, that's right. I heard some rumors that his family is the kind that won't rest until they avenge his death." The man stood. "Come on, the marshal'll be looking for us."

After they left, Antonio finished his tequila then motioned for the old man to come closer. They spoke for several minutes, Antonio asking the man a few questions in Spanish. When finally he had his answers, Antonio gave the man some more money, asked him to take care of his horse, and accepted a key to one of the rooms on the second floor. A few dollars was a small price to pay for a soft, clean bed.

Torreon wasn't anything like Lydia expected. In the dark, kerosene lamps shone in the only building she could make out. By the loud music and boisterous laughter, it had to be a cantina. As they rode closer, the words painted above the door indicated it was the Red Slipper Saloon.

"If you think for one moment that I will step one foot in that . . . that establishment, you are mistaken," Lydia whispered to Miguel as he swung down from his horse and reached up for her.

"What if there is hot water for a bath and a clean bed?" Even in the dark she could tell his eyes were dancing with humor. As soon as he put her down, she pushed away and folded her arms over her chest.

"I've endured riding that beast, eating with my fingers, drinking from my hand, and being assaulted. Now you want me to sleep in a saloon? I'd rather sleep on the ground . . . again."

Miguel heaved a tired sigh. "Perhaps, but I would not, so if you want to take your chances out here . . ." He made a wide sweep with his arm. ". . . be my guest."

When he turned to leave her, Lydia realized that he fully intended to let her do as she'd threatened. For a heartbeat she thought she might make good her escape, but when the swinging doors burst open and two unkempt men staggered out, grinning at her and whistling, she hurried to catch hold of Miguel's arm.

"Surely there must be somewhere other than . . ." She glanced up at the sign and swallowed. ". . . than here where we can stay the night?" Had she not been watching the two men, making sure that they were leaving, she would have noticed Miguel's patient smile. She observed that after he tied his horse to the hitching post, he walked toward the youngest of the men that rode into town with them.

Much to her surprise, Miguel took something out of his pocket and pressed it in the other's hand. The young man looked at it and nodded. Grinning, he took off his hat and untied his serape, giving both to Miguel.

"Here, take off your hat and put this on."

"Why?" she asked, making a face. "How do I know he doesn't have lice?"

"Do not worry," he said, "I borrowed it from the one who took a bath in the river the other night. Look. It's clean." The hat engulfed her, nearly obscuring her entire face. His soft laughter sounded so innocent she smiled when he lifted it off and bade her to put on the serape. Like the hat, the loose fitting garment was too large. It nearly dragged on the ground, but it covered her wrinkled gown quite nicely.

Again Miguel chuckled when he put the hat back on her head. "Now, if we tuck in your hair, no one will be able to see that you are a woman."

He paused when she lifted her head and peered up at him from under the wide brim. His expression was comical. "In fact, I do not believe they will be able to see your face at all." He laughed again and hunkered down, resting his chin nearly on his chest.

"Do this," he ordered, and she did. He took a moment to push her hair up into the hat. "*Bueno,* you look like an old man."

"I'm not going in there," Lydia reaffirmed.

"Scorpions come out at night, and there are probably bats in the bell tower of the church."

She lifted her head in defiance, but the hat slipped down over her eyes. She shoved it up and would have protested further, but the hat slipped again. "I'm not," she repeated, trying to deal with the too-large hat, "going in there."

"Ah, *bonita mia*, you would try the patience of Job. Believe me, there is no place else to sleep that has beds." He paused for a moment, bending a little to see her face under the sombrero. "Unless of course, you prefer to share my bedroll in the barn with the horses."

She wanted to tell him what she thought of his idea, but he grasped her arm and encouraged her to walk slightly before him. "Now, do not speak, *comprende?*"

"*Comprendo,*" she hissed scornfully.

Surprisingly enough, the small room had been worth the embarrassment. A large four-poster bed nearly filled it, but it looked clean and neat, and she was so tired she didn't care by what means Miguel had procured it. The pitcher on the table was full of water, and after she shed her clothing, she washed every inch of herself as best she could with the small cloth and basin provided.

Clad only in her chemise, she used her fingers as a comb to remove the tangles from her hair before braiding it. Weary beyond belief, she pulled aside the comforter and slid in between the cool sheets. The crisp smell of strong soap confirmed that they were, indeed, clean. She yawned, remembering Miguel's warning about scorpions. Instantly, she jumped out, grabbed the lantern and pulled back the covers before she bent down to inspect the floor. Confident that the room held no insects, she climbed back into bed and with a heavy sigh, stretched out once more.

As she listened to the muffled sounds of guitar music, men and women laughing, she began to relax. She thought about escaping, how in the morning she would seek out the sheriff, tell him what happened and finally put an end to her ordeal.

One thought led to another and she felt a pang of worry for Miguel's safety if the sheriff confronted the outlaw.

"Miguel—Antonio—who are you really?" she muttered. She punched the pillow and rolled to her side, forcing any more thoughts of Miguel from her mind. In a short time, she grew quite sleepy.

Several rapidly fired gunshots resounded in the street, causing her nearly to jump out of her skin. A heartbeat later, she heard voices shouting, then more gunshots, one of which came through her open window and shattered the mirror above the tallboy dresser. She ducked under the covers, yelping at the same time. A moment later, the door to her room burst open.

"Get out or I'll scream," she said, inwardly wincing when she remembered that her threat usually wasn't effective. She peeked over the covers, her heart beating so hard she felt certain the person would hear it.

"Thank God you are all right," came Miguel's soft voice.

He stepped inside and closed the door and leaned back against it. It was dark, and even though she couldn't see him well, she knew he held his pistol down low by the side of his leg. She sensed that he wanted a moment to collect himself.

"I heard the glass break, and I thought . . . I—never mind. You are safe and that is all that matters."

She heard him holster his gun, then, to her horror, he came over and sat on the edge of the bed and bounced a little. "Ah, this is *bueno,* no?"

She clutched the covers up to her chin. "If you mean this is a nice bed, then yes. It's very nice."

"And clean?" he asked.

"Yes, it's clean too," she answered.

"*Bueno,*" he said again and gave a curt nod. "It had better be for the price I paid for it." He turned slightly and she could tell he grinned by the muted gleam of white teeth. "I must see to my horse. Do not worry. No one can disturb you. I have the key." He got up and left before she could respond.

Don Fernando Gutierrez filled two glasses with whisky, handed one to the man standing before him, then lifted his own, his expression so dark, the man's hand shook slightly when he accepted it. "You are sure of this?"

The man nodded. "*Si*, as sure as I can be without seeing the body with my own eyes. If Santos said it was Don Miguel, I would stake my life on it. Santos said he died near your *rancho* by banditos. He was shot in the back and the *hombres* who did it left him for the vultures."

"*Dios mio*," Fernando muttered, dragging his hands down his face.

"Do not suffer so, *jefe*," the man cried. "Santos and a man named Randolph took him to the priest. He was buried on holy ground."

Fernando took a drink, turning back to stare out the window. It had been a nearly a year since he had feigned his death and escaped from New Mexico after a near-fatal brush with the law. It was like James Randolph to take the time to make sure a stranger he didn't even know was properly taken care of. Doctor Randolph was a good man. "Tell me again what happened."

Fernando took another sip while he listened. If what this man spoke was the truth, his nephew, Miguel, was dead, killed because he happened to be in the wrong place at the wrong time. His valuable stallion Diablo and the money he took with him to buy horses, stolen by the same men who gunned him down. And so close to the ranch Fernando once owned in a land he longed to return to.

He listened carefully as the man repeated his story, saving to memory the name Antonio Garcia. "You have done well, *amigo.*" Fernando turned back to his richly carved desk, put his drink down and opened a drawer. He lifted out a flat wooden box and opened it. He held out a leather sack heavy with coins. "This is for you and the information you have brought to me."

"I cannot accept it—"

"Nonsense, *amigo*. It is the least I can do." Fernando watched as the man nodded his thanks and left. He sank down into his chair and heaved a long sigh. Tomorrow he would go to his sister's home and give her and Miguel's father the news that their son was dead. Then he would ride north—as far as Santa Fe, if he had too.

It didn't matter that someone might recognize him. The man who killed Miguel had to be found and punished. Miguel's prize stallion had to be brought back to Mexico. "It is the very least I can do," Fernando repeated—this time to Miguel's memory.

The door to his study slowly opened and in stepped a beautiful young woman whose worried smile warmed his heart.

"Fernando, are you all right?" came his wife's voice as she smoothed the loose-fitting blouse over the slight bulge below her breasts.

Fernando stood and opened his arms. "Consuelo, *mi amor*, how is my son?"

"Fernando," she scolded. "If you keep saying that, I fear you will be disappointed if it is another girl."

He placed a kiss on her temple. "Never, but until our son is born," he winked when her head snapped up, "I must call him something, no?"

She returned his smile and patted her tummy. "Very well, our son is fine. It is you I worry about. You look so sad."

"I have just received some terrible news."

"Is it about your friends in New Mexico?" she asked looking up at him after she accepted his kiss.

"Partly, but mostly it is about Miguel."

CHAPTER SEVEN

With the moonlight casting long shadows through the window, Lydia stared at the ceiling of the small hotel room, afraid to go back to sleep. The boisterous men's voices downstairs did nothing to soothe her frayed nerves. As she rested she thought back over the four days she'd been held captive. At least once per day, she'd been frightened out of her wits.

She had begun to think nothing more could happen that would surprise her when she heard someone fiddling with the doorknob. She jumped from the bed and carefully stepped around the broken glass. She snatched up the empty pitcher and tiptoed to the door. A fractured second later, the door opened and a man stepped inside. She shattered the pitcher over his head, jumping back as his knees buckled and he collapsed to the floor. Treading carefully, she hurried to the table and touched a match to the lamp, catching her breath.

"Oh, no," she moaned. She knelt by Miguel's side. He appeared to be out cold, lying on his stomach in a rather crumpled position. With trembling hands she moved the pieces of broken pitcher and rolled him over.

No matter how hard she tried to distance herself, she couldn't deny his masculine charm. Even with a slight shadow of beard, his features were refined, alluring. Where her fingers rested on his chest, she felt hard, warm, masculine muscle. He was exciting, seductive, and . . . an outlaw. She gave a despondent sigh and patted his cheek none too gently. "Miguel, please, wake up."

When he didn't respond, she got up and fetched one of the two pillows before she pulled the borrowed serape off the edge of the bed and covered him with it.

"It's nothing less than you deserve," she muttered as she slipped the pillow under his head and climbed back into the comfortable bed. But as justified as she felt, she also felt guilty— guilty for hitting him, and guilty for wanting him.

Somewhere in the small town of Torreon a cock crowed, drawing Lydia from the warm security of sleep. She had barely opened her eyes when she became aware that she wasn't in bed alone. Gasping, she sat straight up, dragging the sheet up to cover herself.

Miguel rested face down on the other side of the bed, fully clothed except for his boots and gun. Only in the daylight did she notice the small, dark-crimson stain on the collar of his white shirt and the nasty bump on the back of his head, now matted with dried blood.

"Oh, dear," she murmured. She took one finger and gently poked his shoulder.

He didn't move.

Assuming it safe, she slid out of the bed. Her gown hung on the hook on the door. She'd have to walk to the other side of the room to get it. She thought to take the sheet with her, but Miguel's body had it pinned to the bed. Afraid if she kept tugging he'd waken, she dropped it. Her decision made, she ran to the door, carefully avoiding the broken pieces of the pitcher. She lifted her dress off the hook, hastily gathered the material and slipped it over her head.

Miguel slowly opened his eyes. He squinted against the bright sunlight streaming in through the window, but something else caught his attention. Though his head felt as if it would explode, a slight smile slanted across his pained features.

Lydia stood there—before him—her entire, luscious body almost visible through the thin material of her chemise. She struggled with her pantaloons then wiggled into her dress. He smiled again, closing his eyes as he visualized what she had looked like without all the clothes—lying next to him in the moonlight wearing only her silky, thin chemise.

Giving her time to finish dressing, he groaned to warn her before he slowly got to his feet, pressing his palms to his temples.

"You did not have to hit me so hard," he grumbled, sitting on the side of the bed until the dizziness passed.

"You shouldn't have tried to sneak in here," she countered, turning as she fastened the last of the buttons. She came to his side and pushed his hands away from his head. "Let me see."

"Be gentle," he muttered.

"Be still," she countered.

"Where did you think I would sleep, hey?" he pushed her hand away. "I have suffered enough at your hands, thank you very much."

"I was only trying to help." Her expression wasn't as sincere as he wanted it to be.

"You were poking me."

"I had to see if you needed stitches, and you do not."

"*Bueno*. I feel much better knowing that."

Lydia watched him closely for any signs he may have a concussion. He closed his eyes and by his pained expression, she knew his head hurt, but he didn't appear to need any more sleep—a good sign.

"I'm sorry. Really I am. It's just that when you said you had the only key . . . I thought you were keeping it to protect me. You said you were going to sleep in the barn . . . with your horse." She added that last word as an afterthought, hoping it grated on him as it had on her the previous night.

"I fully expected to be left alone. I had no way of knowing you were planning to share the room." She paused for just a moment, searching for a better explanation so she wouldn't appear insensitive. "You have no idea how badly you frightened me."

He gave her a dark look. She awaited a reprimand, but someone pounded on the door. "Wake up, *hombre*. It's time to leave."

"No idea how badly you frightened me," Miguel mimicked in a high voice. He found his boots and tugged them on. When he stood, he swayed a little but motioned her away when she moved to help.

"There's no use holding a grudge," she said, bending to pick up his gun belt at the same time he did. They bumped heads. She inwardly winced when he pressed his palm to his forehead and muttered something in Spanish, flashing another dark look her direction.

"I said I was sorry," she defended, waiting until he finished dressing. She gave him his hat, but instead of putting it on and thanking her for it, he rewarded her with another dark look. Slowly, he looped the straps around his neck, allowing the sombrero to rest on his back.

"After you," he said tightly as he opened the door and motioned her out.

Much to Lydia's disappointment, there wasn't a building, or a house that resembled a jail. Nor was there a sign, either carved or painted, that bore the words Sheriff's Office. In fact, there wasn't even a livery stable large enough where she could rent a horse and carriage, forgetting for the moment that she had no money to do so.

Having been the captive of these bandits for four days, she

resigned herself to the fact that the only way she would be able to escape was with Miguel's help. Perhaps once they reached their destination and she helped whoever needed her help, Raul could be persuaded to let her leave. If Miguel wouldn't take her back, she would try to bribe the youngest of the outlaws. After all, he'd seemed eager enough to let her use his sombrero and serape. Until that time, she'd try to be as inconspicuous as possible, keeping her ears and eyes open so she'd remember the way back.

The only other building with a false front in Torreon was the mercantile. Once inside, Lydia discovered it carried many of the same goods as the one near her father's house in Santa Fe. While the men replenished their supplies, she wandered around, wishing she had money for a few things that would make her ordeal a little more tolerable.

At first she thought to tell the proprietor that she'd been taken against her will, but clearly, the man knew these outlaws and would not betray them. It made sense, she surmised. The men spent money—stolen money—freely, and those who supplied the outlaws without asking questions stood to make a profit.

Even though she couldn't understand most of their conversation, she was beginning to pick up a little of their language. Often they intertwined English into their Spanish. Canned meat proved a favorite apparently, as they asked for it in English, but when it came to a sack of dried beans, she quickly learned that they were called *frijoles,* and potatoes were called *papas.*

Strolling to the far side of the store, she picked up a small brush and comb, turning it over in her hand, admiring the tiny carved roses in the wooden handle. Had she brought her reticule, the outrageous cost of twenty-five cents would have been a small price to pay to have the tangles from her hair, but everything was marked unusually high.

She glanced over at the men—at the way Miguel stood with them, his broad back to her, his dark head bent to the task of filling his saddlebags with supplies—supplies paid for with other people's hard-earned money. She wondered if most of the customers were robbers and thieves. That might justify the high prices.

She put down the brush and looked at some ribbon, lifting the end of her braid and sighing as she glanced at the strip of petticoat she'd used to secure it. Once again, she dearly missed the simple little pleasure of having a colorful ribbon with which to tie her hair. When the men were through paying for their purchases, Miguel came to her and gently grasped her arm.

"Come, *bonita mia*, it is time to leave." He escorted her outside, told her to stay by his horse and not to move.

"Why, where are you going?" she inquired, casting a quick glance at the others.

"I forgot to get some coffee," he said, and went back in for a few moments before he reappeared. Although she'd never admit it, she'd been tense and afraid while he finished his shopping, and was very much relieved when he returned.

After he helped her up onto the saddle, he took the hat and serape she had used as her disguise and gave them back to the young bandit. They spoke for several moments, and though she couldn't always be sure what they were saying, she felt certain they'd said something about her. Her suspicions were confirmed when both of them looked her direction and smiled. She smiled back. After all, if she were to enlist the young man's help, she'd better appear friendly. Finally Miguel came back and swung up behind her.

"So you like Diego?"

She pretended not to hear. "I'm sorry, did you say something?"

"The boy . . . the one you smiled at. I would have to agree

he's a handsome boy, but he's barely seventeen."

She purposely tipped her head to see Miguel's face and tried to feign concern. "My, I had no idea he was so young. He looks much older."

"*Si*, he is only a boy." Without any further comment, Miguel nudged Diablo into a smooth canter down the only street in Torreon and headed south.

Today, especially, she felt glad to have Miguel's strong arms around her. Four days on the trail, making camp in the dark and rising before the sun, took its toll. Not to mention the hell raising that had disturbed her sleep the previous night. Outside of town, Diablo fell into a steady, ground-covering walk, the gentle rocking luring her to sleep.

Weary to the bone, she dozed, holding her hat in her lap, content to be shaded by Miguel's sombrero. When she finally awoke, they were surrounded by angular red cliffs and towering Ponderosa pines. Spiny, round cacti and shaggy yuccas clung to small ledges and crevasses. The sun hung low on the horizon, and a more brilliant sunset she'd never seen. Distant clouds appeared as if on fire—the edges a smoldering yellow, their middles a more muted pink.

"This place is beautiful. Where are we?" she asked, her voice husky from sleep.

"I believe this is the canyon leading to Rio Salado," Miguel answered. He pointed to the top of the cliff. "Look, there are men up there with rifles. They have been watching us."

Raul stopped before a barbed-wire gate and called out in Spanish. Several heavily armed men appeared from behind various rock formations to open the gate. Someone blew into a steer-horn, sounding an alarm. A few moments later, a dozen more heavily armed men rode up on horses.

For a frantic moment Lydia thought to tell them her name and offer a reward for her release, but as if he read her mind,

Miguel leaned closer and whispered in her ear. "If you value your life, as well as mine, *bonita,* say nothing."

"*Buenos tardes,* Raul," a man on a big red horse called. As he and Raul conversed, Miguel translated, until the man looked their way. Lydia guessed the man to be older than Miguel by about ten years. Except for his moustache, he was clean-shaven, his brows and hair dark like Miguel's but tinged with grey. He urged his horse closer, his eyes glued to Miguel. Miguel's hand casually slipped from her waist to rest on his gun.

"I thought you were still in that stinking jail in Cruces, *amigo,*" the man said, his frown turning into a smile as he offered his hand. Lydia hadn't realized she had been holding her breath until Miguel returned the man's handshake. "It is good to see you again, Antonio. I was afraid that you'd be swinging from a tree by now." The man looked at her and smiled. "Raul says you are a nurse."

She felt Miguel's subtle warning not to speak, but obviously Raul had already revealed her identity. "Yes, I am."

Again Juan spoke Spanish to Miguel, and she wondered when she felt the slight stiffening of Miguel's arm what information was exchanged. The bandit leader guided his horse completely around them, and once more she noticed Miguel's fingers flex ever so slightly over the pearl handle of his gun.

"Where did you steal this horse?" Juan asked. "He is *muy bonito,* and so is your saddle and gun—much nicer than those I saw the last time you were here. I suspect some rich man's wife is in mourning, hey?" The thought tightened Lydia's stomach into a sick knot.

"*Si,*" Miguel agreed, smiling slightly.

"You know how it is up here. Sometimes days pass and we hear nothing, then someone rides in and brings us bits and pieces of news. Recently I have heard stories that someone was brave enough to kill Don Fernando's nephew, Don Miguel Estrada. It wasn't you, was it?"

"Me?" Miguel put his hand on his chest. "I am honored that you think I could do such a thing, but only a fool would kill Don Miguel and brag about it, and only until Don Fernando cuts out his heart and feeds it to the wolves, no?"

Juan gave a doubtful laugh. "*Sí.* And we both know that you are no fool. However, if that horse is Diablo, *mi amigo,* you are in a lot of trouble. Don Fernando may not get the chance to cut out your heart, but we all know he will not take it lightly that you killed a member of his family and stole a valuable stallion. He would not like it if we gave you a place to stay or food to eat either. We could all be in jeopardy because of it."

Miguel nodded thoughtfully. "You are right. Perhaps I should not accept your hospitality." Miguel gathered up his reins to leave.

Lydia held her breath. Could it possibly be this easy to get away from these men?

"Wait." Juan shook his head. "Come. It is getting late. *Mi casa es su casa.*" Juan glanced over his shoulder. "At least until I hear rumors that Don Fernando has left Mexico and is looking for Miguel's killer. It is too bad that he is dead. If he had been captured, I am sure Fernando would have paid a hefty ransom."

Lydia frowned. She remembered Miguel's warning about abduction and ransom, and had assumed it applied to her. It was a little unsettling to realize it applied to Don Fernando's nephew as well.

They followed along while the others stayed a while and conversed with some of the men at the gate. She glanced at Juan. He appeared fit, making her doubt that her nurse's skills were really needed. If that were the case, perhaps they would have to stay the night.

"Raul says you are a nurse?" Juan's words negated her hopeful thoughts as they rode along. "My sister's husband is injured, *señorita*. And, several of the women are due to deliver. Maybe you can help them, no?"

"Perhaps," was all she could find the courage to say under his scrutiny.

They rode single file on a narrow trail, crossed a small feeder stream and entered a large clearing. Here Lydia could barely believe what she saw. Adobe houses, built so close together that they often shared a wall, formed a half-circle around a type of courtyard. At the far end stood a tiny church with a whitewashed picket fence that enclosed a small graveyard. In the dimming light it was difficult to see, but she managed to make out a few wooden crosses and one or two stone markers.

The backs and tops of the houses and church were sheltered by tall cottonwood trees. Behind them red, rocky cliffs, turned purple in the fading light. The stream widened at the far end, and there she could see women and children gathering water, while others collected clothes where they hung on trees to dry.

The sound of a hammer on steel drew her attention to a shed where a smithy labored at the task of making a rim for a wooden wheel, and she surmised he chose to work in the cool of the evening rather than the scorching heat of the day. Across the way, the pots and pans hanging from the porch of a mercantile clanged softly together in the evening breeze. This looked like a small town.

They rode up to a large, sprawling house that could, by its size, pass for a hotel. Miguel stepped down, tied the stallion to the post and helped her down.

An old, white-haired woman looked up from sweeping the porch. "*Limpie los pies primero*, Juan."

The big man grinned and went to the straw where he wiped his feet before entering the house. "Since I was a little boy," he said with a sheepish grin, "my mother has been telling me to wipe my feet."

81

He smiled at the old woman and held open the door. "Come, come," Juan urged. "You must be tired and hungry."

A dark-eyed young woman stood in a doorway on the other side of the spacious room, staring at Lydia. The woman's hair was long and black, accenting the olive color of her skin. She wore the type of dress Lydia had seen other Mexican women wear—the white ruffled blouse with the sleeves worn slightly off the shoulders. The skirt was full and as red as the young woman's lips.

Too proud to look away, Lydia raised her chin a little higher, acutely aware of her disheveled appearance as Miguel stepped in behind her and took off his hat.

"Antonio?" the woman cried with eyes wide as if she had seen a ghost. "Antonio!" she repeated, running toward him. *"Mi amor!"* Nearly knocking Lydia over, the woman jumped into Miguel's arms.

Chapter Eight

Stunned, Lydia watched as Miguel caught the young woman or be knocked over. She wrapped her legs around his waist and her arms around his neck and smothered him with kisses, pausing only for a moment before she cupped his face between her hands and kissed him on the lips for a very long time before Miguel pushed her back.

"Salena," Juan scolded. "Let him catch his breath."

With a sultry pout, Salena slowly removed herself, sliding down to her feet, but not completely letting go. Finally, grinning too much, Lydia thought, Miguel pulled her arms down from around his neck. He spoke with her for a moment, but when the woman's gaze settled on her, Lydia didn't think Miguel's old friend agreed with anything he said. The woman turned back to Miguel and spoke so rapidly, it was obvious that she wasn't pleased.

"Salena," Juan called. "Go and bring us some wine. You can spend some time with Antonio later tonight."

Juan motioned to a table and chairs that sat before a stone hearth. The adobe walls were adorned with colorfully painted Mexican masks as well as intricately carved religious artifacts. Ignoring Lydia, Juan sank down into a basket-weave, barrel-shaped chair with a brown leather seat.

"Come and sit down, *amigo*. Tell me how you got out of jail so soon. But first, no guns allowed, remember?" When Miguel hesitated, Juan motioned to an adjacent wall where at least a dozen holsters hung on wooden pegs.

Miguel slowly unbuckled his gun-belt and spoke in Spanish as he motioned to Lydia. She heard her name and Salena's as well, but it wasn't until Juan looked at her and gave another arrogant laugh, that she wanted to strangle Miguel with her bare hands. When the old woman came back into the house, Juan called her over. Son and mother spoke for several minutes before the old woman looked at Lydia and hobbled toward the hallway.

"Follow me," the woman said in broken English. Lydia cast Miguel a quick glance, not completely reassured by his subtle nod. They went down a long corridor to a room with a colorful, but worn, woven rug on the floor. A comfortable-looking bed made of logs and rope supported a thick feather-stuffed mattress. Clean sheets, a blanket and a patchwork coverlet were folded neatly on top.

A carved-log bench squatted near the other wall, and above it hung another crucifix; only this one had been pounded from copper and stamped with an intricate design. Had she not been so concerned with her situation, Lydia could have appreciated the beautiful artwork. Two small matching tables with tattered lace doilies were on either side of the bed. On the table to the right sat a kerosene lamp. There was a small window above the table on the left.

"I will find you something to sleep in and hot water to wash," the old woman said with a hint of a smile. She went to the door and glanced at Lydia once more before leaving.

Lydia stood by the window, waiting for the door to close. When it appeared that the old woman had forgotten to close it, she went to the door, startled by an attractive woman with a little girl as they peeked around the doorway.

"Are you the *Americana?*" the woman asked. Her daughter's eyes danced with childish wonder as it appeared the little girl couldn't take her eyes from Lydia's red hair. "I no speak English so good. Juan is my brother. I am Carmen and this is my *hija*—daughter, Delora. I am . . . how do you say . . . *muy feliz*—v-very happy that you have come."

"Thank you," Lydia replied cautiously. "However, I feel I must tell you that I had no choice. I am a prisoner here."

"*Si*," Carmen said, obviously uncomfortable. "M-my husband is very sick and needs your help."

The child walked closer. "My uncle said that you are a nurse. Is this true?"

"Yes, it is." Lydia smiled as the child's eyes grew round and her smile brightened.

"I want to be a nurse."

"Delora." Carmen motioned for her daughter to return to her side at the same time she spoke rapidly in Spanish, shaking her head and looking at Lydia before saying a few more words to the child.

The child's smile vanished, and taking her place near her mother's side, she looked over at Lydia. "My mama says I am to watch my manners. I am to help you bathe, not waste your time with silly notions. She also wants me to ask you to help my papa, after you have rested."

"How sick is your father?" Lydia inquired.

"Very sick," the little girl confessed.

Her expression looked so sincere; Lydia decided to wait to freshen up. "Tell your mother that I will do what I can for your father." She smiled when the little girl's eyes widened once more.

"May I watch . . . so that I may learn?" Delora asked, as if being a nurse was something wonderful.

"Only if your mother allows it."

Delora turned and spoke with her mother, acting as any child would when her mother shook her head. A loud sigh and slumping shoulders seem to convince her mother to change her mind, and they conversed in Spanish for several more minutes before Delora turned. "My mother says Papa is sleeping. She says we are to help you first. Later, if I do all my chores, I can help you." The child held out her hand. "Come, I will show you the way."

Lydia glanced up at Carmen and when the woman nodded, she accepted the girl's hand. "How long has your father been sick?" she asked as they went farther down the corridor.

"*Dos* . . . two weeks," the child replied, holding up two fingers. "He was shot in the leg."

Lydia tried to hide her surprise. Apparently Miguel had spoken the truth. Every man here appeared to be an outlaw. "How did he get shot?" Lydia asked, morbidly curious.

"He was trying to steal some *vacas* to bring here for us to eat."

"*Vacas?*" Lydia repeated. "What are *vacas?*"

"Cows."

"You live here all of the time? You're not just visiting your father?" Lydia inquired, surprised when the child broke out into giggles.

"Of course. Where else would we live?" They entered a small room dominated by a large fireplace. "See. A long time ago, this used to be a hotel. This room was used by the people to bathe."

A tarnished copper tub sat before the hearth, and two young boys labored with buckets to fill it with hot water from a huge blackened kettle. Clean, coarse towels were neatly folded and piled on a narrow bench.

"Here," the little girl said as she pointed to a linen robe hanging on a wooden hook. "My mother says for you to use that, but you must give it back later. She does not have many nice things and wants to keep it."

"Yes, I shall," Lydia promised. The boys finished, smiled at her, and left the room, closing the door. Delora stood, slightly rocking back and forth with her hands behind her back, smiling. Lydia looked down at the little girl. "Did you want to tell me something more?"

"*Si.* Your are a *muy* . . . very beautiful lady." The child picked up a cake of soap. "Get in. I will wash your beautiful hair. It is also *muy bonito.*"

"What did you say?"

"I said it is very beautiful."

"What does *bonita mia,* mean in English?" she asked, as she started to undress.

"My beauty. Now, do you want me to wash your hair?" the child asked.

"No, thank you." Lydia gave a very slight smile, noticing the child's disappointed pout. "Really, I can manage."

"Very well. Shall I wait outside the door in case you need something?"

"That would be a very good idea," Lydia confirmed, unwilling to decline the little girl's offer.

When Delora opened the door, she cast another glance at Lydia. "You will come and help my Papa, no? I am afraid he will die if you do not help him," the little girl added with a sad expression.

"We'll leave the moment I'm finished." Lydia quickly shed the rest of her garments and stepped into the tub. As she sank into it, she heaved a long, satisfied sigh. The water felt delightfully hot and soothing, but wish as she might for time to soak, she worried about Delora's father. Taking up the cake of soap, Lydia swiftly lathered her hair and gave it a good washing.

With her soapy hair piled high on the top of her head, she scrubbed her body until it tingled, then settled down deeper in the water to rinse. She sank down still deeper to finish her bath in private, letting the hot water soothe her aches and pains.

A few moments later, she wrapped her hair in one of the

towels, dried off and donned the soft white robe. She opened the door and peeked down the hall to see Delora speaking with the old woman. Lydia slipped back into her room, closed the door and locked it, wishing to dress in private.

Turning, she recognized the brush and comb from the mercantile in Torreon. They were placed on a rust-colored riding skirt, a white, long-sleeved lady's shirt, belt, and various other items, all neatly laid out on top of the bed. There was even a pair of soft pantaloons and a pair of white stockings. On the floor sat a pair of brown-leather riding boots.

Delight rapidly replaced her surprise for a few moments before uncertainty clouded her happiness. Should she accept the gifts or return them? After all, proper ladies do not accept gifts from men—especially men with a price on their heads. The fact that they were bought with stolen money further dampened her desire to use them, but her own clothing was badly crumpled and hardly fit to wear. Her hair had become tangled from the scrubbing, and unless brushed, would dry in a frenzied mass of uncontrollable curls. She certainly couldn't be seen in public looking like a wild woman. What could she do? She had a sick man to tend. She couldn't remain in her room forever.

Reluctantly, she sat on the edge of the bed and gave the gifts a closer inspection. After a moment more of indecision, she shrugged her shoulders and slipped on the pantaloons and short chemise. Next came the blouse, the skirt, the stockings and, lastly, the belt and boots. Much to her surprise, everything fit perfectly.

She shook her hair loose from the towel and picked up the brush. At the same time, she noticed several brightly colored ribbons. Only after she had finished with her hair did she catch sight of her hat. Where the ribbon had been torn off, an attractive, brown-leather and silver-*concho* hatband had been attached.

By the time she finished dressing, her hair was almost dry,

falling in soft, coppery curls down her back. Choosing a gold-colored ribbon, she tied it back, and stood before the small chipped mirror on the opposite wall for a self-inspection. Impressed that Miguel had done all this while she bathed, she decided to find him and thank him before going to help Carmen's husband. She reached for the door, jumping when someone knocked.

"Who's there?" she asked cautiously, wondering if Miguel had returned. "It is I, Carmen. My husband is worse."

Lydia followed Carmen and her daughter across the torch-lit courtyard to a small house near the trees. Once inside, Carmen led her to a room in the back where a man appeared to be asleep. Carmen turned up the lamp and knelt beside the bed. She placed her hand on her husband's forehead, whispering something Lydia couldn't understand. The man's eyes slowly opened, and after he forced a weak smile for his wife, turned his glazed eyes to Lydia.

"*Buenas noches, doctor,*" he said in a raspy voice.

"Carmen," Lydia began. "Tell him that I am only a nurse, but I will do what I can for him."

"*Si,*" the woman answered before she spoke with her husband. He nodded, smiled at his wife, and then closed his eyes. Carmen turned. "He says you are welcome in our home, and that he will try to be a good patient."

"Raul has a sack with medical supplies in it. I'm almost certain he won't give it to me, but I believe if Delora asks, he would give it to her." Lydia put her hand on the man's forehead for a moment before she moved the colorful quilt to examine his bandaged leg. "And I will need some hot water."

"*Si,* I will get it, *pronto.*" Carmen spoke rapidly to the child, who followed her mother out the door. In a short time, Delora returned with the sack, stepping into the room as her mother carried in a basin filled with steaming water. Lydia had already removed the bandage and motioned for them to put her supplies on the small bedside table.

"The wound is infected. It must be opened and cleansed so it can drain." Lydia took out a little brown bottle and poured some laudanum into the glass. "Tell your husband, that I must use a knife, and that it will hurt, but only for a little while, and maybe not at all if he drinks what I have put in this glass. Tell him that he must not move until I am finished."

Again the woman spoke to her husband, taking the glass from Lydia and bracing her husband's shoulders while he drank. While they waited for the medicine to work, Lydia washed a small scalpel. "He seems to be relaxed. I think it's time to begin."

Delora took one look at the scalpel and turned wide eyes to Lydia. "You are going to cut him?" she cried in dismay.

"I must so the poison can drain." She watched as the color fled from the little girl's shocked features. "Do you still want to watch?"

The child swallowed. She flicked her gaze to her father's red and swollen leg, then back to Lydia's questioning expression before she motioned to the small pile of bandages. "Ah . . . I think that I should go find more cloth . . . just in case you do not have enough. We would not want to need them and not have them, no?"

"That is a wonderful idea. Your mama will help me."

Relief replaced Delora's apprehension. "*Si,* my Mama will help for now."

An hour later, Lydia gave Carmen's husband an encouraging smile. "Tell him the wound will heal."

"*Tu herida va a sanar,*" Carmen repeated, placing a kiss on the sleepy man's forehead. Lydia stepped out of the room, glancing around at the humble furnishings. A place had been set for her at the small table, and Carmen insisted she stay and eat from a little pot of beef and beans. Delora looked up from the table where she had piled some cloths but now played with a well-worn rag doll.

"My papa is *muy valeroso* . . . very brave, no?"

"Yes," Lydia assured as she sat across from the child. "He is. He's a very nice man and soon, if your mother washes his leg every day, he will be well again." She was unprepared when the child got up, ran to her and hugged her.

"*Muchas gracias, muchas gracias,*" the child cried, swiping at her tears. "Papa, he will repay you someday."

"Delora," her mother chided, saying something more in Spanish.

"My Mama says I should let you finish your beans."

Lydia took a bite, surprised by how delicious they tasted. Carmen brought a basket of warm tortillas and motioned for Lydia to take some. "Delora, ask your Mama if there is anyone here who isn't an outlaw?"

The child blinked up at her. "I do not know what you mean?"

"Is everyone who lives here wanted by the law? You know . . . *banditos?*"

"*Si,* some . . . some are just people." The child spoke with her mother for several minutes and Lydia suspected that she relayed Lydia's concerns. Carmen reached over and put her hand on Lydia's shoulder.

"Do not think we are bad people, *por favor.*" Carmen dabbed at her eyes. "If there was another way, we would . . . how do you say . . . choose differently."

Lydia felt terrible. It had not been her intention to make such a kind woman feel bad. She finished her supper and thanked Carmen for the food. She accepted another hug from Delora before she walked toward the door, pausing a moment to speak. "Your husband should sleep comfortably through the night. If you need me, do not hesitate to send for me."

Carmen nodded and spoke Spanish to her daughter.

"My mama says that a long time ago, she and my papa had a farm and raised our food, but the well dried up and they had to come to Rio Salado to survive. She also says that she wishes she could do something to repay you for your kindness."

Tears burned Lydia's eyes as she reached out to hug Carmen. "Thank you for such a wonderful supper. It was payment enough."

On the way back to her room, Lydia took note of her surroundings. As well as the smithy and the mercantile she had seen before, there was also a large barn with many corrals filled with horses and several donkeys. Chickens roosted on the fence, but hogs and goats were confined to pens. There weren't many wagons, or at least none that she could see herself using to escape.

Never in her life had she felt so helpless. Although she had driven her father's old gelding many times, harnessing one familiar horse to a buggy was far different from attaching a team to a buckboard. Her only other avenue would be a donkey and cart. But she wasn't sure if she could actually manage a donkey, having heard that they were stubborn and willful.

Just as she had the thought, a squeal came from the corral and she turned in time to see one of the donkeys charge a nearby horse, the donkey's ears were flat on its back and its teeth were barred. The horse retaliated by spinning and kicking its hind legs high into the air. Lydia watched the scuffle for several minutes in stunned silence, convinced her fear of riding horseback was justified. However justified she felt, horseback seemed her only means of escape.

"Dear Lord," she muttered in a defeated whisper. "I am totally dependant on Antonio—Miguel—whatever his real name may be—for my rescue."

She heaved a slightly annoyed sigh, promising herself that as soon as she got back home, provided that she ever saw home again, she would purchase a gentle horse and ask Sayer to teach her how to ride.

No sooner had she returned to her room and lit a lamp, than someone else knocked on her door. "Who is it?" she asked impatiently, still distressed about the donkey and horse fight, but mostly because she felt completely weary to the bone.

"It is I, Miguel."

"Go away. I'm sleeping."

"You do not sound like you are sleeping," he countered.

"How would you know what I sound like when I'm sleeping?" she argued. "You know nothing about me."

"Ah, mostly that is true, but you know nothing about me. Open the door and we will get to know each other better, yes?"

She groaned in frustration. "No."

"Only for a moment," he urged. *"Uno momento."*

"Why should I? What do you want from me?" she demanded in a harsh tone.

"Certainly not to stand out here in the hall talking to the door." His curt tone brought a satisfied smile to her lips. Apparently she'd prolonged their conversation enough to strike a nerve, and as tired as she was, it was refreshing to know she could annoy him almost as much as he annoyed her.

"One very small moment," he repeated.

She heaved a loud sigh and threw open the door.

CHAPTER NINE

Miguel nearly filled the doorway. He appeared even more startlingly virile than Lydia remembered from the short time they'd been together. By the strong scent of soap, it was apparent that he also had bathed, shaved, and changed into a clean shirt, one not as elegant as the one he started with, but nevertheless, a shirt that revealed the breadth of his shoulders and chest. His skin looked bronze in the lamplight, and she quickly decided that no matter what he wore, he was definitely too good looking for his and her own good.

The dust had been brushed from his trousers and boots. His shirt lay open at the neck, exposing the elegant little crucifix, and even though she tried not to notice, a few curly black hairs on his chest.

"*Buenos tardes*," he said with his usual superior grin that caused her heart to beat harder against her breast no matter how much she tried to prevent it. "I see the clothes fit?"

He stepped inside without being invited. The way he looked at her as he walked around her made her feel strangely wonderful, even though his behavior bordered on audacious arrogance. "*Si*, they fit you very well."

She turned her back, untying the ribbon in her hair, hoping he would get the idea that she was trying to prepare for bed. "As I said, it's late and I'm very tired."

To her dismay, he gently lifted a strand of her hair, then let it slip slowly from his fingers, "You like the ribbon?"

"Yes, thank you. Now please leave." Would her heart always race when he looked at her like that? Was she insane to react to him—to enjoy it when he said and did nice things? She went to the table and lifted the small brush, pausing a moment before she began to run it through her hair.

"I must make a note," she began, relieved that her voice sounded calm, "to ride back to Torreon when all of this is over and pay for these things with money that wasn't taken from innocent victims with jobs, and families. Honest people who came by their money through hard work and diligence."

His bark of laughter took her completely by surprise—filled her with a peculiar inner fury. He faced her, his eyes dancing with mirth, his smile so crafty she had a hard time resisting the urge to slap his face.

"So, *bonita mia,* you think that I am a bad man, hey? That I robbed a bank and paid for these things with money that was not mine? Is this why you frown so at me?"

She gave him a stiff smile that quickly vanished. "Yes. I certainly do. Although you pretend to be different, you're just like all the men here—thieves, robbers and . . ." She hesitated for a breath of a moment and raised her chin a little higher. ". . . and murderers. Did you gun down a rich man, take his gun and his horse, and his money like Juan said? Or did you simply rob a bank and buy those things with money that wasn't yours?"

"Do you think I could do such things?" he asked, matching her glare.

"I don't know what you're capable of. If I didn't need these items, I would refuse them. But since I have no choice but to accept them, somehow I will see that they are paid for with money that doesn't belong to someone else and taken from them against their will."

"Perhaps you should give your money to the rich investors in

Santa Fe, not the merchant in Torreon, no?" He didn't let her answer as he shook his head. "It is the rich who store their money in vaults, the poor store it in jars . . . provided they have any to store."

"Not always."

"Did you have your eyes closed when you rode in here today? These people have nothing. If you were starving, would you care if the food I found belonged to me or if I took it without asking, as Delora's father did to feed his child?" He gave another little shake of his head at her look of disbelief. "No, under these circumstances, I do not believe you would. So I say, you may believe that I am a bad man, but what matters is that you are no longer hungry."

"What you say is true, under these circumstances. But I have never taken what isn't mine. I do not fault the rich for being rich, nor do I blame them for my circumstance. I am not a thief. I work for my money, and when you and your kind rob a bank, it is the hard-working, honest people in this world you hurt. For some of us do, indeed, keep our money in the bank."

"Does your rich grandmother keep her money in the bank also?" he countered, lifting a dark brow. "How can you pretend to know how it feels to have nothing when you were born with everything?"

She felt as if he'd slapped her in the face. What he said was true. She'd been born into wealth—had never wanted for anything. When she was Delora's age, she had ten dolls, and they each had ten fancy outfits—more clothes than Delora had seen in her lifetime. "It's late," she replied tersely. "I'm tired, and you're not welcome here."

She went to the door and would have opened it, but he put his hand on it.

"I did not come to make you angry. I came to thank you for helping Delora's father."

Lydia swallowed back her desire to order him from the room. "Thank you."

"Aren't you going to ask me how I knew this?"

She glared up at him. "I assume you have spies everywhere."

"When you are angry, your eyes change color," he said, his voice flowing over, soothing her temper much like the hot water of her bath soothed away her aches and pains.

"They change from green to the blue-green of the sea," he added with a small, tender smile.

She continued to glare at him, ever marveling at the intensity of his gaze, yet inwardly ashamed of herself for not being strong enough to resist his overwhelming attraction. Every time his gaze fused with hers, her heart gave a little, jumpy flutter. With him this close, she could almost forget that he was a criminal—a man not to be trusted, especially with her heart.

"I need to get some water," she stammered, grabbing the pitcher and reaching for the knob. He caught her before she could escape.

"Do you think that I am a man who takes without asking?" His breath felt warm and seductive against her neck as he nuzzled her ear. She closed her eyes as tantalizing sensations trickled down her spine. He nibbled the lobe before pressing his cool lips against her neck. "I am waiting for your answer."

His nearness wrecked havoc on her objectivity. "Apparently what I think doesn't matter," she answered hoarsely, struggling to think rationally. She kept her back to him, aware how easy it was to get lost in his captivating gaze.

"Please. Leave me alone," she said desperately, but she made no effort to move away. How could she be so angry one moment and so soft and befuddled the next? "You-you confuse me," she said, her voice tinged with frustration. "Are you Antonio, or are you Miguel? Tell me who you are?"

Again his low laughter washed over her, fraying her nerves.

"Search your heart, *Bonita*," he said, nuzzling her neck again, "and you will know." He moved her hair and kissed the other side of her neck. He began to slide his hands up and down her arms, slowly turning her to face him. He took the empty pitcher and placed it back on the table before he came back to her. When she wouldn't meet his gaze, he put his knuckle under her chin, drawing her eyes to his.

"Ah *bonita mia*, how sad you look," he murmured a moment before he pulled her into his arms and kissed her fully on the mouth.

Oh, God, she thought, melting against him. *If you only knew.* She gave a soft groan, and even though her conscience told her to resist, she couldn't—didn't want to. His hold grew tighter and his kiss became more demanding when she kissed him back, sinking her fingers into the thick hair at his nape.

For a long moment she felt as if she were dreaming—that she wasn't his captive, but his lover, and he wasn't an outlaw, but her knight in shining armor—her champion. Not a man looking for sex, but a man with honorable intentions. When he finally lifted his head, his eyes were the darkest of blue, his breath more harsh, his hold more forceful.

"You are a very beautiful woman," he said, his voice deceptively calm in contrast to the tiny muscle that pulsed above his jaw. "Too beautiful to be here among these men."

His features grew more serious. "I swear to you, *bonita mia*, very soon I will take you back to your family."

His expression was tender, his words filled with promise. With shattering clarity she realized she wanted him, needed him in more ways than to simply rescue her. The thought was startling, wonderful and dreadful all in the same moment.

If she stayed here, her life as a lady—as her father's nurse—was over. Yet if this man took her back to her proper, boring existence, she would lose him forever even if he managed to escape the authorities. Ideas and solutions, like shooting stars, raced through her mind until she remembered something he said back on the trail. *What is important is that you do not, under any circumstances, tell these men that you are family to Sayer Mac-Laren.* She slipped from his hold and turned away, feeling cold as she recalled his warning. *You think that only the English kidnap wealthy nobles?*

"Did you hear me, *bonita?* I will take you home as soon as I can."

His voice broke through her cocoon of her memories. "Will you?" she asked after a moment. Hurt and anger caused her eyes to burn with tears. Slowly, she turned and faced him. "Will you take me back to my father . . . or to my sister's ranch?"

"Whatever you wish. I swear it," he said, his dark brows snapping together.

"For what price?"

"Price?" he repeated. "I do not understand. Why is there sadness in your eyes, yet malice in your words?"

She swallowed past the lump in her throat. "You know who I am?" she asked.

"*Sí.* You are the lovely *Señorita* Randolph. The future Duchess of . . . of someplace I cannot remember. What?" His smile faded. "It troubles you that I know you are the heiress to your grandmother's fortune?"

"Yes. I never said anything about it."

He shrugged his shoulders, but then his dark brows snapped together as if he were trying to remember. "I just know. Perhaps from your brother-in-law . . . Yes. I'm sure he told me about your grandmother and the fact that she is interested in horses."

"Did he tell you specifically that I'm next to inherit?"

"I could be mistaken. It could have been that my father read it someplace. He tends to keep abreast of current affairs more than I."

"Really? I doubt your father can read at all—that is assuming, of course, that you know who your father is."

He placed his fingertip on her lips. Gone was the humor that only a moment ago brightened his eyes. Now his gaze locked on hers with foreboding. "Shush," he said, his smile artificial, his accent more pronounced. "Do not insult my family or me."

She moved away, suddenly aware of the reason she felt so terrible. Even if he wanted a ransom, it didn't matter—nothing mattered—not her life, her family. All that mattered was that she loved him, and deep down inside, she knew he cared for her too.

She stared at a spot on the floor, refusing to look at him. Had he already sent a ransom note? If her family paid, would he give her back? She turned away, wrapping her arms around herself. "Please, get out."

Miguel rose from his bedroll and shook some straw from his bolero. Sleeping in one's clothing wasn't one of his favorite things to do, he thought, grumbling to himself. It would be difficult to explain why he wasn't sleeping with his woman if one of the men came in to check his horse and found Miguel in a nightshirt, snoring away in the loft. To avoid such an embarrassment, he purposely went to bed after everyone else and got up before the village awoke and the boy came in to feed the horses.

He climbed down the ladder and went to Diablo's stall. The stallion snorted a greeting and stepped closer to have his ears scratched. "Ah, *mi amigo*," Miguel murmured. "To be more like you, heh? You love the ladies then they are forgotten. But, me? I am a fool. But it is not my fault. She makes me crazy."

He grabbed the pitchfork and speared a large flake of hay, tossing it into the trough. After he put the fork back, he leaned on the stall door, watching the big horse eat. "When I kissed her, it was as if I were a boy again, struggling for control—

always wanting more. When I closed my eyes to sleep, she was there, taunting me. When I finally do sleep, she invades my dreams."

He gave a disgusted laugh when Diablo lifted his head, looked at his master, and snorted some dust from his nostrils. "Yes, I know," Miguel continued. "You think I have gone mad, no? Perhaps. But know this, *amigo,* when I am away from her, I am a very unhappy *hombre.*"

Determined to clear Lydia from his head, he found a brush and stepped inside the stall, brushing the big black horse until his arm began to ache with the effort. "And now," he grumbled. "She thinks I am after her money. Her money," he repeated with a disgusted grunt. "I have no need of her fortune, I assure you."

When the horse's coat was glossy, Miguel gave him some extra feed then decided to go get some breakfast. Coffee, strong hot coffee, would help him shake his fatigue, and maybe some red chili and eggs. That would taste good, he thought. And while he ate, he would be thinking of easing the hunger-pains in his belly instead of the ache in his heart.

Lydia awoke early to a soft knock on her door. A quick glance at the window confirmed that it was barely past dawn. "Why can't you leave me in peace," she mumbled, assuming it to be Miguel who disturbed her sleep. Donning the borrowed robe, she went to the door and cautiously asked who it was.

"It is us," came a small voice. "Me and Mama."

Lydia closed her eyes in both fatigue and relief. She quickly tidied her hair and opened the door. "What is it? Is your husband worse?" she asked, frowning in concern.

Carmen smiled brightly. "No, he is doing better." She looked down at her daughter and pushed her forward, still smiling.

Delora stepped forward and spoke as if she had practiced her speech. "I am to ask you if you will help some of the other people who are sick. My mama has set up a table on the patio by our house where many are waiting." When she finished, she looked up at her mother and smiled.

Lydia looked at them both for several minutes. "People are there now?" she asked, hoping she'd misunderstood. The sun was barely up. Roosters still crowed in various places around the village, and her bed still looked warm and inviting.

"*Si,*" mother and daughter said in unison. They didn't seem to care that she wasn't dressed and her hair was a mess. Delora looked at her as if she were some kind of angel. But she didn't feel very angelic. Her muscles were still stiff from being dragged over the mountains and across the desert. In fact, if she could, she'd steal a horse, ride away, and never give this place a backwards glance. She tried to smile, but felt sure it must have resembled a grimace as mother and daughter exchanged worried glances.

"Very well," she said, tucking a curly strand of hair behind her ear. "Give me a few moments to dress. Tell your people that I will be there shortly."

Twenty minutes later, Lydia crossed the short distance to Carmen's home. As Delora had said, long, narrow cedar posts had been attached to the side of the house and stretched out, forming a kind of shelter. Delora called it the patio, but the floor was dirt, not stone. A small table had been placed under the shelter and covered with a clean white cloth. On top of the table sat a basket containing the medical supplies Raul had given them last night. Several people stood, while an old man and an old woman sat on up-ended stumps. Two young women sat on a colorful Mexican blanket, holding their babies.

"*Buenos días,*" a toothless old man muttered, smiling. Some of the others followed his lead and mumbled a greeting. Delora ran up to her, taking her hand.

"Come. Mama and I will help you talk with our friends."

Lydia stopped before the old man when he lifted his hand, exposing an inch-long welt that appeared to be festered. On examination, Lydia suspected he'd gotten too close to a large cactus. She found the tweezers and carefully removed the spine, ignoring the man's loud protest. She could only assume that *i-eeeee*, translated to *ouch*. A moment later, he grinned and held his cured hand up for all to see. "Delora, tell him to go and wash his hands very well and to use soap."

"Go *lavese sus manos con jabón*," the child said in a very serious tone. At the same time Carmen carried out a bucket of water, some towels and a large brightly painted bowl.

"These are for you," she said softly, hurrying to help the old man stand.

The old man hurried away, stopping before Lydia. *"Gracias, Doctor."*

Lydia thought to ask Delora to tell her patients that she was only a nurse, but after scanning their eager expressions, decided it would do no good. She quickly determined that the thin woman with the fussy baby was next. After a quick exam and a lengthy conversation between herself, the mother and Delora, Lydia learned the woman was having trouble producing milk. "Tell her I can find nothing physically wrong with her baby—that I think he's hungry."

Lydia waited, rocking the baby while Delora conversed with the worried mother. When she glanced at the young woman, it became apparent that the diagnosis left her very distressed. Huge tears pooled in her big brown eyes.

"What did she say?" Lydia asked Delora as she handed the child back to his mother.

"She said she has little money for food, and no money to buy a cow for the milk."

Lydia watched the young mother leave—so affected by her

plight she didn't realize Delora had tried to get her attention until the little girl tugged on her sleeve. "I'm sorry, sweetie, what did you say?"

The child gave an exasperated sigh obviously taking her job as assistant very seriously. "Your next patient is waiting."

Most of the others were malnourished as well, but one by one, she tried to help them, giving advice, cleaning a small scrape, and lancing a large, painful boil on the old woman's back. And while she tended the sick, she learned that most of the people were trying to make an honest living, that they'd had no choice when Raul came and brought his *banditos*.

It was after noon when she finished. "You were the best assistant I have ever had," she told Delora as the little girl helped her put away the medical supplies.

Carmen came out of the house, wiping her hands on her apron. "I have made tortillas, and there is butter and honey. You two go and eat while they are warm. I will clean this up."

Lydia gave a tired smile, and after she washed her hands, followed Delora into the house.

Miguel leaned against a post in the shade of a cottonwood, watching as Lydia tended to her patients. He'd tried to ignore her when he caught a glimpse of her walking across the courtyard shortly after dawn. He had even gone inside the hotel and eaten, but the whole time, he could think of nothing else. At first he wondered why she helped these people. She'd been brought to Rio Salado against her will and knew no one here would help her, yet she didn't hesitate to help them. But the moment he asked himself why, he knew the answer.

Lydia Randolph did not think of herself as a rich heiress, and that pleased him greatly. She'd been kind to others and considerate of their needs, and that also pleased him. About the only thing about her that annoyed him was her stubbornness, her inability to accept him unconditionally, and . . . he had to stop himself before he became angry all over again.

Heaving a loud, frustrated sigh, he pushed his sombrero off his forehead, wishing it wasn't so hot. He could not let her know he'd been watching, and with nothing to do, he decided to go to the cantina and have a cold beer. If eggs and chili couldn't help him, perhaps beer would.

Diego sat at a table with three other men, and the moment Miguel stepped inside, the young man waved him over. The rest of the afternoon, Miguel played cards, trying to keep his mind off a woman with coppery red hair.

It was dark when Miguel finally left the cantina, having won enough to fill his pockets, buy a few rounds of drinks for the others, and pay for his meal without using his own hidden money. He donned his sombrero and glanced in the direction of the hotel. His woman had been the main topic of the afternoon's conversation, spoiling his best efforts to keep her from his thoughts. Yet there was something more dangerous than his feelings for her. The men he'd played cards with and those he drank with asked many questions about the beautiful *gringa*. It was plain that several would willingly take her off his hands if she became too troublesome.

Troublesome? He thought about the way they had parted. He had not wanted to make her angry. On the contrary, he had wanted to seduce her. He gave a disgruntled sigh, and stepped off the boardwalk. He'd go toward the river where he'd walk along the bank as he had the last two nights waiting until fires were out and rowdy voices grew somber.

"*Hola, amigo.* Where are you going?"

Miguel forced a smile as he turned to face Juan. "To check on my horse."

"Your horse is growing fat on my hay. Come, let me buy you a beer."

Miguel wanted to refuse, but to do so might rouse Juan's suspicion. He nodded and the two of them went back into the cantina, found a place to sit and ordered beer. Miguel accepted a few lewd jokes about returning to the cantina when he should be bedding his woman, nodding and trying to smile. If his life hadn't depended on playing the role of Antonio, he would have gladly bloodied his knuckles on several of his so-called *amigos*.

Juan lifted the glass and took a drink, dragging his hand across his face. "Alberto is doing much better, thanks to your woman."

Miguel just took a sip of beer, declining to comment.

"Today she tended several of our people. She is a good nurse. When you leave, what do you plan to do with her?"

Miguel shrugged his shoulders. It was a question he'd been asked more than once in the last few hours. "She is mine, and she will leave with me."

"But what if she wants to return to her family?"

"She has no family," Miguel stated calmly.

"And if she decides she likes it here and wants to stay—you will take her against her will?" Juan asked, narrowing his gaze.

"Why not? I took her the first time." Miguel took another sip of beer. "This time is no different."

"You both should stay here in Rio Salado. We could always use another gun and a good nurse."

Miguel grinned. "You have no bank, and no stage or train comes close. What would I do with nothing to rob, hey?"

"I see your point," Juan muttered, giving a soft laugh. "Many days I think the same. Sometimes I think I should give this town back to the people and go and find someplace more exciting, but . . ." He shrugged his shoulders. ". . . where would I go?"

To hell? "It is getting late." Miguel put down his unfinished beer and stood.

"The night is still young, *amigo,* where are you going?" Juan protested. "I was hoping for a game or two of cards."

Miguel paused at the swinging doors. "Maybe *mañana.* I'm tired of playing cards." Several more lusty remarks from Diego's table nearly turned his stomach. "First I must check my horse, and then . . ." He turned and grinned. "Then I must go and make love to my woman."

"Oh, *si,*" Juan said sarcastically. "One's horse should always come before one's woman, hey *amigos?*" he asked the others, waiting until the laughter died down. "We saw the marks on your face when you rode in. Perhaps she will be more willing tonight, no?"

Miguel gave a dry laugh and stepped outside, too disgusted to reply. He swore under his breath and headed for the barn, just in case Juan watched.

"God help me if I have to spend one more day in this place," he muttered as he opened the door and stepped inside. After a brief check of his stallion, he blew out the lamp, opened the squeaky door, but remained inside. A quick glance confirmed that he had not been followed.

He glanced over at the ladder to the loft, shaking his head, wondering if Lydia enjoyed the clean room and especially the soft bed. And the special room where she could enjoy a hot bath—did she like that also? he wondered as he stepped outside to wash in the horse-trough.

CHAPTER TEN

Lydia crept into the main room where all the guns hung on the wall. She lifted Miguel's, checked to see if it was loaded, and slung it over her shoulder. With her hat in her hand and a small bundle of supplies under her arm, she quietly stepped out into the night. The courtyard appeared to be deserted. She put on her hat and glanced up at the stars.

A childhood memory flashed into her mind—how she and her sister had often picked out a single star and wished for something special. One particularly bright star stood out among the others, and for a fractured moment she wished for a miracle—that Miguel was who he said he was and that he had honorable intentions and didn't want to ransom her back to her family.

But another memory shattered the first. The memory of his handsome face on the wanted poster. For a moment, she wondered where he had gone, but then Salena's laughter drifted over from the cantina enforcing Lydia's decision to sneak out of town on her own.

Keeping to the shadows, she had just about made it to the barn where she hoped to steal Miguel's canteen and bedroll, when someone grabbed her roughly around the waist, covering her mouth with his hand. She bit his palm at the same time she stomped her booted foot down on the man's arch. She heard him grunt in pain, but he only shifted her position, never letting go as he hoisted her up under his arm, half-carrying, half-dragging her toward the back of the barn.

She clawed at the hand on her mouth, struggling to breathe. His grip was powerful, unrelenting, as she tried to pry herself loose to keep from being dragged inside. She kicked and squirmed as hard as she could, her heel striking his shin. The next instant, she was tossed into a pile of hay that choked her when she gulped in air to try and scream. This time when her assailant muttered something in Spanish, his voice sounded so familiar, she froze.

"M-Miguel?" she gasped, trying to spit out bits and pieces of hay before she choked again.

"Who else would be up at this hour protecting you, hey?" he asked, his voice soft yet threatening. "What in the name of the blessed Mother are you doing, trying to break my leg?"

She strained to see in the dark, but she couldn't. She jumped when a match flared, momentarily illuminating his dark scowl. After he lit a kerosene lamp, he braced his booted foot on a stall rail, and rolled his pant leg to look at his shin. "*Ay caramba*, you kick harder than my horse." He rolled down his pants, and held up his hand, showing her the marks her teeth made on his palm even though it was difficult to really see them. "And look at this."

She brushed some straw out of her face. "I'm sorry about that—"

"Keep your voice down. Do you want us both to be shot?"

"No, no of course not, but you shouldn't have frightened me like that. I simply reacted the only way I knew how."

"They teach women how to fight like wildcats in English schools?" he challenged.

"Do they teach bank robbing and murder in Mexican schools?" she countered.

He paused, momentarily rendered speechless by her quick wit. He glared at her, only slightly bemused when she lifted her chin a little higher in blatant defiance.

"Where did you think you were going?" he demanded in a harsh whisper as he hung the lamp on a nail. He picked up his gunbelt and shook it in her face. "And this, what were you planning to do with this, hey? To shoot the guard at the gate?"

"I'm not the one who can so easily take another's life," she snapped, anger replacing her relief.

She dusted off her clothing, trying to keep from screaming at him. He was the criminal, for heaven's sake, not she. His shirt lay open at the neck, and his hair was tousled, giving him a carnal, untamed appearance. Though she tried not to let it happen, she remembered how his hands had felt on her body, how his touch had made her feel wildly alive.

"I cannot stay here any longer," she said in a voice tinged with bitterness. "I-I—"

"Do you think that you can just walk away?" he asked incredulously. As she watched, his expression grew softer. "Do you think, after what has happened between us, that I can let you go?"

She took a step back. "You don't have any say in the matter," she countered, inwardly cursing the fact that as angry and confused as she felt, she ached for him to hold her—to make her forget their circumstances for just a little while longer. "And, nothing has happened."

He took a step toward her. "Oh, yes it has, *vida mia*. And, yes, I do have a say because I love you."

She took a step back, startled and confused by his statement. "No. You mustn't say that. You . . . and I . . . what's happening is a mistake . . . a terrible mistake brought on because of our circumstances."

She turned away, unable to meet the intensity of his gaze. "We . . . I cannot stay here and live like this."

She spun back around, angry that just being this close to him could so completely destroy her control. "You don't understand. Even if what you say is true, there's a price on your head." She pressed her palm to her forehead, trying to control her rampant emotions. "You've robbed and killed, for God's sake, yet I . . . I—"

Fury boiled up inside her, twisting and tangling with the painful knowledge that they had no future together. "I'm not going to give my heart to a man who kills because he wants another man's horse."

She would have left, but he caught her wrist, and pulled her up against his chest.

"You . . . you knew I was vulnerable. You took advantage of me—made me care for you."

She didn't resist when his mouth came down on hers in a savage kiss. As his tongue demanded, she opened for him at the same time he pressed her back against the wall. His hands were everywhere, working at the buttons of her blouse, slipping inside to caress her breasts.

She moaned as her nipples grew taut against his palms. A moment later, he caught her hands, held them prisoner above her head while he kissed her throat, her cheek, arousing her to the point of pain before kissing her lips. Inflamed, she hungrily kissed him back, groaning when he let go of her hands to cup her cheeks.

"I love you, and nothing short of my death will change how I feel. Yield to me, *vida mia*," he breathed against her mouth, kissing her deeply.

She tore at his shirt, slipping her hands inside, brushing her fingertips across his ribs, up his chest, and around his back to hold him closer. As if it were the most natural thing to do, she pressed her hips against his arousal, delighted that she could have such a potent effect on the man she loved.

Slowly, she became aware of strong arms pushing her back,

holding her steady until her gaze fused with his. His eyes were dark, glinting with what, she didn't know, but she sensed it to be something far more primal than anything she had ever experienced before. He took a step back, holding his hand out to stop her from coming any closer.

"You make me crazy," he said gruffly, raking his fingers through his hair.

Her heart hammered against her breast as she forced herself away from the wall and turned her back on him. With trembling fingers she straightened her clothing and buttoned her blouse. He stooped and picked up his gun-belt and her hat, holding it out to her, but she refused to look at him when she accepted them.

"Go back to the hotel," he ordered.

And she obeyed, running to the door.

Lydia spent the morning and most of the afternoon in disgruntled thought. Lying on the bed, she stared up at the ceiling, concentrating on all the good things she had back home—remembering her family, her work and her comfortable, peaceful life. Her peaceful, unexciting life, she amended.

When her thoughts drifted to Miguel, she refused to let her heart dictate her reaction. Yet it wasn't easy, forcing her lusty thoughts to the back of her mind. She would have preferred to remain alone, but footsteps outside the door and a few muffled voices banished the thought at the same time someone rapped softly on the door.

"Just a moment," Lydia said with a sigh. She rose, straightened her appearance and opened the door fully prepared to refuse the intruder's request. Much to her amazement, the old man from whom she'd removed the cactus spine stood in the hall holding a large, fat chicken. Delora stood by his side, smiling. The old man grinned, yanked off his battered straw hat and at the same time put the squawking chicken in Lydia's arm, ignoring her protest as well as the chicken's.

"Delora," Lydia gasped, struggling with the hen. "What is this? I don't want his chicken." The little girl's smile vanished and her eyes grew wide, but Lydia had little time to notice as the hen wiggled one wing free and flapped it wildly, scattering several feathers.

"You cannot refuse," she said in a small voice. "To refuse his payment would . . . well, I do not know the word, but it would not be good." The child nodded as if to reinforce her statement, then calmly reached up and grabbed the hen, tossing it on the floor in Lydia's room.

"Payment?" Lydia repeated, watching as the chicken instantly quieted and began to explore. "Payment for what?"

Delora gave an impatient sigh. She cast a quick glance at the old man, smiling briefly as if to reassure him, and leaned closer to Lydia. "For fixing his finger, remember?"

Lydia took her gaze from the wandering hen to glance at the old man. He nodded as if he'd understood the whole conversation, but she knew he didn't speak a word of English. "Payment . . . *si* . . . ah . . . *gracias*," she stammered. When they both turned to leave, she frantically caught Delora's arm halfway down the hall. "I can't keep his chicken," she hissed. "Think of something. Tell him there's no need to repay me. Tell him I have no place to keep a chicken. Tell him anything you can think of. Just help me get rid of that hen."

Delora shrugged her shoulders. "He will not take it back. And, there are more outside. Mrs. Lucero has a rooster you can slaughter for soup, and six eggs, and Mrs. Montoya has fresh tortillas and beans, and—" Delora caught Lydia's hand and pulled her toward the front door. "Come and see for yourself."

Lydia stepped outside and was greeted by all the people she'd helped. As Delora said, there were two more chickens, a small basket of eggs, some goat's milk, tortillas, small sacks of coffee and flour, topped off with a generous sack of dried beans. All were given with large smiles and muttered words of thanks, some in Spanish and some in broken English.

Overwhelmed by the gifts, Lydia returned their smiles and carefully accepted the two chickens, tucking one under each arm. Delora helped with the other items, and after several more thank you's, headed back to her room. The moment she stepped inside, she released the chickens and watched in horror as they deposited several little chicken poops on her clean floor.

"Do not worry," came Miguel's voice from the open doorway. "I will clean it up. But first . . ." He came in and turned her to face him. ". . . we must think of a way to dispose of them without hurting anyone's feelings."

Delora put the eggs on the table, along with the tortillas. "I'll go get the beans," she said brightly as if having chickens indoors wasn't anything to bother about.

"How?" Lydia asked. "How do I do that?" She swallowed hard. "I cannot . . . will not ring their necks, if that's what you're thinking." He pretended to shudder, and for a moment the thought of wringing his neck was almost pleasing.

"The thought never entered my mind. No, I thought we could build a little coop by your window, and every morning at dawn the rooster could wake you up? He would see that the hens keep laying eggs. A rooster can be very helpful."

She turned from watching the rooster chase a hen under the bed to tell him he was crazy, stopping the moment she saw his expression. His eyes were alive with mischief. "A coop? Outside under the window?" she repeated, matching his good-humored smile. "I think I have a better idea."

He feigned insult. "Better than mine?"

"Most definitely."

Lydia sat at the small table at the young woman's insistence. Miguel stood, leaning against the doorjamb in his usual relaxed, terribly handsome way, holding the woman's baby in the crook of his arm. "He is a handsome boy, no?" he asked when the woman left to make coffee from the sack of supplies they'd given her. "He will have milk and his Mama will have food."

Lydia felt Miguel's charming smile wash over her. And charming he was, as she watched him apply his charm along with some fancy talking as he convinced the young mother to accept the gifts. In the end, he'd won, but not before the young mother threw her arms around him and kissed him several times on the cheek, before she turned and hugged Lydia so tightly, it took several minutes before she could draw a proper breath.

"And she'll be able to make some chicken soup when the beans run out," Lydia added, happy to have helped a person in need. "No?" she replied doubtfully when Miguel slowly shook his head. "She won't make soup?"

"No, *vida mia,* but do not despair. The chickens will have a much better use."

"Fried?" she asked cautiously.

"Are you hungry?" he asked frowning.

"No, of course not. I was just trying to think of a better use for the chickens."

He shifted the baby to a more comfortable position over his shoulder, patting the infant's back. "Eggs. Two chickens, one rooster. Soon there will be more chickens and more eggs and our little baby here may never be hungry again."

"Yes, of course," Lydia exclaimed. "Eggs and chicks, and this turned out better than I'd hoped for."

The baby's mother returned, put two cups of coffee on the table before she took her son from Miguel.

"Sit," she said with a bright smile. She conversed with Miguel for several minutes, and in that time Lydia understood several words. *Mujer* meant woman, and when she heard it, the young mother glanced at Lydia and smiled, then asked, *"Usted tienen casa aquí?"*

"Sí, nos gustamos aquí mucho." Miguel took his place across from Lydia, leaning forward so only she could hear. "All this talk of chickens and soup . . . I think that I am hungry now," he added playfully. "Dine with me?"

"Do I have a choice?" she countered. "After all, I am thought of as your woman, am I not?"

Miguel cleared his throat. "Yes," he said in a more somber tone, taking a drink of his coffee.

Lydia lifted her cup. "She said I am Antonio's woman, to be precise, and there was something about a house . . . or home."

He met her gaze over the rim of his cup. "That is correct. Your Spanish is improving."

"But you're not Antonio. Or at least that's what you want me to believe."

He let out a slow sigh. "Yes, that is what I want you to believe."

Lydia would have pushed the subject, but the young woman returned from the stove with more coffee. "No, *gracias*," Lydia replied with a smile, using the interruption as an excuse to leave. She nodded to Miguel. "Please tell her for me that I must be going."

Miguel stood, but she turned and hurried out the door.

"His woman," Lydia muttered in exasperation. She glanced around the sleepy little village. In a very short time, she'd come to know some of the people, and they all seemed to know Miguel, only as Antonio. But for now, she had a mission. She needed to find Delora and find out what *Usted tienen su casa aquí* meant.

★ ★ ★ ★ ★

"You will make your home here," Delora confirmed with a knowledgeable nod, and her face brightened. "Is it true? You and Antonio will stay?"

Lydia's heart sank. Apparently Miguel planned to stay at Rio Salado, leaving her no recourse but to find her own way home. She wasn't foolish enough to think she could do it alone. She'd have to procure someone's assistance. She had seen Delora riding a horse with some other children. Surely if the children could master their equestrian skills, so could she.

"*Señorita.*" Delora smiled at her as she sat on the boardwalk next to Lydia. "Because of you, my papa is feeling better. If you and Antonio stay, I will never have to worry that my papa might get sick again."

Lydia returned the child's smile. "I can't stay. I have a papa too, and I'm sure he misses me." She paused and took the child's hand. "Delora, how would you feel if you were taken away from your papa?"

"I would be sad," the child responded.

"Yes, and I'm sad. That is why I was hoping you might help me with something. Something I've been meaning to do for quite some time and just never got around to it."

"What is that?"

"Well, to find someone who could assist me with a suitable mount."

"A what?" Delora asked with a bewildered frown. "I do not know what that is."

"A gentle horse. I wish to learn how to ride. Then maybe I could visit my papa."

Delora beamed with understanding. "I can teach you." She pulled Lydia to her feet and ran ahead of her toward the barn. "Come. My papa's horse is very gentle. His name is Poco."

CHAPTER ELEVEN

Just before the sun vanished completely, Lydia sank into a hot tub of water. Every muscle in her body seemed to protest at the same time, especially those of her thighs, hips and bottom. "I'll never escape," she moaned as she closed her eyes and slipped deeper into the water.

Her first lesson had been a disaster. Her fear was far greater than she first expected. She lifted her hand and looked at her nails. Two were much shorter than the others as a result of clutching the horn so tightly they simply snapped off when the horse suddenly shook a fly from his neck. And even after hours on the horse's back, she never got up enough courage to do more than walk around in circles with Delora leading the poor beast with a rope.

"Are you still in there?" Delora asked, knocking softly.

Lydia gave another soft groan. "Yes. But the water's cold. I'll be right out." She stood and after she dried, slipped on the robe. When she opened the door, Delora's worried expression only served to add to Lydia's mortification. What had she said previously that day? If a child could do it, surely she could? *Fool*, Lydia scolded herself.

The child followed her to her room, taking a seat on the bench while Lydia sat gingerly on the bed, picked up the brush and dragged it through her hair.

"I saw you ride in with Antonio," the child began cautiously. Her eyes were wide with innocence. "I thought you were his friend and that you wanted to ride on his horse with him. I did not know that you were afraid and missing your papa."

"I am not his friend, Delora. I am his prisoner."

Delora fell quiet for a long time and heaved a sigh. "I do not understand. Antonio looks at you like he used to look at Salena. I suppose that explains why he chooses to be all alone when the other men are playing cards and dancing with the women."

"Perhaps he doesn't know how to play cards or dance," Lydia replied as she shifted her weight, wincing just a little. Her frown deepened when the little girl laughed before she heaved another despondent sigh.

"No, it is not that. He knows, 'cause I have seen him. If what you say is true, that you are not lovers, I think that perhaps when they captured him, someone must have hit him on the head."

Lydia was speechless. Lovers? Is that what everyone thought? Inwardly she gave another groan in spite of the fact that her heart gave a silly little jump.

Delora looked over at her from where she stood by the window. "My mama told me that sometimes when a person gets hit real hard, they forget. I think Antonio forgot to be mean and now he is nice."

Lydia nodded, amused by the child's words and her own recollection of breaking a pitcher over Miguel's head. "I suppose that could be true. Was he mean before?"

"*Sí.*" Delora looked at the end of her braid, fixed the ribbon, and grinned up at Lydia. "I think he loves you. That must be why he sent Salena away tonight. She is *muy enojada.*"

Lydia put aside the tray. "Delora, what did you say?"

"Oh, I forgot that you do not speak Spanish so good." She thought about it for several moments before she nodded. "While you were taking a bath, I went for a walk. Antonio sat in the shade of a tree by the river talking to Salena. She wanted to know why he slept in the barn last night when he could have slept with her. I did not mean to listen, but Antonio and Salena, they had a, how you say? A fight. Antonio told her he no longer wanted her to be his woman. She is *muy enojada* . . . very angry."

"Really?"

"*Si*," Delora replied, nodding her head. "She wanted Antonio to go to her casa, but he wouldn't. He sent her away, but he did not look happy. Are you sure you are not lovers?"

Feeling the child's gaze glued to her, Lydia cleared her throat uncomfortably. "Isn't it getting to be past your bedtime?"

Delora shook her head. "Aren't you wondering where Antonio is tonight?" she asked. The child walked to the door. "I will tell you anyway. He is getting drunk. Come and I will show you."

"I don't think I should," Lydia replied, but the little girl ran back and picked up her hand.

"Come. No one will care. There is a big fire outside. Everyone is dancing, even Antonio. He is funny to watch. I will wait until you get dressed."

A short time later, Lydia followed Delora out into the courtyard, more than a little bit curious. Bales of straw were scattered around to be used by the dancers as benches. Several of the men strummed guitars and one played a violin. All four of them sang as they played. Men, women and even children danced to the slow, pleasing music. Older couples stood and watched, some holding hands, others cradling their grand-children while parents danced. Although Lydia knew how to waltz, the Mexican way of dancing was far different.

If she had to put their style into words, she would choose *sensual* or *seductive*. The men were dashing and wore arrogant smiles, the women alluring and provocative. The enchanting music, in combination with their intricate dance steps, was fascinating.

Lydia accepted a warm, rolled tortilla and blended in with the small crowd as Delora rushed ahead. As she nibbled the flat bread, she looked for Miguel.

He was easy to find, as he was taller then most of the others.

"Antonio, Antonio, dance with me," Delora cried joyfully. Miguel stood conversing with another man, and only when Delora ran up to him did he turn. It quickly became apparent that he'd been drinking as he swayed ever so slightly, smiling down at the little girl as he said something that Lydia couldn't hear.

The music turned livelier and another dance began. Expecting the child to be turned away, she wasn't prepared when Miguel took her small hand and twirled her around. Bemused, Lydia sat on a bale of straw in the shadows where she could observe without being seen. As Miguel danced with Delora, Lydia couldn't keep her eyes off of him—the way he smiled, or the way he moved to match the child's shorter steps.

He was unlike any man she had ever met—bold and powerful one moment, kind and considerate the next. She remembered how his hands felt around her waist, how his lips felt on her skin when he kissed her neck. She shivered, but not from cold.

The music grew softer and while she watched, Miguel escorted the little girl to her mother, bowed and kissed the back of the child's hand. What he said to her wasn't important. It was the dreamy look on Delora's face that filled Lydia with inner warmth. How could someone so completely charming be a ruthless outlaw?

She sighed, once more wishing it weren't true when suddenly he turned and strode toward her. She thought to flee, but realized it would appear as if she were afraid. Perhaps she was . . . a little. But she'd never let him know the spell he had cast over her heart.

Another song began, only this time the music was slow and strangely alluring. As if she were watching herself from afar, she accepted Miguel's outstretched hand, shivering ever so slightly as the rough pad of his thumb brushed over her knuckles.

He stepped back, pulling her out into the center of the other dancers. He never said a word, his gaze locking with hers in a way that made her wonder if he could read her mind. His lead was easy to follow and they danced well together, almost as if they had practiced the steps before.

Near the end of the dance, the crescendo rose as he twirled her around and caught her quickly in his arms, pressing her tightly to his chest—his mouth so close to hers, she expected him to kiss her and was strangely disappointed when he didn't.

"You have danced to this song before," he challenged, his breath sweet with tequila and warm on her skin. He released her when another man came over, but held tightly to her hand. The man offered Miguel a bottle, conversed for a moment then left. The others began to leave as well. One by one, couples, arm in arm, strolled toward the buildings. Delora called to Miguel, blowing him a kiss before she ran and caught up to her mother, glancing at him dreamily one more time before she went into her house.

"Ah, do not look so sad," Miguel said, smiling at Lydia. "It is understandable for you to be jealous."

His accent sounded heavier than what she had grown accustomed to. She looked over at him and noticed the half-empty bottle of tequila clutched in his fist.

"After all . . ." He made a wide sweep with his hand. ". . . look around. Am I not the most handsome?" He answered before she could. "Indeed, even the little *señorita* is smitten."

"Smitten?" Lydia asked, slipping her hand from his. Could she be the cause of his overindulgence?

"*Si, si.* Did you not see it in her eyes?" He gave a haughty nod and took a sip from the bottle. "Is it not the same with you?" His expression mocked her.

She raised her chin just a little. "I wouldn't go as far as smitten." She shook her head. "Grateful, perhaps, for saving my life, but . . ." She shook her head again. ". . . smitten is not the word I'd choose."

"Really?" he asked, raising his brows. "How about charmed? Or . . . how do you say . . . infatuated! *Si,* that is it. Infatuated."

"No, that's not it either." She turned to leave, but he caught her arm in a firm but gentle hold.

"Come and walk with me, while I think of another word."

She pulled away, surprised and a little disheartened by how easily he let her go. When she looked at him, his shoulders seemed to sag ever so slightly.

"Please," he whispered. Aware that some of the men were watching, she swallowed her pride and took a step closer. He tucked her arm into the crook of his and they strolled along the river's edge. She refused when he offered her a drink from his bottle. He laughed and muttered something about propriety, apologizing for not having a glass.

"If you are not smitten, and you say you are not infatuated?" He raised his brows in question until she shook her head, frowning once more. "Very well, give me a moment to search for the perfect word."

He fell quiet for several moments, his fingers entwining with hers as if this were a normal occurrence between them. They stopped, and once more he graced her with one of his wide, enchanting smiles. "I think I have it."

When he didn't continue, she felt compelled to ask, "Well, are you going to tell me?"

"Perhaps . . ." he replied, releasing her to take another drink. They were at the place in the river that widened, where the women washed their cloths in the daytime.

"I'm waiting," she prompted.

"For what?" he asked, nonchalantly.

"For your answer. I'm waiting for you to tell me how I feel."

"Oh," he said, as he pulled her into his arms. He tried to kiss her, but she moved her head back out of his reach. *"Amor,"* he murmured with conviction. "I am sure of it, now. I saw it in your eyes when we danced."

For a moment she could only stare at him while what he said registered on her befuddled state of mind. How could he know? Was she that transparent?

"Amor?" she gasped, pushing him back. He swayed precariously until she felt obliged to grasp his arm to steady him.

"Si. It means—"

"I know what it means," she replied impatiently. "Come, you're drunk and delusional." She guided him back toward the hotel. "I do not love you," she said with more conviction than she felt. "I admit that I'm attracted to you, but that's certainly not love."

She cast him a quick glance. "My attachment is due to our circumstances."

"Did we not speak of this before?" he asked, his words slurred slightly.

She shook her head. "No."

He stopped. *"Si,* we did. I remember."

"I assure you. We have not. I would have remembered."

"No, *bonita mia,* I remember. I told you in the barn how I felt, and you told me about our circumstances." He lifted the bottle for another drink, but she took it from him and poured the rest on the sand before she urged him on.

"Ay caramba," he groaned. "Why did you do that?"

"You are well into your cups already," she shot back as she urged him forward.

"My cups?" He made a show of looking around. "I do not have a cup. I was using the bottle you have tossed on the ground." He shrugged his shoulders. "No matter. Where were we?"

She gave an exasperated sigh. "What do you mean?"

"I mean, what were we talking about?" he asked, pulling her to a halt. His expression became unreadable, but in the moonlight she could see his brows crinkled.

"Oh, I remember." He flashed her a grin. "You said you were attracted to me, no?"

She gave an embarrassed groan. "Yes, I did, but—"

"Then you admit it?"

"Admit what?" she cried, annoyed that they hadn't made any progress toward the hotel.

"That you love me."

She stared at him expecting to see his eyes twinkling with teasing humor, but what she saw was much more unsettling.

"That's not what I meant," she countered, trying to think of a way out of her predicament. It wouldn't do to tell him the truth. He was already too proud, too sure of himself.

"No?" he asked, pulling her around to face him. "What did you mean?"

"I-I meant that I might rely on you for certain things, but that is most definitely not to be confused with something as . . . as complex as love."

"Complex?" He took her hand and hooked it over his arm as they resumed their walk. "Love is not complex, *bonita mia*," he said matter-of-factly. "It is a simple thing. A bond between a man and a woman. Surely as a nurse, you would know this."

"What has love got to do with me being a nurse?" she demanded, baffled by his words.

"I would think that you studied such things in school."

"I studied anatomy and how the human body functions. We did not spend a great deal of time on emotions, especially love."

"Why not?"

"Because it wasn't important. Love cannot heal a wound. Love certainly has nothing to do with consumption or . . . or nausea."

"Nausea?" he repeated, making a face. "I beg to differ. Once, when I was much younger, I fell in love with the most beautiful *señorita* I ever saw. She was twelve and I only eight. One day, she brought over a basket of *biscochitos*. That's a very delicious Mexican cookie."

"Yes. I know. I've tasted them."

He stopped once more. "You have?"

"Yes, at a party I attended." A soft breeze carried the sweet smell of the flowering bushes to them.

"You attended a party in Mexico?" he asked.

She laughed at his expression. "No. A friend of ours, Don Fernando Gutierrez—"

"You know Don Fernando?"

"Yes, I knew him," she said growing impatient. "He was a very kind man, and a lot like you." She coaxed him to walk, delighted that they were almost back at the hotel where she could escape his questions and seek the sanctuary of her room.

"Really? In what way?"

"He too was a splendid dancer, but, unfortunately, like you, he was a good man on the wrong side of the law. It cost him his life."

Miguel frowned as if thinking about this, shrugged his shoulders. "Where was I?" he asked, but began without preamble. "So there I was, a boy in love, and to show her how much I loved her, I ate all the cookies, right there in front of her. Later that night, I was very sick. So, you see. Love can make you nauseated."

She groaned in frustration.

Miguel gave her a concerned look. "Are you feeling sick, *bonita mia?*" His grin was scandalous.

"No," she very nearly shouted.

He grimaced. "I think I am, but then, it could be the tequila."

She heaved an impatient sigh. "May we discuss something else?"

"Of course. However, it was not I who brought up the subject. You did."

"I never—"

His warm fingers pressed gently against her lips, and his expression was heartbreakingly tender. "I know, *bonita mia,* and that is why you deny it so vigorously. It is nothing to be ashamed of. In fact, I am ardently looking forward to teaching you."

She had the strong urge to kick him, but decided against it as another couple strolled by, holding hands and looking very much in love. "Deny what?" she demanded, keeping her voice low. "And what's this nonsense about teaching me? What could you teach me?"

He leaned close, his warm breath tickling her ear. "That you are in love with me . . . and how to show it. What else?"

A frustrated groan tore from her breast. "You are impossible," she hissed as she pulled her arm free of his. "I'm tired and I'm going to bed. Good night, Mr. Garcia." She would have escaped, but he caught her by the arm, pulled her back against his chest and kissed her. She melted against him wondering why she felt so safe and secure.

After he had ravished her mouth, he lifted his head and gazed deeply into her eyes. "Love sometimes comes very slowly, when we are prepared, or very fast, taking us by surprise."

She took a step back yet couldn't drag her gaze from his.

"Buenos noches, bonita mia."

He left her at the door, and as he walked toward the barn, an odd feeling came over her. The security and contentment she'd felt in his arms had vanished, replaced with emptiness and dismay.

CHAPTER TWELVE

Lydia punched the pillow and stretched out on the bed to glare at the ceiling. How had everything become so complicated? she wondered, recalling Miguel's words the very next moment. Love is not complex, *bonita mia.* It is a simple thing. A bond between a man and a woman. Disgruntled, she tossed the light coverlet aside and rose, thinking a breath of fresh air might take her mind off Miguel.

She donned Carmen's robe, left her room and quietly stepped outside. She strolled to the balustrade surrounding the wooden porch and rested her hands on the cool lumber. The sky seemed to be a multitude of stars, and while she gazed up at them, she closed her eyes and took a deep cleansing breath, listening to muffled male voices as they softly sang while the fire dwindled across the courtyard.

She recalled how she and Miguel had danced, how his warm fingers had splayed across her waist and ribs. She visualized his expression when he gazed at her after they shared a kiss. A warm breeze tugged several curls loose, and brushing them back, she turned and stepped inside just as Miguel walked out of the kitchen with a towel draped around his neck.

"Why are you here?" she demanded in a desperate voice.

"Shush. You will wake the entire household. It is very late."

"I don't care if I wake the devil himself. You nearly frightened me to death. I thought you went to the barn. How did you get in here?"

"I walked in a little while ago to take a bath. Bathing is not only for women." He went to the table in the center of the room and a moment later a candle flickered to life, casting the room in dancing shadows.

He had his back to her, and he was naked from the waist up. The sight of his golden body sent strange yet familiar sparks shooting through her. Though she knew she shouldn't stare, she couldn't help it. He was magnificent; the only marks on his smooth skin were the stitches on his left upper arm. When he turned, she knew she should look away, but she couldn't.

It was a mistake. Like his back, his chest was smooth and broad and muscled. His stomach was hard and flat. She swallowed and quickly looked away, feeling the heat of a blush as she had felt the warmth of the evening breeze just moments ago. He came closer.

He caught her hand and led her down the hall to her room, opening the door for her to enter. "There is no reason to be so upset, *bonita*. If I do not pretend to sleep in here with you, there will be uncomfortable questions to answer in the morning."

"I don't care if there are questions in the morning. You cannot sleep here."

He shrugged his shoulders. "Where can I sleep if not here?" He touched the flame to the lamp then blew out the candle.

"In the barn . . . or with Salena," she shot, remembering how the young woman attacked him when they arrived—remembering the sting of jealously. "I'm sure she'd be agreeable." He covered his heart with his hand, but she spoke before he could. "I know, I've wounded you."

"*Sí,* you have, and deeply. I do not know Salena like I know you," he said with a smile.

"Well, according to Delora, she certainly knows you well enough." When he turned her to face him, his clean scent washed over her.

"You are jealous."

"I am not. I care very little that . . . that hussy threw herself into your arms. It's apparent that she's done it before by the way you kissed her, so why deny it now?"

"That was days ago, and she kissed me." He gave a long, tired sigh. "It is as I told you. I am not who they think I am. She, like the others, knows Antonio Garcia, not me."

His confession stirred up another, almost forgotten, memory. *Perhaps it is better, for now, that you do not have all your answers.*

"Besides, is it not time for you to remove these annoying stitches?" He lifted his arm and inspected her handiwork. "They are beginning to bother me."

"Tomorrow." She tried to move him toward the door. "I care very little about what name you wish me to use. All I know is that it isn't proper for you to be here, and if you don't get out, I'll-I'll scream."

His soft laughter infuriated her. "Among my people, *bonita mia*, a woman screaming is not always a bad thing."

She gave an audible gasp. "You're impossible."

"You are a prude." He sat on the bed. "Ah, this bed feels good, no?"

"Yes, but don't think for one minute—"

If only he wasn't a bandit. His easy manner, his endless patience. He was everything desirable—everything she had ever dreamed a man could be—tall, well built and sinfully handsome. She was naked under the robe and felt a gush of warmth in response to her thoughts.

"Very well, if you won't leave, I shall."

He stood and caught her before she could reach the door, trapping her in his embrace. "I wish I could leave you alone, but I cannot."

"Why?" she cried irritably, aware that the longer he stayed, the more difficult it became to send him away.

"Because, I am in love with you."

His repeated confession left her speechless. He caught her chin between his thumb and forefinger, holding her gently. The kiss was long and intoxicating, drawing her closer to him. "Say you love me as I know you do."

She pushed away from him and pressed her fingertips against her temples. "Yes," she cried, turning to face him. "I do. I love you. There you have it. Satisfied? But, that's not all I feel. I'm angry and jealous, and confused."

Her gaze fused with his. His features softened with an understanding smile, and he reached for her, brushing a kiss on her forehead and another one on the tip of her nose. "Anger can be soothed. Confusion turned into understanding. But love? There is nothing for us to do except give in to it."

His gaze raked over her, his emotions mirrored in his dark eyes. "Yield to me, *vida mia.* Say you will be mine forever."

Liquid fire surged through her. Suddenly she ached to feel his skin against hers. She loved him, and the moment she said the words, something erupted inside. No longer did she feel restrained. She reached up and kissed him, and was surprised at his reaction.

He groaned, low in his throat, as he quickly took control and molded her to the hard contours of his body. She seemed to fit perfectly in his arms and he in hers. He intensified the kiss, teasing her to open to him with the persistent tip of his tongue. The moment she complied, he plunged into her, causing a lingering swirl in the pit of her stomach.

Her fingers glided over his back, his ribs, grazed over his chest, teased his nipples to harden against her palms. The feel of his flesh excited her, acted like an aphrodisiac, and while his mouth left a trail of kisses from her ear, down her neck, she unbuckled his belt and unbuttoned his pants, sliding the tips of her fingers just under his waistband.

His arousal was instant, his gaze so hungry and powerful that it nearly took her breath away. It should have been against the law to look so seductive, to be so alluring, but he was all that and much more. He untied the belt of her robe, tossing the garment aside, touching, caressing. He kneaded her breasts, drawing the rough pads of his thumbs across the sensitive nipples.

When she was completely naked, he pressed her back on the bed. His gaze slid down every inch of her body and he smiled a smile that only made her want him more. Unashamed, he finished undressing then joined her on the bed. The ropes groaned under his added weight, but she barely noticed. He kissed her on the mouth, on the eyes, the tip of her nose, burning a path down her throat to her breasts. He circled her nipples with his tongue, scraping his teeth lightly over the soft peaks, suckling until she clung to him and moaned his name. His touch became soft and painfully teasing, like fire and ice twisted together and touching her skin at the same time.

She squeezed her eyes tight in pleasurable anguish as his fingers explored and massaged her moist feminine folds. She writhed beneath his touch. Masterfully gentle. Intimately arousing. Slowly, she opened her eyes, sank her fingers into his hair, and when he lifted his head from her breast, their gazes locked.

"Love me," she breathed against his lips a second before he kissed her senseless. He braced his weight on his elbows, cupping her face between his hands as he whispered something in Spanish and moved over her. She instinctively arched against him when he entered her, thick and hard.

She froze, her eyes widening.

"The pain will pass, *mi amor*. I swear."

And she believed him, for even as he waited, she felt her body adjust to this new and glorious intrusion. Slowly, he began to move within her, deeper, withdrawing, driving deeper yet again. He soothed her with whispered words of love and adoration both in English and Spanish between ardent kisses. Slowly at first, she began to move, growing more and more restless. His ardor was extraordinarily tender, meticulously restrained.

All thoughts except those of him vanished.

Miguel sank his fingers into her luscious hair and looked down at her. She felt like velvet beneath him, hot and tight. Her eyes were hooded, smoldering with the fire that ignited between them. The scent of her filled his nostrils as he moved his hips in rhythm with hers, deeper, into her moist heat until he felt as if he burst into flames. She moaned and raised her hips to meet his, drawing on him, surrounding him. He spoke her name, using every ounce of his will to hold on to his control as he watched her climax.

Lydia couldn't hear; she couldn't see. She could only feel. She felt hot, then cold and empty, then complete with each driving force of his body into hers. She burned and ached inside, shivering with a strange new euphoria that started slowly and climbed to match the frenzied beat of her heart. His muscles bunched under her fingertips, and she heard him groan, felt his body shudder.

Only after he found his release did reality crash down around her. How many times had he teased her about being a nurse, and here she was, making love to him without a care about conceiving his child. Yet even as the thought whispered through her mind, it didn't frighten her. She loved this man, good or bad, right or wrong. If something happened to him . . .

He must have sensed her dismay, for slowly he lifted his head and kissed her gently on the mouth. When he looked at her, he grinned, mischief dancing in his eyes. "You are a very beautiful woman."

"You said that before," she murmured.

"I did?" His skeptical expression acted like a balm to her spirits.

"Yes."

He grew quiet for several minutes, then caught her face between his palms. "Well, I meant it. You are the most beautiful woman I have ever met. But do you want to know something else?"

She smiled. "I'm not sure if I do."

"I will tell you anyway."

"Somehow I knew you would," she said a moment before he kissed her. Slowly he raised his head and his expression was unlike any she had witnessed before.

"You are even more beautiful now that you are mine."

She entwined her arms around him and accepted another kiss, hoping he couldn't hear how his compliments had started the rapid pounding of her heart, the tingling in every limb. When they parted, her fingers brushed at the stitches on his arm.

"I should remove these."

His gaze followed hers to his arm. "Very well, if you insist."

He rolled, and leaned toward the table where he picked up her medical sack, plopping it on the bed. He pulled out a small pair of scissors and gave them to her. A few moments later the deed was done. Before she could protest, he pulled her back against his chest and nuzzled her ear.

She leaned her head back, exposing her neck. "What are you doing?" she asked softly.

"What do you think I am doing?" he countered, his voice thick with humor . . . and something more.

"I know what you're doing," she said trying to push him away. "You're trying to seduce me again."

"*Quédate tranquilo, yo me encargo todo,*" he said, the lamplight dancing in his eyes. "And just because I know it makes you angry when I speak Spanish, I will translate." He kissed the tip of her nose. "Relax; I will take care of everything."

And he did, arousing her to the brink of insanity before sharing another heart-shattering climax. Long after he slept, she lay in his arms, gazing at his face, memorizing every line. She moved a lock of ebony hair from his forehead, and gently traced a path down his slender nose, around his moustache and across his lips. She snuggled close, gleaning his warmth, and wishing they could stay like this forever.

The next morning, Lydia awoke early, aware that Miguel had already gone. She sat up, glancing at the smear of blood on the sheets, remembering how gently he had loved her.

They were lovers. For Miguel, she had cast aside her proper upbringing and had absolutely no regrets. Even as she thought about him now, she missed him, wanted him.

She dressed and, while she tied her hair back, remembered her plan. She needed to take full advantage of her pre-arranged riding lesson with Delora. She had to focus on her escape—refusing to acknowledge that it meant leaving Miguel.

When she arrived at the barn, she froze. He sat there, saddling his horse while Delora held the reins of her father's horse. They were talking, and Delora glanced her way.

"Look, *señorita*, Antonio has come to take you for your first ride away from the corral."

Lydia lifted her chin a little higher when Miguel flashed a wily smile.

"I see," she replied. So this was why he was in such a hurry to leave her bed. Part of her felt delighted, the other part dismayed and another part scared to death. "Perhaps you and Mr. Garcia should ride today instead," she suggested cheerfully.

"Oh no," Delora declared as she caught Lydia's hand. "You need it much more than me."

Lydia reluctantly accepted the reins.

"Shall we?" Miguel asked as he led his stallion outside.

Lydia balked. "I'm not ready to ride out. I prefer to ride in the confines of the corral."

"*Si*, she isn't very good," Delora added with a knowledgeable nod.

Miguel's smile widened. "Then we must endeavor to help her improve, no?"

Delora gave him a dreamy smile. "*Si*."

Miguel turned to Lydia. "You cannot learn how to ride going in circles."

"You were watching?" she gasped, suddenly embarrassed.

"What else do I have to do?" He heaved a very indignant sigh. "It is very . . . what is the word . . . monotonous to play cards and drink tequila all day. But no matter, hey? It is as Delora said, you are not very good. But I . . ." He put his hand on his chest, his eyes brilliant. ". . . I am . . . I am an . . . how do you say . . . ?" he teased.

"An equestrian?" she asked.

"*Si*." He leaned a little closer where only she could hear. "I am a very good teacher, no?" His smile became sinful. "With my excellent instructions and careful guidance, soon you will be an equestrian too." He lifted her to the gelding's back and handed her the reins, holding her hand a little longer than necessary. "Come. We will take a ride along the river. We will not go faster than a walk. I promise. Poco is a good horse. He knows what to do. All you have to do is listen to everything I say."

Lydia swallowed down her trepidation, too proud to refuse, too intent on holding on to the saddle horn to notice his roguish grin. "Very well," she replied with a serious frown. "Lead on."

Miguel swung up on the stallion's back and smiled. "I prefer to ride beside you."

"What if they don't like each other? Are you sure it will be safe?" she asked.

Miguel's smile was reassuring as he moved his horse alongside hers. "Look, they are fine. There is nothing to worry about." The gelding matched the stallion's stride and together, Miguel and Lydia rode along the bank. As they left the village behind, she did, indeed, began to relax. She pushed all her worries to the back of her mind and listened as Miguel told her how to cue her horse to do certain things. Stopping was the first lesson, and they stopped many times when he told her to gently pull back on the reins.

"That was easy, no?" he asked.

"Yes, but we've only just begun."

Guiding the big horse around a log wasn't as difficult as she'd guessed it would be either, and soon, even though she protested, Miguel urged her to let the animal trot as they approached a small sloping hill, explaining that by increasing his speed, the horse could more easily maneuver the incline. At the top of the hill they stopped again, and she felt much more in control.

And so she followed his advice, mile after mile, her confidence growing. Just when she thought they should turn back, Miguel swung down and hobbled Diablo before helping her out of the saddle. When the horses were munching on the tall grass by the bank, he took a sack from his saddlebags, caught her by the hand and led her to a shady spot under a large cottonwood tree.

"Sit. Are you hungry?"

She smiled up at him after she sank down on the blanket. "As a matter of fact, I am."

"*Bueno*, for I have brought some food and some wine."

Sitting beside her, he pushed his sombrero off and let it hang from the leather strap to rest on his back. He reached into the sack and pulled out two small cloths, draping one on his knee and one on hers. He handed her a rolled tortilla, filled with thinly sliced meat and cheese, then took out two tin cups and filled them with wine from a kidney-shaped skin.

"There is a story the old women tell to the young ones," he said while they ate. "It is about two lovers and how their love at first seemed impossible, but in the end prevailed."

His eyes filled with mischief, yet his smile appeared as sweet as the wine. He took a bite of his food, chewed slowly in enjoyment, then swallowed. "These lovers, this man and this woman, lived during very difficult times. Often there wasn't enough food to go around. The girl's father was a farmer and had many other children."

He finished his meal, took a drink and moved closer—his shoulder nearly touching hers. "One day while walking with his little daughter, a young, wealthy nobleman rode up. One look at the child's beauty, and he knew he must have her even though he was many years older than she. To bind his proposal, he paid the man with gold. Enough gold to build a better house, buy pigs and goats and even a horse to plow his field. Compared to the other men in the village, the betrothal made the farmer a very rich man."

Miguel turned slightly and brushed a strand of hair away from her face. Though his touch was brief, the fire it stoked to life grew hot and fierce within her. Her food forgotten, she gazed into his eyes.

"So," he began again, his voice a little huskier. "Many years passed and the little girl grew up in the village with the other children. The proposal was forgotten. She befriended a young boy, but he was very poor. Money did not matter to the girl, but it mattered to the boy. He knew she would have a better life with the nobleman, but his love for her was too great to let her go."

Lydia finished her food, brushing the crumbs from her skirt. Aware that Miguel watched her every move, she picked up her cup and took a sip of wine. When she turned her head to see why he didn't finish his story, she knew the reason—it showed in the smoky allure of his eyes.

He cupped her face between his palms and very slowly, purposefully, kissed her. When he finished, he traced his fingertip across her lips.

"Miguel, please," she murmured, aroused by his sensual touch.

"What is it you fear?" he asked softly. "You tell me no, but I see yes in your eyes."

"You see what you want to see," she countered, looking away on purpose.

He was quiet for several moments, heaving an impatient sigh. "Very well, but at least let me finish my story."

"I'm sure you had every intention to finish with or without my permission."

He gave her a stern look. "*Si*, it has a moral. One that may explain many things. Now, where was I?"

"She had a friend—his love too great—"

"Oh yes, yes. Now I remember." His expression grew more serious, but she could tell he thoroughly enjoyed himself. "So, one night they ran away. When the nobleman came to collect his bride, he was furious. He declared the young man to be a *bandito* and put a price on his head. The young man was forced to leave the women he loved and join a band of outlaws to survive. Then, after one of their adventures—"

"Adventures?" Lydia gave him a skeptical look. "Is that what you call it when you rob a bank? An adventure?"

"Shush," he said harshly though his eyes danced with mirth. He picked up a small stone, rolled it around between his thumb and forefinger and tossed it into the water. "The young man only pretended to be an outlaw. He learned about the *banditos*, their ways, and how to be very fast with a gun. One day, the

nobleman was out riding with his bride-to-be. They were attacked by three vicious *banditos*. Terrified, the nobleman did not
know what to do. Then the young man appeared. Unafraid, he
shot them, killing two and wounding one, but not before he
himself was wounded."

"This is a terrible story," she protested. "I like happy end-
ings." She stood, but Miguel caught her hand and pulled her
down to sit on his lap.

"So do I, so sit and listen," he said, pressing her hand between
his. "Well, the rich nobleman was very grateful and insisted that
the young man be rewarded with anything his heart desired.
Much to the old man's surprise, the young man asked for the
girl. The nobleman refused. They argued, neither one paying
the *banditos* any attention until one of the *banditos*, who was not
too badly wounded, grabbed the nobleman, took his gun and
threatened his life. 'Kill this *bandito*, and I will give you the girl,'
the nobleman cried to the young man, but the young man was
bleeding badly and growing too weak to obey. When he collapsed, his gun slipped from his fingers. Desperate, the girl
picked up his gun and fired, killing the evil *bandito* instantly."

Lydia turned and looked up at the man who had stolen her
heart. His hands felt warm where they held her, and his eyes
glittered with hunger. Once more she felt as if nothing mattered
but being with him—not her meticulous upbringing or her
grandmother's uncompromising principles. Not even the fact
that their future together would be bleak at best. The only thing
that mattered was that this man loved her, and she loved him.

He took her hand and placed a kiss in her palm. "So you
see," he whispered, "the moral of the story is, if you love
someone enough, you can accomplish the impossible." He
smoothed his knuckles over her cheek and sat quiet for several
moments. "I can love you like that, *vida mia*. Marry me."

A lump formed in her throat. She had learned enough Spanish to know that he said she was his life. She wanted to return his vow, but a niggling fear of the unknown deep inside stopped her.

"Miguel, please," she murmured, pushing away. She stood and focused on the shimmering reflection of the sun on the water, trying to gather her thoughts, to find the right words, yet uncomfortable with the rush of feelings he brought to life. "It's getting late, and we still have a long ride ahead of us."

She heard him stand, half-expected him to come up from behind and try to kiss her again, but he didn't. Instead, he gathered up the remains of their picnic and put them back in the sack.

"I had no idea a little outing would wear you out so much," he said, and by his tone, she knew he was teasing. Relief rushed over her, but she knew it was only a temporary reprieve.

"It had nothing to do with that. I didn't sleep well last night," she confessed.

"No?" His eyes were filled with insolent humor. "Perhaps I should have stayed awake and been more . . . how do you say it—"

"Oh, please," she moaned, covering her ears with her hands. "Why do I always have to come up with the words?"

His laughter became contagious. "Because you are so well educated and I . . ." He covered his heart with his hand. ". . . I am just a poor Mexican boy with little or no understanding of your language."

She laughed. "You spoke French well enough." As soon as she said the words, they struck her as odd.

"Only a few words, I assure you." He caught her horse and after lifting her to the saddle, gave her the reins.

"You seem to have English down rather well also."

"Only with your help, *bonita mia*. Without you, why I would be . . . how do you say it?" His laughter told her he teased, but she couldn't resist answering.

"Hopelessly lost?"

"*Si, si,* hopelessly lost." He put the sack back in the saddlebag, then took the hobbles off Diablo. Once on the stallion's back he nudged the animal closer to Lydia's gelding. "Perhaps hopelessly in love is a better choice of words."

He picked up her hand and kissed its back, smiling when he finally let her go and urged the stallion toward the trail. She nudged Poco and fell in behind, grateful Miguel hadn't repeated his proposal. She began to let down her guard.

He glanced at her over his shoulder and their eyes met. "Do not think that I am a man who asks a woman to be my wife and then is content to be ignored. Maybe you are not prepared today, *vida mia,* but soon, very soon, I will want an answer."

She wanted to tell him how she felt, but he turned to guide his horse down the path leaving her no recourse but to follow.

CHAPTER THIRTEEN

Antonio Garcia kept his sombrero well down over his face while he rode out of Albuquerque. The four days he'd spent there had given him time to buy supplies, some clothing, and to catch up on some rest. He filled his belly with good food and at night his pockets with other men's money, expertly cheating at cards. All the while his beard grew to further disguise his features and hide his scar.

He had thanked the old man and given him a few extra dollars for his help—a little assurance that no one would be the wiser about his whereabouts. If the rumors he'd heard were true, a rich white woman, Lydia Randolph, had been kidnapped by some Mexican *banditos*. There was only one he knew who would be so foolish to go directly to Rio Salado with his prize: Raul.

"*Idioto,*" Antonio muttered as he shook his head. He turned southward at the fork, wondering if Raul even knew of the woman's identity. If he and Juan were planning to ransom the woman back, Antonio wanted a share of the money.

The morning felt warm and promised to grow warmer as Lydia stepped outside with a bundle of laundry under her arm. Clad in the dress Delora's mother had sent over, she took a long, cleansing breath and let it out slowly. Somewhere someone baked, and with the aroma of fresh bread, the air smelled sweet and slightly scented with the fragrance of cedar smoke. Carmen had done her laundry before, but today Lydia wanted to do it herself. After all, she had been there nearly ten days. It was time she tended to her own chores.

Sounds of women's laughter drew her attention to the river where she and Miguel had strolled along the bank the other night—where he had treated her to a picnic yesterday. Now it was crowed with women washing their clothes while their children splashed and played in the shallow water. Wet clothes hung on ropes strung between the trees.

"*Buenos dias,*" Delora said as she skipped beside her mother. Lydia returned the child's smile.

"Are you coming to the river to wash?" Carmen asked.

"Yes," Lydia replied stepping off the porch. Carmen carried a large bundle of clothing, some she recognized as Miguel's. The little girl's mother smiled, and said something in Spanish to her daughter.

"My mama can speak some English, but not as good as me. She says since you want to do the wash, you can use our soap if you'd like."

Lydia smiled at Carmen. "*Gracias.*"

Lydia followed Delora and her mother to the bank, somewhat surprised when the older woman bent down and grabbed the back of her skirt, pulled it through, between her legs to the front, tucking it into her waistband. She grabbed an armful of laundry and waded out into the water.

"Come," Carmen encouraged. "Sit on that rock and Delora will pull off your boots."

"I-I can't do that," Lydia protested as she stared at the other women. "It's not proper to show off your legs."

Delora looked confused. "Who is doing that?" She glanced at the women. "They are not showing their legs, they are cleaning their clothes." The child lifted one of Lydia's feet and tugged off the boot. When the other dropped next to the first, Lydia glanced around, feeling a little embarrassed.

Slowly, watching the others, she slipped off her stockings and stood. Following Delora's instructions, she reached under and grabbed the hem of her skirt, pulled it through her legs and tucked it into her waistband. Swallowing back her unease, she followed the little girl's guidance and inched into the water. The muddy bank felt pleasantly cool, but as they waded deeper, the water grew much colder, stealing her breath. Several of the other women giggled. Delora's mother smiled, then spoke to Delora. The child, still on the bank, picked up Lydia's blue-checked gown and tossed it to her.

"Watch my mama, and she will show you how."

It wasn't long before Lydia felt completely at ease, washing the sheets off her bed, rinsing them, wading ashore, and hanging them among the ropes. She finished her own pile and began to help Carmen, paying no attention as she grabbed one of Miguel's shirts. She scrubbed it well, and was delighted to see it bright and white once more.

She never noticed that some of the women grew quiet, that even a few moved farther downstream. In fact, as she dragged her arm over her sweat-dampened face, she didn't even recognize Salena until the woman purposely stood in her way, blocking the path to the trees.

"Excuse me," Lydia murmured as she tried to step around.

Salena planted her hands on her hips. "Antonio is mine." She snatched the wet shirt out of Lydia's hands. "I should be the one to wash his clothes, not you."

Salena ground the clean garment into the mud before she threw it back at Lydia.

Lydia caught the shirt, but not before it splattered mud over her blouse, face and neck. Anger flashed in the depths of her eyes.

"Very well," she replied a little too sweetly. She bent over and picked up the soaking wet shirt, throwing it and hitting Salena directly in the face. "You want it so badly, you wash it."

The woman squealed in rage, glaring at Lydia. *"Puta,"* Salena hissed.

Lydia cast a quick glance at Delora, whose eyes were wide with shock.

"What did she say?" Lydia demanded.

"My mama won't let me say things like that," the child protested, shaking her head.

"What's the matter, *gringa, no comprende?*" Salena replied with a haughty toss of her head. "I said you are a whore."

She gave Lydia a self-important smile, then said something else in Spanish that caused several of the women to gasp.

None too gently, Lydia shoved Salena aside and stepped out of the water. "Perhaps when you're through washing that shirt, you should wash out your mouth."

Salena curled her long fingers into fists. "You, you think because you are *Ingles* you are better than me?"

Lydia lifted her chin. "My being English has nothing to do with it. If I were a monkey out of South America, I would still be better than you."

Delora's mother, along with several of the women giggled the moment Delora translated. Lydia glared at Salena and feigned a superior smile, but before she could retrieve her boots to leave, Salena grabbed her by the arm and pulled her around.

"Puta."

Lydia fought the urge to slap the young woman across the mouth, using every ounce of control she could muster to keep her anger in check. "Name calling is childish."

Salena flicked at a loose strand of Lydia's hair. "The other day, when Antonio rode away with you, did he make love to you?" she asked, smiling at Lydia's shocked expression.

"He is a very good lover, no?" Salena twisted her fist in

Lydia's hair causing her to yelp in pain. "He is mine, *gringa*, and if I see you making advances to him again, I will slit your throat, *comprende?*"

Lydia lost her balance when Salena pushed her away, landing on her backside in the cold river. Before she realized what she was doing, she scrambled up and lunged, shoving Salena backward into the water. The woman splashed and cursed until Lydia spread her fingers over her face and pushed her under.

"*Puta,*" Salena spluttered the moment she surfaced and caught her breath.

A sinister smile curled the corners of Lydia's lips as she shoved her under again. When Salena's struggles weakened, Lydia grabbed a handful of hair and dragged her toward the bank, just close enough to grab the borrowed cake of soap.

"*Puta?*" Lydia hissed through clenched teeth, giving Salena a good shake. "That, I'm told, is a very bad word." Salena sank to her knees, but Lydia followed and shoved the soap into Salena's mouth. "And there are children present."

Salena began to struggle, but Lydia gave her a good scrubbing before she dunked the young woman into the water to rinse her.

"Now, never use that word again, *comprende?*" Lydia said firmly. She'd just dunked her again for good measure, when someone grabbed her by the arm and yanked her up. She spun, her fists tight, her eyes ablaze with fury until she realized it was Miguel.

None-too-gently he escorted her to the bank. "Do not move," he warned where only she could hear. He turned and stepped back into the water, grabbing Salena and dragging her to her feet. She coughed and choked, and pretended to cry at the same time trying to catch her breath. She tried to throw herself into Miguel's arms, but he wouldn't let her.

Long black hair clung to Salena's face, reminding Lydia of a half drowned cat. She snarled something in Spanish, but never finished it as Miguel pulled her around roughly and answered in his native language before he gave the woman a little shake.

Salena wrenched her arm free, grabbed a fistful of sodden skirts and clambered toward the cantina. Casting an angry look over her shoulder, she muttered something Lydia couldn't discern as she sulked away. Lydia took a long, deep breath and brushed her wet hair from her face as Miguel picked up the sodden shirt, rinsed it out and tossed it over a branch.

"She started it," Lydia defended, not sure why she felt the need to explain. "She called me a—"

"I know what she called you. Are you all right?" He looked at her—the way her wet clothing hugged her curves; the way her wet hair clung to her smooth face, making her eyes look even bigger. He stepped closer and gently caught her trembling chin between his thumb and forefinger, gazing deeply into her rebellious eyes. "You are not like Salena, *bonita*," he muttered, keeping his voice low.

"Aren't I?"

She moved away and he knew by the defiant angle of her chin he had somehow offended her. He reached for her arm to escort her back to their room, but she took a step back, glowering at him.

"I have slept with you. I think that qualifies me as a—"

He held up one hand, stopping her before she said something that he couldn't bear to hear. "No. Never."

She stared at him; hurt flickering in the depths of her wretched gaze. Again he grew quiet for several moments until he finally took her hand between his own. He gave her an understanding smile, but sensed it was not enough to lift the heaviness from her heart. "A few days ago, I asked you to be my wife. When will you give me an answer?"

Her expression cut into him, and when she slipped her hand

from his, he didn't try to stop her. He watched in silence as she retrieved her boots and walked away.

"She is a very feisty woman, no?" Juan's voice reluctantly drew Miguel's attention. "I can see why you have rejected Salena for her."

"What do you want?" Miguel asked, refusing to allow Juan to goad him. "Certainly not to stand here in the mud discussing women?"

Juan laughed, but the humor didn't quite reach his eyes. "*Sí, amigo.* It is time that you paid your dues."

Miguel flicked some mud from his thigh. "My dues?" he questioned, aware that if he didn't pretend to know what the other man meant, it could be a deadly mistake. "I have not forgotten." He motioned for Juan to look at his clothing. "I am wet. After I change I will meet with you and we can discuss it over a glass of tequila."

"Finish with your woman, *amigo,* but do not keep me waiting too long."

Miguel ignored Juan's lecherous grin, turning in time to see Lydia disappear into the hotel. The sight of her renewed the heaviness in his heart. She loved him, of that he felt sure, and the knowledge was so exhilarating, it almost blinded him to the fact that she still thought him to be an outlaw. Should he chance telling her the truth? Another question clouded his mind. Why couldn't she trust him? Hadn't he shown her he wasn't like the others? And as soon as he thought it, he realized why her words had hurt. In her eyes, he was just like Raul and Juan, and many of the others—a *bandito,* an outlaw.

Swearing under his breath, he headed toward the hotel. It was time to make her believe that he was Miguel and not Antonio.

Alone in her room, Lydia shrugged out of her wet clothing.

After she dried, she wrapped her long hair in the towel and slipped on the only clean thing she had—a thin, silk chemise. Still angry, she sighed, sat on the side of the bed, and plotted her escape.

"Dear Lord," she moaned, dragging her hands down her face. What was happening to her? It had only been a couple of weeks since she'd been kidnapped, and already she had cast aside everything for a man who was almost a stranger. She closed her eyes and groaned in despair. But something else bothered her more deeply. Though she had denied what Salena insinuated, inside she knew it was true.

Yesterday, by the river, when Miguel had kissed her, she'd wanted more than his kiss. She'd wanted him to press her back in the soft grass and make love to her again. She hungered for him, wanted him each time she looked at him. She closed her eyes again and saw her grandmother's stern features, her superior smile fade to one of disapproval.

Lydia gave another despondent sigh, feeling miserable. Her gaze fell on a few pieces of Miguel's clothing, recently brushed and neatly folded beside hers on the bench. Feeling terribly alone, she slipped her arms into Miguel's bolero and pulled it tightly around herself, noticing a slight bulge in the pocket. Her fingers brushed against a leather wallet. She pulled it out and opened it, blanching at the sight of so much money. Was it stolen? She continued her search, noticing a folded paper carefully tucked in the back. When she opened it, it was a wanted poster with his picture on it.

The doorknob jiggled. *"Bonita?"* Miguel called. "Let me in."

"No. Go away." Her fingers shook as she put the poster back into the wallet and shoved his wallet back in the pocket of his bolero. After she slipped it off, she put it back on the chair.

"There is no time to argue. Open the door, *por favor.*"

"No."

Muttering under his breath, Miguel angrily raked his fingers through his hair, frustrated beyond measure. "You do not understand. Carmen put my clothes in there. I need to change as quickly as possible. I must meet with Juan very soon."

"I'm not finished dressing," came her reply.

"*Ay caramba,*" he muttered, heaving another impatient sigh. "*abierto la puerta, bonita, por favor.*"

"Speak English," came her stern reply.

He clenched his teeth, hoping to control his rising temper, but to no avail. "Open the door before I break it down." The last few words he nearly shouted. He had just braced his shoulder against the wood, when she wrenched it open, glaring at him as he stumbled inside.

He would have vented his resentment, but she wore only her chemise, exposing her long shapely legs. Her hair had been wrapped up in a towel, giving him a tantalizing glimpse of her neck and shoulders.

His anger vanished at the sight.

Although her eyes spat fire as his gaze slid down her full length, her nipples hardened, straining against the thin material.

"Oh, *Dios,*" he grumbled dragging his fingers once more through his hair.

"Don't you dare swear at me," she muttered, slamming the door.

"I was not swearing," he said, his voice more husky than it had been a moment ago.

"Then if you aren't swearing, you must be complaining, and I'll tell you right now, I'll have no more of that either."

She turned away, and at the same time, pulled the towel from her hair. Soft, coppery-curls tumbled down her back. Once more he could not take his eyes off of her. The sight of her feminine curves through the thin material of her chemise was more stimulating than anything he could have imagined. He

151

muttered something under his breath, but stopped the moment she spun and glared at him.

"I was only saying that I wish I could postpone my meeting with Juan," he replied honestly. He took another calming breath, but this time not for his temper, but to squelch the pounding of his heart and the surge of heat through his body.

"Why?" she challenged. "So you can have a little fun with your *puta?*"

The moment she said the word, his expression changed and something flickered in the depth of his eyes. A muscle jumped above the tight set of his jaw, but he didn't speak. He picked up his clothing, then retrieved his wallet. He pulled out several large bills and pressed them in her hand. "Take this and buy some supplies. Be discreet."

"What for?" she asked cautiously.

"There you go again, questioning everything I ask you to do." He heaved an impatient sigh. "I ask you to be discreet so none will be the wiser that we are planning to escape."

"You mean you're going to take me home?" she asked with a mixture of dread and relief.

He tucked his wallet back inside his bolero. "I will return soon. Then I will explain."

CHAPTER FOURTEEN

Miguel stepped into the cantina, hesitating a moment as his sight adjusted to the dimly lit, smoke-filled room. Juan sat at a round table with Raul and Placido, drinking tequila and laughing. Several others, sitting at various places around the room, glanced his way, but went back to their business. When he approached, Juan kicked out a chair and motioned for him to sit down, tossing a fifty-dollar gold piece on the table.

"So, *amigo,*" Juan began, lighting a cheroot. He puffed on it for several moments. "Raul said he got five-hundred dollars from Wells Fargo. Should I believe him?"

Miguel glanced at Raul. The bandit swallowed audibly and squirmed in his chair. So this was what Juan wanted. Miguel inwardly breathed a sigh of relief, glad that he'd had the foresight to bring some money.

"We are *banditos.* Can any of us be trusted?" Miguel countered with a grin. He took his place and pulled out his wallet. When the bartender came over, he ordered a beer, frowning when he noticed that the folded poster he had so carefully placed on the left side of his wallet was now on the right.

Raul heaved a loud sigh. "You charge too much, Juan. In Albuquerque, I can get a room for a month and a woman to boot for that price."

"Do no look so unhappy, *amigo,*" Juan chided. "I only ask for a small amount." Juan motioned around the room. "It is how I pay for your comforts, and a small price to pay for my protection during your stay, no?" Juan turned his attention to Miguel. "What do you think, *hombre?* Is ten percent too much?"

Miguel shrugged his shoulders. "It is not for me to decide." He pulled out three one-hundred-dollar bills and placed them on the table. Juan's eyes grew round, as did Raul's and Placido's.

"You have done well for one who's supposed to be in jail," Juan confirmed, gathering up the money and stuffing it inside his shirt.

"Why do you think they were so anxious to catch me, hey?" Miguel countered with a grin.

Juan laughed as he motioned to the bartender. "Drinks for my *amigos.*"

"Not for me," Placido said, pushing away from the table. He nodded his respects, his gaze pausing on Miguel's hand. "I do not remember you wearing a ring before, *hombre.*"

Miguel looked at the ruby on his finger. "It is a little something I recently acquired." His smile grew sinister. "The man I took it from was rude and ill-mannered." Miguel raised his gaze to lock with Placido's. "He was staring at me."

Placido smirked. He retrieved his sombrero and left the cantina.

Raul pushed away from the table, stood and pulled up his sagging pants.

"Where are you going?" Juan asked.

"I'm going back to Torreon. There is a little woman there that is better company than all of you, and not nearly as expensive."

Juan chuckled. "I had better get his gunbelt before he steals one that's better." He finished his drink and motioned for Miguel to join him as he strolled toward the door.

Placido stood several yards away talking with Raul, but when Juan and Miguel came out, Placido glared at them, tossed his cheroot in the dirt and walked away. Raul followed along like a lost dog.

"That one has never liked you much."

"This should matter to me?" Miguel asked.

Juan laughed. "Perhaps. Perhaps not. Placido is a little crazy, but I do not think he will challenge you openly. But, if I were you, *amigo,* I'd watch my back."

Miguel put on his sombrero and stepped down off the boardwalk. He glanced around, half expecting Placido to return, but he went into the barn with Raul. Nevertheless, Miguel couldn't shrug off the feeling of dread that came over him as he headed toward the mercantile. As he had expected, Lydia stood there. Just the sight of her caused him to smile and filled him with pride.

"You don't understand." Her voice carried over to him as he leaned against the door to watch. She picked up a canteen and shook it at the shopkeeper. "How much?" she said in a loud, clear tone. When the man only frowned and shook his head, she repeated her question a little louder.

"I do not think he is deaf," Miguel said as he came up behind her. She spun around. Her eyes were vivid, but once she realized who had spoken, they softened and she almost returned his smile.

"I-I didn't assume he was," she replied. "Tell him that I didn't realize I shouted at him, and that I apologize."

Miguel conversed with the proprietor in Spanish, pulled out his wallet and paid for the canteen as well as several other items she had laid on the counter.

"There," he said, placing his purchases in Lydia's hands. "You have made good choices. We will have a long way to travel and these things will come in handy." He lightly grasped her elbow and escorted her toward the door.

"When are we leaving?" she asked, trying to sound cheerful.

"As soon as—"

"*Señorita* Randolph," Delora called, waving as she raced toward her, her big eyes wide with concern. "My *amigo,* Alfonso, he fell out of a tree and hurt his leg. Come . . . come. I know you can help him."

"Where is he?" Lydia asked as she took the child's hand.

"Come, I will show you."

Lydia hurried to keep up with the little girl. By the time they were in the shade of the trees, several women were standing around, blocking her view of the boy. They parted when they saw her, but much to her surprise, Miguel moved ahead and knelt down and braced the boy's weight.

"See," Delora cried. "Is it broken?"

"I'll have to touch him to tell," Lydia said as she gave Delora her package. Lydia tried to get closer, but the child's mother refused to move. Miguel glanced up and spoke to the woman. Reluctantly, she scooted back so Lydia could have a look. The frightened child tried to move away, but more tears trickled down his cheeks. Miguel leaned a little closer to the boy and whispered in Spanish, nodding and grinning when the child looked up at Lydia before he answered in his native tongue.

"What did you tell him?" Lydia asked as she examined the little boy.

"I told him he would be the envy of all the other little boys to have such a beautiful nurse care for him." It warmed her soul the way Miguel's eyes glittered with mischief. She would have scolded him, but the child cried out when she pressed gently near his ankle. Both the child and the child's mother spoke at the same time, but after a few moments, Miguel had them settled down.

"See how helpful I can be?" he asked, grinning. "We are good together, *no?* I, with my charm to calm them, and you with your skills as a nurse."

She gave him a skeptical look. "Tell his mother that I don't think it's broken, but he will have to stay off his ankle for several days."

Lydia smiled at the little boy while Miguel relayed the information. Again, several women spoke at once, and it took several moments for Miguel to settle them down. Finally the mother ended with a heavily accented "thank you."

Miguel placed the child in his mother's arms, and as Lydia explained how to care for him, Miguel translated the information into Spanish, ruffling the boy's hair when he finished.

Lydia dusted off her skirt, glancing at the boy, who stared at her with a silly grin on his face. She gave him a gentle smile and turned to leave.

She heard Miguel approach—didn't resist when he caught her arm and matched her quick pace. "I think the boy is in love with you for saving his life," he began, walking with her by the river.

"Oh, please," she began, refusing to look at him. "Can't you find something else to speak of?" She pulled her elbow from his gentle grasp. "Better yet, can't you find something better to do than to . . . to torment me?"

She refused to smile, even when he covered his heart with his hand and gave her a pathetic look.

"You wound me," he said, his smile melting her indifference. "Did you not think I was helpful? Did you not think that I have a natural gift . . . that I could be your . . . how do you say it—"

"Say what?" she countered, reluctant to play his game. "I haven't any idea what you want me to say."

"It is simple," he stated with a firm nod. "I could be your assistant." His smile faded when she turned away.

"Delora is my assistant. I've no need of another," she replied. "The two women who were pregnant had their babies on their own without an assistant."

"Not exactly," he said with a shrug. "They had the help of a *curandera.*"

She stopped and put her hands on her hips. "What, or should I say, who, is a cur . . . curan—"

"*Curandera,*" he repeated. "They are healers, women who grow herbs and make potions for the sick." He motioned to Raul's mother, who, in spite of the heat, swept the boardwalk. "She helped the women with their babies."

"Why didn't she help Carmen's husband?"

"Alberto?"

"Do you know everyone here by name, for heaven's sake? Oh, never mind. If Juan's mother is a-a—"

"*Curandera.*"

"Healer," she nearly shouted, angry that he finished her sentence, "then she should have tended Alberto's leg more carefully."

"I am sure she did the best she could. You see, *bonita, curanderismo* is old village medicine—part science and part superstition with lots and lots of candle lighting and prayers. Some patients get well, while others do not."

Lydia gave a despondent sigh. "Well, regardless, I have no patients, and therefore I have no need of an assistant." She turned and together they headed toward the hotel.

"Of course you do. Once we are back in Santa Fe, you will have many. I am sure of it . . . especially if they shoot every stranger who rides in."

She cast him a skeptical look over her shoulder. "It will be difficult to be my assistant once you are captured and put in jail."

"Do not be so certain, *bonita.* I am innocent until proven guilty, *no?*" He gave her a crafty grin. "You can teach me what I need to know."

"I see." She paused for effect. "First you'll have to learn how to deliver babies, then—"

"Me?" He held up his hands. "I am no *curandera*. I thought that I could perhaps boil water or fold bandages. However, I have a very good voice and could sing to the babies after they are born."

"Really?" she asked. "It isn't as profitable as robbing banks."

"Must you constantly accuse me?" he asked, his smile fading. "Have I not given you reason to trust me?"

"Trust?" she cried. "It's as if you're two different people. There is Miguel, the one who maintains he's innocent, and insists that I blindly trust him—the man I love. Then there is Antonio, a stranger to me, yet known to these people, and who cannot be trusted."

"Please," he said, but she wouldn't let him speak.

"Who are you, now, this moment? Are you the kind, considerate man I fell in love with, or are you Antonio, the man who robs banks and murders innocent people? Can you tell me? Because I'm totally confused. When I look at you, my eyes tell me that they are both the same person."

The subtle change in his expression told her she had hurt him, but his tone sounded expertly controlled, his fingers gentle when he picked up her hand. "What does your heart tell you?"

She gazed into his dark eyes; wishing for several long moments that things could be different. Finally she took a shuddering breath, blinking back her tears.

"I don't know," she said flatly, pulling away. "I need some time alone, to think and sort out my feelings."

Expecting an argument, he surprised her when he gave her an understanding smile. "I will leave you to your thoughts." He walked away, and for a moment she wished she could take back what she'd just said, but part of what she said was true. She needed to sort things out.

Yet when she glanced at Miguel, she felt as if she had done

something hateful, even though it had been unintentional. Heaving a despondent sigh, she sank down on a fallen log and stared at the water as it slowly drifted by.

Miguel headed toward the cantina, thinking that a cold beer would taste good and might take his mind off Lydia. Perhaps if she had some time alone, she would realize he thought only of her welfare. He wanted to tell her the truth, but more importantly, he wanted her to trust him enough to know that he would never do anything that would hurt her.

Preoccupied with his thoughts, he didn't notice Placido standing in the way until he pushed open the swing doors, striking Placido. Before Miguel could apologize, Placido shoved him back.

"Watch what you're doing, *cabron.*"

Miguel kept his anger in check, choosing to ignore the obviously drunken man. He stepped around Placido, walked up to the bar and ordered a beer. "Where is Juan?"

The bartender shook his head. "I do not know for sure. I think that maybe he's in the back."

"Hey, *hombre.* I was talking to you," Placido interrupted, staggering up to Miguel from behind. "Are you deaf as well as stupid?" Placido tried to grab Miguel's arm, but Miguel caught his wrist in a vice-like grip.

"Go sleep it off, *amigo,*" Miguel warned. "You are drunk, and I have no desire to fight you." Miguel let him go and turned back to pay for his drink. "Go and get Juan, tell him I—"

"I think you are a stinkin' coward." Placido turned to several others sitting at the nearest table. "The Antonio I knew was no coward. He was a man . . . a man who would take what he wanted, not go around sniffin' at his woman's skirts beggin' for a little—"

Placido never finished his sentence. Miguel had a tight hold of his throat. "Enough," Miguel said in a voice so low, only Placido could hear. Slowly, Miguel let go, and while Placido caught his breath, Miguel slapped several coins on the bar and turned to leave.

"Your woman," Placido began. "Though she acts as if she is too good for us, she is just like the other *putas.*"

His voice washed over Miguel like a foul smell as he described in detail what he would do if he got Lydia alone. The room grew quiet, and several of the men sitting at the nearest table slowly got up and moved away.

"I do not know why you speak such filth, *amigo*, but I assure you, I will not tolerate it." Miguel took a step closer to Placido, his expression cold as steel, his stance deadly. "I am a very jealous man. When you insult her, you insult me."

Miguel shoved Placido out of his way, heading toward the door before he could lose his temper and beat the man to a bloody pulp. He was just about out when he realized it had been a mistake to turn his back on Placido. A chair came crashing down on his back, sending him to his knees. Slightly dazed, Miguel shook the fog from his head at the same time Placido pulled a knife from his boot.

"*Cabron*, stand up and fight like a man."

The crowd scattered when Miguel slowly got to his feet.

"Do you think you can take me?" Placido taunted, slashing the air.

Placido lunged, but Miguel dodged the deadly blade, catching Placido on the chin with his fist. Placido stumbled backwards into the table. It toppled and Placido pitched to the floor.

"Think about what you are doing, *hombre*," Miguel warned. "You are drunk. I have no wish to see you dead."

Placido slowly got to his knees. He dragged his hand across his mouth, glancing down at the smear of blood. Enraged, he scrambled to his feet and charged.

Lydia shielded her eyes as she watched several of the villagers run toward the cantina. Already the door filled with spectators, shouting what she thought were words of encouragement. Curious to see what had captured their attention so completely, she stood at the same moment the crowd parted. She saw Miguel step down from the boardwalk, carrying a bottle of tequila.

Several men slapped him on the back, and even though they spoke in Spanish, she sensed that they were congratulating him. But before she could get his attention, he headed towards the hotel. She thought to follow, but several men came out carrying the limp body of another man.

"Dear Lord," she gasped as she hurried over to them. "Let me through," she demanded, trying to get to the injured man. Juan caught her arm and forced her to stop.

"You are too late, señorita. He is dead."

"How . . . I mean . . . what happened?" she said in dismay.

"Antonio killed him. You should be pleased."

"Pleased?" she repeated in a breathless whisper. "H-how could I possibly be happy that a man is dead?"

"Because," Juan added with a grin. "Placido insulted you. Antonio defended your honor. He never did that for Salena."

"He what?"

Juan heaved an impatient sigh. "Antonio defended—"

"I heard what you said," she nearly shouted, jerking her arm free from Juan's grasp.

"Well then, you should understand that Placido deserved what he got," Juan stated smugly.

"No," Lydia cried, taking a step back. "No one deserves to die because they say bad things."

Juan's bark of laughter nearly shattered her fragile control. "Perhaps, but now I do not think the others will be so eager to speak unkindly about you." He shook his head as if the sight of her displeased him and stepped off the boardwalk. "If I were you, I would go and thank Antonio."

Although the sun was high and the day quite warm, Lydia shivered with the thought that she might be the cause of Placido's death. The next instant she became furious. Surely Miguel could have handled the situation without lowering himself to violence.

"Miguel, wait!" she cried, but he wouldn't stop. When she caught up with him, she thought he would stop, but he didn't—he kept walking, a bottle of tequila resting in the crook of his arm.

"How could you?" she demanded, trying to keep pace with his long strides. "You tell me that you're different, that you're not like the others, but now a man is dead because he said something that made you angry."

"He insulted you before the others."

"Do you think I care what these men think of me?" She nearly ran into him when he stopped.

"You do not understand. I cannot fight them all for you. If I let Placido talk about you like that, they would think that I no longer care what happens to you. They will think there is a chance that they can take you from me, *comprende?*" His voice sounded harsh, and was tinged with something more than anger.

"There had to be another way."

"I tried to stop him—"

She gave a skeptical laugh. "Oh you did, indeed. You stabbed him."

"Do you think I would kill a man simply because I was angry? *No, vida mia.* I am not like that. He was drunk. He attacked me and when I defended myself, he fell on the knife."

He went into the hotel. Again she followed as he continued down the corridor toward their room. After he put the bottle on the table, he grabbed a small towel and held it to his middle. Only then did she notice the blood. "My God, you're hurt. Why didn't you tell me?" she asked. One quick glance at his expression gave her the answer. She reached for the towel. "How bad is it?"

"It is nothing. A scratch."

"Nothing?" she said tightly. "Let me see." She helped him remove his bolero and unbuttoned his shirt. She took the cloth away, examining a six-inch cut on his abdomen. "Thankfully it isn't jagged or deep. Lie down and hold this over the wound," she ordered as she urged him toward the bed.

Much to her relief, he obeyed and even allowed her to remove his boots. He muttered something in Spanish when she took a wet cloth and bathed away the blood, and she instantly felt bad for not being as gentle as she should have been.

"Here, keep pressure on this." She rose and dug around in the sack with her father's medical supplies until she found a small jar and some clean bandages.

"A fire dances in your eyes when you are angry."

She looked at him a long moment before she smeared some salve over the cut and he sucked in his breath.

"You could have warned me," he protested. "It hurts worse now than when it happened."

"You could have been killed," she scolded.

"You always smell clean," he said, drawing in a deep breath close to her hair.

She moved slightly away. "And you always manage to change the subject."

"Was it your father who wanted you to be a nurse?"

"No. It was my mother's wish that I study medicine. However, my grandmother refused to allow me to become a doctor. She believed it to be a profession too messy for a lady of my standing."

His soft laughter startled her.

"Did I say something amusing?"

"No, not really. I was just wondering what your grandmother would say if she could see where you are now."

She heaved an impatient sigh. "My grandmother is a high-born lady of impeccable moral character. I'm sure she would be shocked and disappointed that I have stooped so low as to . . ." She glanced at his face; his slight smile had vanished. ". . . to let myself get caught up in the circumstances."

"When I meet her, I will be sure to bring a copy of my, how do you say it . . . ah . . . perhaps ancestry will do, *no?*"

"I rather doubt she'd recognize any of your, *how should I say it,* brothers . . . comrades? Names like, Billy the Kid and Black Bart are not frequently used in my grandmother's social circle."

Once more he gave a soft laugh, only this time his gaze held less humor. "Nevertheless, when we meet . . ." He caught her hand and forced her to meet his gaze. ". . . and I swear, *bonita,* one day your grandmother and I will meet."

He let go of her hand, wincing when he shifted his weight. He grabbed the tequila and took a long drink, pausing as if it burned his throat. "When that time comes, I will be sure to tell her how I admire your strength and temperance," he replied with a sarcastic edge to his voice.

She thought to comment, but she knew that the sooner she finished, the sooner she could get away from his overpowering appeal. But where would she go? And how would she be able to defend herself if the danger was as real as he led her to believe? She covered the wound with a clean bandage and held it in place as she asked him to sit up so she could wrap the ends around his waist. Another mistake, she soon realized, aware that standing so close to his muscular chest made it quite difficult to remain focused.

She secured the bandage, took the bottle from his grasp and

165

poured some into a cup, appalled at the way her hand shook—that just being this close could unnerve her so completely. She bade him drink then helped him lie back down, making sure the bandage stayed in place.

"You can take this off in a day or two."

"Good, because I told Juan we are leaving."

"And he agreed?" she asked, gathering up her supplies. "But what about—"

"Alberto is well. There is no reason for you to stay, and Juan knows he cannot keep me here."

She nodded, yet couldn't fathom why his news wasn't as exciting as she expected it would be. "That's wonderful," she murmured. "When?"

"Tomorrow."

A heaviness settled in her breast as she picked up the empty water pitcher. "We'll be in Santa Fe by the end of the week?" She glanced at him before she went to the door.

"*Sí.* There is something else I will tell your grandmother when we meet," he began before she could leave. "I will tell her how much I love her granddaughter, and if her granddaughter would only trust me, she wouldn't be so unhappy."

CHAPTER FIFTEEN

Raul tied his horse to the hitching post in front of the Silver Slipper Saloon. Tired and thirsty, he pushed the swinging doors open. He paused for a moment, waiting for his eyes to adjust to the bright light.

"*Hola, hombre,*" Antonio Garcia said, pressing the cold steel of his Colt .45 against Raul's neck.

Raul swallowed audibly. His hands shook ever so slightly as he raised them up and turned. "Antonio!" he gasped. "It cannot be. I left before you . . . and yet here you are . . . and you have a beard." His voice faded away in confused awe. "That stallion must be faster than the wind."

Antonio's sinister smile faded. "What are you talking about?" He un-cocked his gun and dropped it back in its holster.

"You, and that black demon you stole from Don Miguel. You know . . . the horse . . . Diablo." Raul swallowed again and tried to touch Antonio's beard, but his hand was slapped away.

"If I knew what you were talking about, *idiota,* I wouldn't have asked. Now, tell me why you are muttering about the devil and looking so surprised to see me?"

"Si, but . . . but . . . I just saw you, two days ago, back at Rio Salado. You killed Placido, but . . ." Raul took his finger and drew an imaginary line across his shirt. ". . . you were cut and bleeding."

He started to touch Antonio's middle, but again his hand was slapped away. "Stop it. Are you *loco?*" Antonio growled. "Now,

167

what of Placido? Who killed him?"

"You did. I was there. I saw it with my own eyes. You both fell to the ground, but not before he cut you . . . there."

Once more Raul pointed at Antonio's ribs. With a look of disgust, Antonio slowly pulled up his shirt, exposing his smooth abdomen.

"Eee," Raul moaned. "How can this be?" He shook his head and sank down in the nearest chair. "I think I need a drink."

Antonio snatched up the bottle. "First tell me what you are doing here, and why you are talking crazy, then you can have a drink."

Miguel shifted his weight and opened his eyes. He glanced down at his side. Tiny little splotches of blood had seeped through the clean bandage. By the shadows on the wall, the sun had started to rise. Lydia slept next to him, her unruly hair spread over the pillow in a blaze of orange. He rolled over and placed a kiss on her cheek. Her eyes fluttered open and she blinked up at him, causing his heart to beat a little faster. "You are very beautiful while you sleep."

She sat up, brushing her hair away from her face. "How are you feeling?" she asked as she slipped into her robe and filled the basin with fresh water.

"Still a little sore," he replied truthfully. "But not so bad that I cannot ride."

She splashed water over her face before drying it with a towel. When she looked at him he had bunched the pillows behind his back and was watching her. She put aside the towel and sat on the side of the bed. She touched his shoulder. "This is healed nicely."

"I had good care," he murmured, dragging his finger down her cheek. She looked away, still troubled by how easily he could make her want him.

"Now what?" he asked, his voice flowing over her like the softest velvet. "After we are safely away from here, will you choose to go home without me?"

She gave an uncomfortable laugh and refused to look at him—afraid of what she'd see. "I can't very well take you home to meet my grandmother, can I?" She glanced down at her hands, missing Miguel's understanding smile. " 'Grandmama, I'd like to introduce you to a man who is rather well known . . . sought after by many a prominent businessman.' " She gave a little laugh to hide the pain in her heart. " 'But you must not tell anyone his name, Grandmama. You see, he's wanted by the—' "

"*Bonita*, look at me." He smiled when she met his gaze. He held out his hand, and when she took it, he pulled her close and kissed her for a long time, sinking his fingers into her hair. Slowly, he held her back, gazing deeply into her sad, green eyes. His expression changed, grew tender. "Soon, everything will be all right." He grasped her hands and gave her fingers a squeeze. "Marry me. You are my life, *mi amor*. And for you, I would do anything."

Her eyes filled with fresh tears. "Please, don't say that."

"Marry me," he repeated, refusing to let her up.

"Are you mad?" she said softly.

"*Sí*, madly in love with you."

She pulled her hands free, and shrugged out of her robe. "This is absurd."

"You think so?" When she looked at him, his brows were tightly together. "Then, like me, you are very good at pretending."

"I'm not pretending," she snapped, pulling on her chemise.

"Yes, you are, for you say something quite different from what I see in your eyes."

Dear Lord, he wasn't making it easy. Her chin quivered, but

169

she managed to blink back her tears as she stepped into her skirt and pulled on her blouse. "Love is one thing. Marriage is quite another, especially to . . ."

"A man like me," he finished.

"Yes!" she cried. "Do you think living our lives on the run is acceptable? I assure you it is not. I would rather—"

"Would rather what," he challenged.

"Stay here like the other women and wait to see if you return alive." She turned away, unable to meet the intensity of his gaze as she tucked in her blouse and tugged on her boots. "Marriage right now is impossible."

"Do you not remember my story? Nothing is impossible."

"Some things are, Miguel." She pulled her hair back and secured it with a ribbon.

"Why?" he demanded.

"Because," she stated glumly.

"Because why?" he asked impatiently.

She turned and raised her chin. "I could never condone what you do, no matter how badly we needed food . . . or . . . or shelter. I could never take what isn't mine, or accept it from you." She spun around, yet hesitated at the door. "No matter how I feel about you, or what you see in my eyes, our union would destroy my family, and I care too deeply for them to let that happen."

Out in the hall, Lydia leaned back against the door, telling herself it was best this way. For whom? she asked herself. Certainly not her. When she was with him, she couldn't think—felt hot and cold at the same time—ached to have him hold her.

"It's better for the family," she murmured, closing her eyes and seeing her grandmother's wrinkled features. She was an old woman. Could she endure the disgrace?

And what of Rebeccah and Sayer? Then there was her father, Santa Fe's respected and revered doctor. Could he bear the whispers? The gossip? Even the newspaper had focused on their family's good name. "Miss Lydia Randolph . . . not only beautiful, but sound and level-headed . . . an asset to the community." What would they print once they found out that the future Duchess of Wiltshire had run off with a man wanted for murder? She pressed her trembling fingertips to her lips to suppress the urge to shout the injustice of it. She drew in a shaky breath, determined to remain aloof. Yet that little voice kept nagging that he was just too irresistible—and she too lonely.

The rest of the day, Lydia spent with Carmen and Delora, helping them with their chores, teaching them more English as they tried to teach her more Spanish, while Carmen taught her how to make tortillas. They had finished that chore and moved to weed the small vegetable garden when Miguel came through the gate with his arms full.

"Here," he said. "Try this on." He gave her a brown and green serape, smiling when she slipped it over her head. "It fits well, *no?*"

Delora giggled, but both she and her mother agreed with Miguel.

Lydia glanced down at the garment that nearly engulfed her. "How could it not?"

His laughter soothed some of her trepidation. "It will keep you warm at night and will blend more easily with the rocks and trees." He pulled out a similar one for himself and tossed it over his head. "How do I look?"

"*Muy apuesto,*" Delora said with her usual dreamy smile.

"Yes, I agree," Lydia replied. "Very handsome, indeed. However, red and black is not the same as brown and green. I doubt you'll blend with anything on the trail."

"*No?*" The twinkle in his eyes made him even more appealing and teased her as he took off the serape and helped her out of hers. "Perhaps in the daylight, but we will be sleeping when the sun is high, traveling at night."

"It is true?" Delora said sadly. "You are leaving tomorrow?"

Miguel bent down, reached into a cloth sack and pulled out a small, elegantly dressed doll. "*Si, mi belleza pequena.* But, I promise that someday I will return."

The child nodded, then fell quiet for several moments while Miguel gave Carmen a sack. "This is for you." When the woman tried to give it back, Miguel refused. "Where is Alberto?"

"*Hola,*" Alberto said as he walked out of the house with the aid of a cane. Miguel acknowledged the man before he pulled out his wallet. The two men spoke for a while before Miguel pressed several bills into Alberto's hand. Alberto tried to give back some of the money, but Miguel persisted.

"What are they saying?" Lydia asked.

Delora looked up and smiled. "Antonio bought Poco for you. He gave my father much money, more than Papa thinks the horse is worth, but Antonio said he wanted to make sure Papa had enough to buy an even better horse, and a saddle, too."

Afterward, when they had accepted some of the tortillas and cheese, Lydia walked with Miguel toward the hotel. "When did you make the decision to leave?"

He stopped and looked at her for several moments. "When I saw the pain in your eyes. Pain I have caused you."

They walked in silence for several moments. "What else did you buy?" she asked.

"Some dried meat and dried fruit for our journey. They will keep better in the saddlebags. With the supplies you purchased, we should have nothing to worry about."

"Can horses see in the dark?" she asked.

"Better than we can," he said. He caught her hand. "Do not worry. You have learned very much. Poco will follow Diablo, and I will take care of everything else."

"Antonio, wait up."

Miguel swore softly under his breath, and put his finger on her lips to keep her from speaking. Slowly he turned and faced Juan. "*Hola,*" he said with a forced smile.

"So you are really leaving us?" Juan handed Miguel his gunbelt.

Miguel accepted it. "I cannot stay here forever, *amigo.*"

Juan shook his head. "No, I suppose not." His gaze landed on Lydia for several moments before he turned back to Miguel. "Take care. I would not want to see some *hombre* shoot you in the back to collect the reward."

Lydia sat on a flat rock near the river, deep in thought. They had left before sunup, and now it was nearly noon. Miguel insisted she rest while he watered the horses at the river. She thought about what lay ahead. Not so much about the journey, but what she would do once they arrived in Santa Fe. Was there a chance he could be tried and sentenced to jail instead of the gallows? How would her family react once they learned she had fallen in love with an outlaw?

She sighed and tossed a twig into the slowly moving water. When she glanced up, Miguel stood there. He had removed their saddles and hobbled the horses to let them graze. He sat next to her, their backs touching as he took off his hat and balanced it on his knee. "I have everything we need in my saddlebags to catch some fish. Would you like that?"

His question brought a smile to her lips. "Yes, I would. My sister says there is nothing better than freshly caught trout, roasted over hot coals."

He laughed. "*Bueno.* Come, help me collect some rocks." Soon, Miguel had a small fire burning in the circle of rocks they had made. He reached into his saddlebags and pulled out some ͏ne and a hook. He took his knife and cut a long narrow limb from a nearby tree and to one end fastened the line. "To be a good fisherman, one must use the right bait," he said.

She watched as he went back to his saddlebags and pulled out a small cloth. In the cloth was a chunk of salt pork, from which he cut off a small portion, which he skewered on the hook.

"Here," he put the pole in her hands and tossed the line into the water with an audible plop. Placing his finger over his lips, he motioned for her to sit down on the grass near the river. He sat beside her and leaned closer. "Now we wait."

Lydia held the pole. She only pretended to watch the line, watching him through her long lashes. Each time she looked at him lately, her heart twisted painfully with the knowledge that these precious moments would soon be lost forever.

She didn't have too much time to dwell on their future as the line jumped and she nearly dropped the pole. Miguel moved behind her and placed his hands over hers.

"Easy," he said softly, helping her land her first trout. "*Eee-ho-la.*" He grinned. "He is *muy gordo, no?*"

"Is that how you say slimy in Spanish?"

"No," he laughed. "It is how you say very fat." He held the trout up. "See for yourself. He has eaten a lot of worms and is very fat."

"Worms?" She made a face. "I rather think I shall pass on the trout."

Again his soft laughter made her smile.

He cut another piece of pork and slipped it on the hook. "Now that you have caught my dinner, you better catch your own."

"Oh, don't worry about me. You eat him." She glanced around the area. "I'll go find something else to eat."

"I will teach you how to do that, tomorrow." He pushed her down and put the pole in her hands. "Do not worry, *bonita,* it tastes much better than it looks. Remember the rabbit? You were skeptical then, too."

He pulled out his knife and went downstream as she turned her attention back to the line dancing in the river. By the time he returned with the gutted fish, she had caught another. He constructed two forked sticks that he stuck into the ground on either side of the fire. When the second trout was cleaned, he put both fish on another stick and placed them over the fire, resting the ends on the first two sticks.

"Very clever," she commented as she sat beside him on their saddle blankets. "You've never met my sister, Rebeccah, but when we were children, she was always the reluctant one. By this, I mean that she never wanted to learn anything new—wouldn't take any chances. I, being the elder, often teased her for being set in her ways." Lydia sighed. "Now, here I am, more set in my ways than ever I thought possible. If it wasn't for you, I would have never survived . . . nor would I ever have got on a horse. And, quite frankly, that was my first fish."

"No," he said, shaking his head. "I would have never guessed."

"Miguel, be serious."

"Does your sister ride?" he asked.

"Oh yes. Sayer insisted she learn. He even taught her how to shoot." She heaved a despondent sigh. "I, on the other hand, have no experience with pistols either. I'd probably be afraid to shoot one if I had one."

Miguel put his arm around her shoulders. "Do not be so hard on yourself. I know many women who do not ride, nor do they shoot guns." He placed a kiss on her cheek. "If it makes you feel better, after we are married, I will teach you all about horses as my grandfather taught me, *si?*"

She smiled at his sincere, yet boyish expression. "And will you teach me to shoot, also?"

His dark brows snapped together. "I will have to give that

more thought."

"Why?" she asked, amused by his worried expression. "If Sayer taught Becky, surely you could teach me. It can't possibly be that difficult."

"Yes, that is true. But I am not sure it would be wise to teach you how to shoot a gun."

"Why not?"

"Does your sister have red hair?"

"No, she's a blonde, but what has that got to do with learning how to shoot?"

"It has everything to do with it, *bonita*. Surely you as a nurse know these things?"

She gave an impatient sigh. "Will you stop assuming that because I am a nurse I know more than other women. Now quit being so evasive and answer my question."

"There, you have answered it yourself," he countered, looking over at her. "You are angry, *no?*"

"Yes. I am getting angry, and it's your fault. I ask a simple question and you . . . you speak in riddles until I am so frustrated I could . . . could choke you with my bare hands."

He turned, his eyes alive with mischief. "Precisely why I would prefer you never learn to use a gun."

She laughed with him. "Very well, but I still think it would be a good idea, especially since you are a wanted man." She sensed his good mood had vanished.

"Do not worry, *bonita*, I will teach you everything you will need to know." He leaned closer, slipping his hand behind her neck to pull her closer to receive his kiss. "Look what you have learned already."

She accepted another kiss, then whispered in his ear, "The food is burning."

He turned quickly to see to it.

"Perhaps I will teach you how to cook," she said with a

superior grin.

"We will have a maid," he countered. "You will be too busy learning how to ride and shoot to do much cooking."

His answer conjured up another question, a possible solution to her dilemma. "Where are you from?"

His grin was back to being cocky. "Mexico."

"I knew that," she scolded, even though his answer delighted her. He would be safe in Mexico, and, in time, she could learn to love it as much as she did the Territory of New Mexico. "Where do you live, what part?"

"I have a modest hacienda on five hundred acres in *Zaragoza*. It is small, but joins my uncle's *rancho*. He wants me to assist him with the breeding of horses and raising cattle. Diablo has sired many foals, all as dark and as beautiful as he is."

Though she doubted the validity of his statement, she decided not to challenge him. "I miss my family, too," Lydia said with a tinge of sadness in her voice. "My sister just had her baby a few days before I was captured."

"What did she have, a *chico* or a *chica?*" Miguel asked as he tested the trout for doneness.

"I'm assuming you said boy or girl?" She accepted a small piece, savoring the taste as he put the stick back over the coals.

"*Si,* you are getting better with your Spanish."

Lydia laughed, totally aware that her Spanish was awful. Once they were in Mexico, she would have plenty of time to improve. "She had a darling little girl."

"*Vamos a tener muchos bebes hermosos*—we will have many beautiful babies." He handed her the stick and kissed her temple. "Mostly *chicos*. Boys."

She smiled and shook her head. He made it easy to push aside the seriousness of his situation, and now that she had decided where they would go, she felt as if a great weight had been lifted off her shoulders. With her fortune, Miguel would no longer have to rob banks to survive. "How many children do you want?" she asked cheerfully.

He shrugged his shoulders as he pulled off a piece of meat and popped it into his mouth. "Let me see. If we are married very soon and we stay married for twenty years . . . I would think we could have fifteen . . . maybe twenty little ones, *no?*"

"Fifteen or twenty?" she repeated in shock as he took another piece.

His eyes glittered with roguish humor as he pulled off another piece and fed it to her. "Do you want more?"

"No," she cried in disbelief. "I-I—"

"Good," he said with a wink, pulling off more of the savory trout. "I must tend to the ranch some of the time." His expression softened and she knew he'd grown serious as he chewed and swallowed. "I will be content with just you, *vida mia.*"

"And I with you," she said, accepting his kiss. "But a family . . . someday . . . will be nice."

"*Si,* perhaps a daughter for you and a son for me."

She liked the sound of that. When they were finished, he stood and took the stick with the leftover trout and tossed it far away from their camp. "Tonight, some animal will finish our feast. But now we must rest or we will be too tired to continue on our journey."

Chapter Sixteen

Raul slipped out of the barn after putting his tired horse into a stall. Although he was tired and didn't want to make the long trip so soon, Antonio had insisted that they ride back to Rio Salado the very next morning. While Antonio waited in a copse of trees, Raul entered the compound with a message for Juan. The sun squatted on the bluff when Raul banged on Juan's door.

"What are you doing back so soon?" Juan asked. "Mama is about to put supper on the table. I will talk with you later." He would have closed the door, but Raul put his hand on it.

"I have a message from Antonio."

Juan frowned. "He left early this morning. What could he possibly have to say?"

Raul shook his head. "No. This message is from the real Antonio. He is waiting outside the gate to speak with you."

"He is back?" Juan asked as he grabbed his sombrero off the hook.

"He was never here," Raul said with a worried frown.

"What in the hell are you saying?"

"I am saying that the man who calls himself Antonio is an imposter. He is really Don Miguel Estrada."

Lydia stretched and yawned. The sun slipped behind the distant mountains, turning the landscape a brilliant orange, but also dropping the temperature.

"It is beautiful here, no?" Miguel asked as he tossed a saddle on Diablo's back and tugged the cinch tight.

"Yes, it is," she said wistfully, shrugging on her serape. He finished saddling the horses and reached for her. She leaned into his arms, delighted with the way he held her for several moments before helping her into the saddle.

"You are sore?"

"A little," she confessed. "I think I still prefer a horse and buggy."

He gave her a patient smile and swung up on his stallion. "We will only ride for a little while and then rest for a little while until you are more used to it."

She followed him along a narrow trail. "It's a shame that the people in Rio Salado don't send Juan and his outlaws away and reclaim their village. I already miss Carmen and her family."

"Who would feed them?" Miguel asked. "It is the money Juan collects from the *banditos* that supplies the people with food."

"I suppose, but if Juan wasn't there, someone like . . . like Carmen could manage the hotel, rent rooms to travelers."

"I do not think many people know where this place is hidden in the canyon," he replied as he tossed her a glance.

"A sign on the trail would remedy that. Carmen and her husband could make a good, honest living there with just a little encouragement."

She smiled when Miguel gave her a proud smile. "You are a very intelligent woman, *bonita*. My father will like that trait."

"It's your mother that worries me. What if she doesn't like me?"

"She will love you. Especially your courage. Though the men in the Estrada family are good providers . . . and lovers," he added with a sly grin, "it is the strength of our women that holds the family together."

He nudged Diablo a little closer and gave her a quick kiss. "You are a fearless woman. I knew it the moment you took a swing at the men who attacked you near your sister's ranch."

They rode a few more hours, unable to converse as the trail became steep, and in the dark it looked treacherous. Lydia clung to the saddle horn, straining her eyes. "Are you sure the horses can see?"

"It is as I told you," he said. "They can see better than we. You must learn to relax. The more time you spend on Poco, the better equestrian you will become. And," he continued, "look how many miles we have traveled with two horses instead of one."

"Miguel," she said when the trail grew a little wider and she encouraged Poco to walk beside Diablo, "I've been thinking. If we were to stop at the next town, I could send my family a telegram telling them that I'm safe. Then we could go south toward Mexico to your ranch . . . and get married."

He pulled his stallion to a halt and Poco stopped without her asking. In the dark, she couldn't see Miguel's expression, but sensed he was pleased. "Is this what you want, *vida mia?*"

"Yes," she said.

He was quiet for a long time.

"Very well. Do you remember passing an old abandoned ranch?"

"Yes, but why is that important?"

"If we go to Mexico, it would be wiser to follow the river, and in order to do that, we must go back."

"But that was an hour ago."

His soft laughter floated over her as he turned Diablo back the way they came. "If you want to go to Mexico, it is the price we must pay."

Juan motioned for Antonio to take a chair at the table in the darkened corner of the cantina at Rio Salado. "Sit. I do not want anyone to see you."

"Who will see, hey? Not even Raul could recognize me with this beard."

Juan stared at Antonio for several moments and shook his head. "The resemblance is amazing." Juan poured his old friend a shot of tequila, watching as Antonio tossed it down his throat.

"I assume you are speaking of this *hombre* who looks like me?" Antonio stated, dragging his hand across his mouth.

"If you were standing side by side, perhaps I could tell the difference." Juan continued to stare at his friend, pointing at his eyes. "Now I see it."

"See what?" Antonio growled.

"It is here, in the eyes. His are like the blue on the barrel of a gun." Juan shook his head. "The *cabron* will rue the day he tricked me."

"He is no *cabron, amigo*. He is Don Fernando's nephew, and Don Enrico Estrada's only son."

Juan's brows snapped together. "You do not look particularly worried about this, yet we both know that Don Fernando will avenge his nephew if anything should happen to him."

"*Si,* that is why we must make sure nothing happens, at least until we want it to." Antonio leaned a little closer, lowering his voice so the others in the cantina wouldn't hear. "That is not all. Raul said he was with a woman."

"*Si,* a very beautiful redhead . . . a nurse."

Antonio gave a sinister smile. "I have learned that she is Lydia Randolph, heiress to her grandmother's fortune." He grabbed the bottle and refilled the small glass.

"Are you certain of this?"

"*Si.* Her grandmother is a noblewoman from England. I overheard two deputies talking about her in Albuquerque. They were looking for her, said she had been kidnapped by me." He lifted his glass and took a sip of tequila. "Once I heard my name, I listened very carefully."

Juan grew quiet for several moments. "This is very interesting, *amigo*." A slow smile spread across his features. "If what you say is true, we could be rich men very soon, no?"

"*Sí*. Very rich," Antonio agreed.

"But there is a problem we have not considered." Juan wiped his hand over his whiskered chin. "If we ask for ransom and their families pay it, then we must let them go."

Antonio laughed. "Why must we do that?" He filled Juan's glass. "You act like we are men with honor." Both men laughed.

"If we kill them, what will stop Don Fernando for avenging his nephew's death?"

"An ocean, *amigo*." Antonio raised his glass and admired the golden liquid in it. "I, for one, have always wanted to live in Spain, and with the ransom money we get, we can both soon do so."

Juan hesitated for a moment then grinned. "I see," he said, nodding. "I had not thought of that before now." He called over the barkeep. "Another bottle for me and my *amigo*."

Antonio shook his head. "Not for me. I need a clear head. We must leave immediately. The sooner we capture Miguel and his woman, the sooner we will all be rich."

Juan stood with him, catching his arm. "What about Raul?"

"We will need Raul and a few others we can trust to help."

"But if we do that, we will have to promise to share the money."

Antonio shook his head. "After Miguel and the woman are our prisoners, and once we collect the ransom, we will simply break our promise, no?"

Juan frowned at first, and then he smiled. "I like your plan, but do me a favor and shave. I want to see Miguel's expression

183

when he looks upon the face of the real Antonio Garcia."

Sayer swung down from Rounder and tied him to a stout tree. He scanned the area before he crouched down and inspected the remains of a long dead fire. He stood with a sigh, dusting his hands off on his pants. "No telling how long ago this happened," he growled when Fergus came over. "We've been on the trail over a week with very little to show for it."

"There are a few tracks over there, but nothin' goin' in any particular direction.

"Well, this is as good a place as any to make camp." Sayer tossed some twigs on the ashes, stopping when Rounder suddenly spun and gazed off in a different direction.

Sayer and Fergus exchanged glances before they went to the horses, untied them and led them behind the cover of the rocky cliff. Sayer drew his Army-issue Colt, and carefully glanced around the rock to get a look at the approaching riders. Fergus came up behind him.

"How many?" Fergus whispered.

Sayer held up two fingers. He motioned for Fergus to stay put, then carefully made his way around to the other side, using the thick sage as cover. Two Mexican horsemen rode into the small clearing. Dressed in coarse-wool serapes and large sombreros, their faces were hidden from view. The leader spoke to the other in Spanish, and for a moment Sayer thought he recognized the voice.

"Hold it right there," Sayer warned as he stepped out from his hiding place with his gun drawn. The smaller man raised his arms, but the leader ignored the command.

"I do not believe you would shoot an old friend, Colonel." The leader pushed his sombrero back off his forehead and grinned. "*Buenos tardes, mi amigo.* It has been a long time, no?" Both he and the other man climbed down from their horses.

"Well, I'll be damned," Sayer replied, holstering his gun. "What in blazes are you doing way out here?"

Fernando motioned to his companion. "This is my *amigo,* Jorge. And, this is the man to whom I owe my life, Colonel Sayer MacLaren."

Fergus came around and eyed Fernando. "I thought you were dead."

Fernando gave the sergeant a wide grin. "I was only pretending." He handed his reins to his comrade. "As you can see, I am alive and well."

Fergus gave a disgusted snort frowning at Sayer. "Would you like tae explain?"

Sayer patted Fergus on the back. "After you help Jorge with the horses."

By the time the fire had turned into glowing red coals, Fergus and Jorge were asleep and snoring in their bedrolls. Sayer heaved a tired sigh as he and Fernando sipped the last of the coffee and exchanged information. "I'm hoping when we get to Torreon tomorrow, there will be a telegram waiting from Doc Randolph saying Lydia's home, but I'm not holding my breath either."

"Jorge and I will ride with you," Fernando stated.

"I'm not so sure it would be wise to show yourself."

"No one will know me." Fernando's frown deepened. "I must avenge my nephew and help you find *Señorita* Lydia. I have heard of these men, Antonio Garcia and his cousin Raul. Both of them are ruthless *cabrons* who cannot be trusted. They would kill each other for the right price. If *Señorita* Lydia has been with them this long . . ." Fernando shook his head. "I pray she has not."

Sayer heaved a tired sigh, feeling the need to think of something other than Lydia and her grim situation. "I'm sorry about your nephew. I looked forward to making a deal to have his stallion breed a few of my mares in exchange for Rounder breeding a few of his mares." Sayer put down his cup and reached into his saddlebags. "Look at this."

"What is it?" Fernando asked absently. He unfolded the poster, leaning closer to the coals for better light. *"Dios mio,"* he breathed. "There must be some mistake? This is Miguel, but—"

"Look closer. What does it say?" Sayer waited until Fernando finished reading. "Your nephew's eyes weren't brown, and I don't remember any scar."

"No, they are . . . they were a dark blue. You remember my mother, no? She was born in Spain and her eyes are blue as are my sister's." Fernando shook his head sadly. "Miguel was their only son. Enrico took the news badly." He handed the poster back to Sayer. "So why did you show this to me?"

Sayer shrugged his shoulders. "I've been thinking that the men who took Lydia are most likely the ones who killed Miguel. If that's true, they might still have his horse."

"*Si*, Diablo. Enrico gave Miguel the black colt for his twenty-first birthday."

"If I recall, he's no ordinary animal. Someone's bound to remember seeing him."

"And if they do, we will know we are after the right *hombres.*" Fernando leaned back against the log. "I will not rest until I see his killer hang." Fernando fell quiet for a very long time. "So, here we are, *amigos* once more, only now you are married and have a baby daughter that, I am sure, looks just like her beautiful mother." Fernando shook his head and smiled. "I am happy for you, *amigo* . . . more than you know."

"Yeah, my life turned out all right," Sayer replied, yawning. "And you? Did your wife take you back?"

Fernando's smile was answer enough. "*Si*, she took me back and more. We are expecting our third child in a few months."

"Congratulations."

"Pray it is a boy. With the girls, my mother and my wife, I am surrounded by women."

Sayer laughed at his friend's expression and held up his cup. "To a boy—make it twin boys."

Fernando drank to Sayer's toast, and then heaved a very satisfied sigh. "I am a lucky man."

"Yeah," Sayer repeated, his voice tinged with sarcasm. "Lucky and rich." He grinned when Fernando flashed him a wounded look. "You, my friend, are a very imaginative man. First you dress your men up like Indians, fooling everyone including myself, then you hide the loot in the last place anyone would want to look." Sayer shook his head. "Yeah, as I think back, I must admit. I never would've searched the casket for the stolen money."

"I gave most of it back," Fernando defended. "I had to have a little . . . to rebuild."

"A little?" Sayer countered. "I reckon you had enough to buy half of Mexico."

"Only a few thousand acres, I assure you. Think of my unborn son, my daughters. They will need an inheritance, no?" The two men laughed again. "And what about you, hey? I have heard about the Duchess of Wiltshire and the fortune she brought from England. I remember you saying a soldier's pay was nothing to brag about. Did you use the money I left behind to buy my *rancho?*"

"That went back to the people you stole it from. Rebeccah's grandmother bought the ranch and gave it to us as a wedding present. Seems the old gal kept a secret for a long time—a dream to raise horses."

"No, a lady of her standing?"

"Yup. We're partners. And, surprisingly enough, the old gal has a good eye for sound horses. I supply Rounder and the know-how, and she supplies the money to purchase breeding stock. We split the profit fifty-fifty."

Fernando's expression grew serious. "Diablo was imported from Spain." Fernando stood and stretched. "Jorge and I will help you find *Señorita* Lydia. And perhaps you will help me find the man who killed my nephew and stole his horse. I will give you one of Diablo's sons as a token of my appreciation." When Sayer tried to protest, Fernando held up his hand. "Miguel would have wanted it that way. He also had a dream to raise fine horses."

"I'm thinking if we find his horse, we'll find the man who murdered him." Sayer stood and kicked some dirt on the dying coals. "We'll head out at first light and be in Torreon by nightfall."

CHAPTER SEVENTEEN

Before Lydia realized it, the outline of a barn and a house could be seen in the distance.

"There, *bonita,* your castle awaits."

Her hopes dwindled at the sight of what was once a large adobe home. Now mostly in ruins, the glass was broken in the windows and the front door hung askew. A windmill groaned in the breeze to the left of the house, but by the rust on the pump's handle, it had been a long time without use.

Miguel swung down and lifted her off her horse. She winced and spread her fingers over her back. "Do you want help with the horses?"

It felt good to walk beside him—to work some of the stiffness out of her legs while she and Miguel unsaddled the horses before turning them loose in the corral. When the horses were munching the abundant weeds, Miguel found a bucket and led her to the pump.

He worked the handle, and after a little while, the water ran clear. She pulled the ribbon from her hair and washed it as best she could, enjoying the feeling of cold, clean water in the warmth of the morning sun. When she finished, she cupped her hands and drank. Together they watered the horses, and after Miguel washed, they went into the old house. Lydia glanced around and righted a still usable stool. "Well," she said, dusting off her hands. "It's not too awful, is it?"

Miguel glanced around. "Not bad at all." He inspected the

stone hearth. "It's too dark to tell if there is something living in the chimney, but—"

"What could possibly live in there?"

"A bird could have made its nest, or some mice could—"

"Mice?" She cast a cautious glance around. "Do you think there are mice in here?"

Miguel smiled as he took her hand and pressed it between his own. "Of course not. Why would they want to live in this dusty old house when they have everything they need outdoors?"

She jerked her hand away. "Don't mock me. I hate mice."

He raised his brows innocently. "I would never. However, if I were a mouse, I would probably think this old house would make a very nice home for me and my family."

"There's probably more than one. Is that what you're saying?"

"If there are, *bonita*, they will be as frightened of you as you are of them."

"I'm not afraid of a silly little thing like a mouse," she lied. "I just don't like the way they scurry about. Now, why don't you try and find us a nice fat rabbit while I tidy up a bit?"

"That is a wonderful idea." He checked his revolver, then kissed her forehead.

Lydia's stomach rumbled, causing him to give her one of his lazy smiles. "I will hurry, *vida mia.*"

After he left, Lydia bent to the task of clearing off the table and making a place where they could sit and eat. She found an old broom and swept away a little of the dust and dirt, but the house appeared to be in hopeless disarray. When she stooped to pick up a broken board, a mouse scurried away into a dark corner. She jumped back, taking a deep breath to calm her nerves, jumping again when she heard a distant gunshot.

Cautiously, she gathered enough pieces of a broken chair to fill the hearth and make a good fire. Afterwards, she swept off the raised stone hearth, deciding that it would be nice to sit there while they ate.

A little while later, Miguel came in with a skinned rabbit, skewered on a stick. Together they made a fire, sitting together on the hearth while the meat cooked, filling the room with its luscious aroma.

"It's rather frightening to think that a family used to live here, isn't it?" she asked watching as Miguel turned the stick.

"*Si*, we are lucky compared to others, no?"

She scooted closer and leaned her head on his shoulder. "Yes, we are."

She watched as he roasted the meat. After it started dripping juice, he took his knife from his boot and tested the meat for doneness, then gave her the stick to hold while he cut more meat.

"Here," he urged, holding it while she took a bite. "*Bueno, no?*"

"Yes, it is very good and *muy caliente.*" She blew on the meat to cool it off.

"See, soon, you will be able to speak my language as if you were born in Mexico." They ate, and after they had their fill of roasted rabbit and tortillas, Miguel went outside and carried in a bucket of water. He found a small kettle and set it on the coals before he left her to wash while he tended to the horses.

The hot water felt good as she washed her hands and face. She heard his footsteps and asked if he'd like any of the water, but realized when she glanced his direction that he had washed outside.

"Come. It is too hot in here to sleep." He caught her hand and led her toward the barn where he had spread the saddle blankets over a thick bed of straw. "It isn't much, a little cooler, but better than sleeping on the ground. And," he added, "I chased away all the mice. Diablo hates mice too."

He pulled her into his embrace. "This has been the best two weeks of my life."

She gave a small, doubtful laugh. "Oh yes, you've nearly been killed twice, we've been dragged across brutally rough country, imprisoned in that . . . that outlaws' fortress, yet it's been the best two weeks of your life?"

"*Si,* you finally agreed to marry me."

She tried to smile. "Miguel, please, can't you be serious for even a moment?"

"Listen to me, *vida mia,* I may tease about many things, but marriage—never. I have never asked any woman to be my wife. I want to spend the rest of my life with you." He touched his fingertip to her mouth when she started to speak. "I know there will be obstacles ahead of us. We are, for a fact, from two different countries, both of us with family obligations."

His expression softened as he kissed her slowly, sensually, pressing her close. He paused for several moments and his expression grew more serious. He took off the delicate chain and cross, caught her hand and placed it in her palm.

"If we should get separated, *vida mia*—"

"Separated?"

He touched his finger to her lips again. "You can take this to my family and they will know that I have given you my heart, and they will take care of you." He folded her fingers over the cross.

His tender words brought tears to her eyes. "I have no intention of letting you out of my sight," she said, trying to give him back the crucifix.

"Shush," he whispered. "Keep it. It will keep you safe, and by God's grace, should you already carry my child, he is entitled to all that I own."

His explanation shook her to the core. Tears burned behind her eyes as he took the chain, turned her around and fastened it around her neck, pausing only to kiss the spot his fingers had touched.

"Let me see," he added, his smile dissolving some of her fear. "It looks better on you than on me, no?" He didn't give her time to answer as he pulled her down, stretching out beside her.

Lydia raised her head and glanced around. At first she felt a little disoriented, but quickly realized that they were still in the old abandoned barn. She got up and brushed a few bits of straw from her skirt and serape, then tucked a wayward curl behind her ear. By the pink light coming through several broken slats, she saw it was barely dawn as she gathered up their blankets and Miguel saddled the horses.

"Ah, good you brought the blankets. I thought that we would get an early start. Later when the sun is high, we will stop and eat."

"That sounds good to me," she agreed, shaking the blankets before she rolled them to be tied behind their saddles. Afterward, she accepted his help to mount. He swung up on Diablo and motioned for her to follow as they rode out of the barn. "Come, it is a beautiful morning. See for yourself."

"*Buenos tardes, hombre.*" With a sickening feeling, Miguel recognized Raul's voice. When he turned, six others, men he didn't recognize, stepped out of the old house with a variety of weapons aimed in his direction.

"There is no need for guns," Miguel said with a forced smile. "Tell me why you are here."

"I think you know, *amigo.*" Juan's voice was laced with contempt as he came from the side of the barn and walked toward them. He cradled a rifle in the crook of his arm. "Both of you get down, slow and easy."

"You are making a big mistake," Miguel began as he slowly dismounted. He turned and helped Lydia down, keeping himself

193

protectively between her and Juan.

"Do you think so?" Juan challenged. "I think you have been keeping something from us. Something that can make us very rich, no?"

"Let her go. She is not who you want," Miguel replied, taking a step toward Juan. One of the men from the six surrounding them stepped forward. Slowly he lifted his head and pushed back his sombrero. It was like looking in a mirror. Instead of waving his pistol around and hollering insults like the others, the bandit's dark eyes never left Miguel's, nor did his finger ever leave the trigger of the weapon he pressed against Miguel's chest.

Antonio Garcia stood before him, and by the way he stared at Miguel, he saw the likeness too.

"My God," Lydia whispered as her mouth went dry.

"So, you are Don Miguel Estrada?" Antonio asked. Without warning, he hammered his fist into Miguel's middle, doubling him over. "I do not like it when someone uses my name."

"Don't do anything foolish, Antonio," Juan ordered. "They are no use to us dead. Get the *puta* inside, and don't let her out of your sight."

Lydia began to struggle until she looked at Miguel.

"Go," he encouraged. He tried to give her a reassuring smile, but he knew by the terror in her eyes he had failed. "Go," he repeated. "They need us both alive, *bonita*. Everything will be all right."

"No. Tell them who I am." She glared at the man who held her. "My name is—"

"We know who you are," Antonio replied contemptuously.

"Say nothing," Miguel warned, turning his attention to Antonio. "Harm her and I will—"

Antonio backhanded Miguel across the face. At the same time, Lydia renewed her struggles with even more energy.

"Leave him alone," she cried.

"She is a feisty one, no?" Antonio leered.

Miguel wiped the blood from his mouth. "My family is very wealthy," he said, the tiny muscle above his jaw pulsating spasmodically. "Let her go and I will arrange for—"

"For what?" Antonio sneered. "A ransom?" Antonio laughed, as did Juan and the others.

"You do not understand." Miguel took a step, but stopped when he heard guns being cocked.

Antonio's expression grew even more terrible when he grinned, his eyes glinting with malice. "As you pretended to be me, I will pretend to be you."

Raul came and stood beside Antonio. *"Eee-ho-la,"* Raul said grinning as he looked at his cousin then back at Miguel. "See, it is like I said, no? He looks just like you."

Miguel never looked away, matching Antonio's stare with one as steady.

"Take off your clothes, *cabron,* and give them to me," Antonio ordered. He cast a quick glance at the others. "I will look good dripping in silver *conchos, si?"*

"Si," they all agreed.

Miguel took off his serape, exposing the weapon strapped to his hip. Once more the men made threatening comments.

Juan grabbed Lydia's arm and pulled her back a few steps as he motioned with his rifle. "Take his gunbelt and hide his horse in the barn. Tie the animal well, he's too good a horse to lose."

Raul spat on the ground. "Too fine for a dead man, hey?"

Antonio raised his pistol and dragged the barrel across Miguel's cheek. "I think, when you and I trade clothes, no one will know who the real *bandito* is, no?"

"Hey, Antonio," one of the men called, drawing the leader's attention. "Dressing like a gentleman won't make you one." The

195

others joined in with several lewd remarks and boisterous laughter.

"I bet I could ride up to the front door of Don Fernando's rancho and be treated like family." Antonio walked over to Lydia and grasped her chin between his fingers. "Who knows? Maybe even your woman could not tell the difference."

"I can see a definite difference," she hissed. "You're a pig." She turned her face away as the others laughed and tossed in their remarks.

"Let her go," Miguel began, relieved when Antonio turned away from Lydia. "When my uncle comes for me, and I assure you, he will come . . ." He paused, his gaze never wavering. "I will ask him to spare your life."

Antonio stared at Miguel then tipped his head back and laughed. "I do not think he will be looking for you. You see, he thinks you are dead." Antonio grinned. "Once I have your clothes and your horse, and we send them back to him, I am sure he will agree that there was a mistake. He will be eager to pay for the return of his favorite nephew. And we cannot forget your father, Don Enrico. I wonder how much he will pay for the life of his only son. Now, do as I say and take off your jacket, and your ring as well."

While the men teased their leader, Miguel slowly took off the ring and dropped it in Antonio's hand. The bandit quickly put it on and raised his hand to show the others. Next, Miguel began to remove his bolero, and without warning tossed his serape at the horses' heads. They reared at the same time he drew his gun and fired point blank at Antonio—the bandit died with a bullet between the eyes before he hit the ground.

Lydia wrenched free, spun and kicked Juan as hard as she could. He howled in pain, jumping on one leg. Another man grabbed her, slapped her hard and dragged her toward the barn.

Miguel fired again, his bullet grazing Juan's shoulder. Juan sank to his knees, groaning in pain. Miguel dropped and rolled under an old wagon, shooting one man in the leg and another in the chest. Using the wagon wheels as cover, he fired two more shots, dodging as return fire sent dirt and bits of gravel into his face.

Trying to find Lydia through the dust, he quickly reloaded and fired again. His first shot missed, but his second hit dead-center in the last man's chest. The bandit staggered a few steps and fell. Miguel rolled out from under the wagon then ran toward the cover of the house. He heard Juan shout and a bullet zinged past his head. He cast a quick glance over his shoulder and saw Raul scramble up on Lydia's horse. A moment later, he heard the sound of hoof beats gaining on him.

"*Cabron,*" Raul shouted, "you killed my cousin."

Miguel barely had time to jump out of the animal's way. He hit the ground hard, his gun knocked from his hand. Dazed, it took him several moments to get to his feet. But Raul turned, charged and fired. A bullet tore into Miguel's upper left chest knocking him to his knees.

"*Cabron,*" Raul repeated and fired again.

Pain exploded in Miguel's head before everything went black.

"*Cabron,*" Raul repeated as he stepped down from the prancing horse, his smoking gun still clutched in his hand. "Get up," he growled. Furious, he kicked Miguel in the ribs. "Get up," he said again. When Miguel still didn't move, Raul kicked him again.

Juan clutched his wounded arm and slowly got to his feet. "Stop it, you fool. If he isn't already dead, we need him alive."

Raul swore in Spanish, and pointed his gun at Miguel, his finger tensing on the trigger. "He's alive, but I should kill him for what he has done," he snarled.

"Kill him, and Don Fernando will never rest until we are both dead, and you know it. Go and hitch some horses to that wagon. We will take him and the woman back to Rio Salado."

Raul sniffed and slowly let the gun fall to his side, where he slammed it back into his holster. He dragged his sleeve over his eyes.

"Perhaps you are right," he grumbled as he walked away. "A quick death is too good for him."

CHAPTER EIGHTEEN

Miguel couldn't tell how long he'd been lying face down in the dusty straw. He vaguely remembered being thrown in a wagon, and hearing Juan explain to Raul why there weren't any guards at the gate of Rio Salado. They had said something about a woman missing, but now all he knew was that he felt hot and thirsty. The buzzing of insects seemed to reverberate through his head, and when he dragged his hand up to rub his eyes, his fingers came away sticky with blood, and his shoulder began to throb.

"*Ahhh Dios*," he groaned as he rolled onto his back. He tried to open his eyes, but the light was too bright, the pain in his head and shoulder more intense.

"Get up, *hombre*."

In spite of the annoying light swinging above his head, Miguel forced his eyes open at the sound of Raul's voice. He dragged himself upright, leaning back against the railing of Diablo's stall while Raul took another drink from a bottle he had clutched in his hand.

"Where is Lydia?" Miguel demanded past the revived agony in his skull. "What have you done with her?"

"She is none of your concern."

"Harm her and I will—"

"What will you do, hey? Nothing," Raul spat, swaying a little.

"There is nothing here for you," Miguel replied, trying to think past his pain. "You are a wanted man. I told you before,

199

my family will make you rich, but first you must take her to them."

"Do you think I am a fool?" Raul grabbed a fistful of Miguel's hair and jerked his head back, ignoring his painful groan. "Look at me," Raul snarled, his breath foul. "I could kill you now and be done with it and still collect the ransom. But that wouldn't make you pay for killing my cousin."

Miguel fought the urge to pass out, drawing in several painful breaths. "M-my family will come for me. There will be no place for a dog like you to hide."

Raul planted his boot in Miguel's middle. *"Cabron,"* he shouted. He kicked out again, but in his drunken state, his boot only grazed Miguel's cheek.

Another man came in, grimacing at the sight of fresh blood on the prisoner's face. He shoved Raul back before he rolled the unconscious man over and pressed his ear to his chest. "Lucky for you, he's still kicking or Juan would have your head. Juan's *muy enojado* about losing the woman. He sent me to take him to the jail in case she tries to rescue him."

"The *puta* will be crawling back here as soon as she gets hungry. She is too weak to survive alone." Raul gave a disgusted grunt and spat on the ground close to Miguel.

"Why did you do that for? You got spit on my boot." The man gave Raul a dirty look and shoved him back. "Get away from me." He stood and with a grunt hoisted Miguel over his shoulder.

Lydia sat huddled on the ground. Her heart hammered against her breast, but that was nothing compared to the visions of Miguel, motionless in the wagon, covered in blood, next to the body of Antonio Garcia. She angrily swiped at a tear, wincing when she touched her bruised cheek, silently scolding herself for not taking a gun when she'd had the chance.

If only she had been faster, more aggressive, perhaps she could have been more help. But, instead, she had been afraid. Afraid the guard struck by a stray bullet would waken before she could escape. But when she saw he was dead, she had donned his serape and sombrero and stayed in the shadows until she could get to the scattered horses. She had found Poco and scrambled up on his back, digging her heels into his ribs.

She vaguely heard Raul and Juan calling her name, but she paid them no mind. She had fooled them, and they were angry. But she only rode a short distance, watching from some cedar trees as they tied Diablo to the old wagon. After they were a safe distance away, she followed.

When at last she made it to Rio Salado, it was dark, but close to dawn, and though she wondered why there weren't any guards, she gave the matter only a passing thought. She hurriedly unsaddled Poco, hiding the tack under some bushes, before she put the animal in a corral with other horses, praying he wouldn't be noticed. Now, hidden between two rain barrels behind the hotel, she felt safe for a while—at least until she could figure out how to rescue Miguel.

As the day wore on, she crouched down under her stolen serape, pulling the guard's sombrero farther over her face as Miguel had shown her when they were in Torreon. With darkness came despair. She touched his crucifix, offering prayer after prayer. When she couldn't keep her eyes open any longer, she dozed, ignoring the hungry rumbling of her stomach—the pain in her heart too intense to think of anything but helping Miguel.

Salena dried her tears and gazed down at the ring she had taken from Antonio's cold finger. A hundred stubby candles flickered on the wall of the church, casting the room in dancing shadows. The women who had washed his body and prepared him for burial had left, and now she was alone with only this small token.

No wonder the man she thought to be him had spurned her; he had been an imposter. Did he think because he was a rich nobleman that he was too good for her? Sniffing loudly, she picked up Antonio's bolero and took out his wallet. She took all the money and slipped it in her pocket with the ring. As an afterthought, she kissed her fingertip and touched it to her lover's cold lips.

"*Adios,*" she murmured.

She slipped outside, covering her long black hair with her colorful shawl. Staying to the shadows, she stepped into the barn and went directly to Diablo. Speaking softly in Spanish, she led the stallion out of his stall.

Miguel tried to move to a more comfortable position, but each time he stirred, the pain in his head and shoulder intensified. He opened his eyes, but his vision was cloudy. There were bars all around him, and in his befuddled state of mind he couldn't determine his whereabouts.

"*Agua,*" he rasped, trembling with cold. He waited for what felt like an eternity, but no one came. Submitting to the desire to sleep, he curled his knees up to his chest and prayed that Lydia was safe.

Lydia awoke with a start and pushed the sombrero back off her forehead. The sun appeared to be a fiery orange ball on the horizon turning the adobe houses a bright gold. She stood slowly, wincing as stiff muscles rebelled. Keeping to the backs and sides of the building, she carefully scanned the area, then hurried to Delora's house and knocked softly on the door.

"*Señorita?*" Delora asked, rubbing the sleep from her eyes. Her mother said something in Spanish and after the child answered, she stepped aside. "Mama says to come in."

Delora's parents were sitting at the table in the small kitchen, and when she entered, they exchanged worried glances. Lydia lifted her chin a little higher, unsure of what they would do.

"Carmen, I need your help," she said frantically. "You've got to help me. The man who you've been calling Antonio, he's really Don Miguel Estrada."

Carmen spoke in Spanish with her husband. "Alberto says he knows, that when he saw them bring two men back in a wagon he went over and spoke with Juan."

"Did you see where they took Miguel?" Lydia cried. "Is he alive?"

Again Carmen spoke with her husband. "He is alive, but he is badly hurt."

Lydia sank down on a wicker chair as all the stories her father had told her about head wounds flashed through her mind. Alberto seemed very concerned, tugging at his wife's sleeve until she gave him her full attention.

"Mama?" Delora said in a small voice. "Anto . . . Miguel was very nice to me. He gave me a new doll."

Carmen and Alberto conversed, and soon they seemed to agree. Carmen gave her husband a kiss on the cheek, went to the cupboard and filled a cup with hot coffee, pressing it into Lydia's cold hands.

"Do not worry, *señorita*," Carmen said, and turned to speak with Delora.

"My Mama says her brother will not search for you here. My Papa and Mama will help you, but we must wait until dark."

"But they don't understand. Miguel needs immediate attention."

"*Si*, I know." Delora spoke with her mother, and Carmen's expression filled with understanding as she conversed in Spanish with her daughter.

"Mama says it is too dangerous to try to help now. Tonight, my Papa's cousin guards Don Miguel."

Carmen put her hand on Lydia's shoulder as Delora continued. "My Papa's cousin owes my Papa a favor, and we can trust him to keep a secret."

Salena rode the stallion into Torreon. It was very early, still dark outside, but after she woke the boy at the livery and gave him a dollar, he agreed to unsaddle the big horse and put him in a stall.

"I will take those," she said as the boy lifted off the saddlebags.

She snatched them away, sat on a bale of hay and searched through them. With only the light of a single lamp, she lifted out a fancy black wallet, gasping when she looked inside. She quickly shoved the wad of bills into her pocket, then returned the wallet back to the bags.

Tossing it over her shoulder, she decided to get a room at the hotel to rest for a while. With so much money, she could even open up her own cantina, maybe in El Paso, somewhere far away from Rio Salado.

Sayer looked past Don Fernando as a young Mexican woman stepped inside the hotel, went to the bar and spoke with the owner. A few moments later, the man accepted some money and gave her a key. The richly carved black saddlebags over her shoulder nearly engulfed her, but she hoisted them to a more comfortable position and climbed the stairs, disappearing from his view.

"What are you looking at?" Fernando asked as he sipped his coffee.

Sayer turned his attention to Fernando. "It's kind of strange to see a young woman traveling alone, wouldn't you say?"

Fernando shrugged his shoulders. "Perhaps, perhaps not."

Fergus and Jorge stood. "We'd better go and get the horses ready. We'll be wantin' tae be gettin' an early start." They had only just entered the barn when Jorge ran to a stall and pointed, yelling in Spanish.

"Now, now, calm down," Fergus encouraged. He glanced around and noticed a boy raking some hay into another stall. "You, there. Who brought in this animal?"

"A woman . . . just a little while ago, *señor.*"

Jorge said something, and the boy pointed to the rail. "Well, what's this?" Fergus asked as he followed Jorge. A large, dusty black saddle straddled the rail. Fergus ran his fingers over the rich leather, stopping on the heavily carved skirt. Embedded in the corner was a sterling silver E. "Come on, lad. We'd better go get Don Fernando."

Salena stepped out of her room. She needed some supplies, a hairbrush to take the tangles from her long black hair, and food for her journey. She glanced over the balcony rail, pleased to see the cantina empty. Though she felt sure Juan wouldn't chase after her, she needed to be cautious. Once outside, she shielded her eyes against the bright sun and crossed the dusty street toward the mercantile.

"*Hola,*" she said, unaware that Sayer watched from behind a stack of flour sacks. Salena pulled out the ring. "How much will you give me for this?" She spun around when it was taken from her fingers, only to find herself staring up at a very handsome American.

"Where did you get this?" Sayer asked as he stared at the ring.

"That is none of your business," she snapped, trying to snatch it back. "It is mine. Give it to me." Her lips turned up in a sultry smile. "Unless you'd like to buy it?"

Sayer held it out of her reach. "How much?" he asked.

"Fifty dollars."

"It is worth ten times that." Fernando stepped inside. He grabbed the woman, glaring at her while they conversed in Spanish. Only when she kicked him and tried to run did Sayer act.

It was no easy task to catch her, dodging her nails and kicking feet. But, finally he managed to pin her arms to her side as Fernando grabbed her feet. Together, they tied her in a chair. Winded, Fernando grasped her chin. "Now, I will ask you only one more time. Where did you get the ring?"

"I will only speak with Don Fernando Gutierrez."

"I am Don Fernando."

She spat in his face. "Liar."

Fernando moved as if to strike her, but was stopped by Sayer's firm grip on his arm. "Maybe it's better if she doesn't know who you are right now," Sayer said softly. Fernando swore under his breath, then moved away, too angry to speak.

"Who gave you the ring?" Sayer asked.

"What if I told you I took it from Don Miguel?"

Growling with rage, Fernando turned back and once more started to slap her, but Sayer caught his hand.

"I would suggest you give us some straight answers," Sayer urged softly, "or next time I won't stop him. Now, let's start with your name."

She glared at Fernando and smiled at Sayer. "He is angry because he believes Miguel is dead, no?"

Sayer nodded. "Yes, that and the fact that you spat on him." Sayer waited until she turned her attention back to him. "But, you know differently, don't you."

She gave him a coy smile. "He is alive, but—"

Fernando broke away from Sayer and grabbed her shoulders, giving her a good shake. "His horse is in the barn, now where is Miguel?"

"If you kill me," she cried, "you will never find him."

Sayer put his hand on Fernando's shoulder and walked with him to a stack of blankets. "We're not going to get anywhere frightening her to death." He motioned for his friend to stay put before he walked back to the woman. "I'll protect you, but you must cooperate, *comprende?*"

She continued to glare at Fernando, but nodded her head.

"All right," Sayer began. "Let's start over. What is your name?"

She smiled at Sayer. "Salena."

"Miguel gave you his horse and the ring?"

"Not exactly. I took them from Antonio."

Furious, Fernando groaned and raked his fingers impatiently through his hair.

Sayer gave him a hard look and turned his attention back to the girl. "Antonio?" Sayer hesitated for a moment, took the wanted poster from his shirt and unfolded it. "This Antonio?"

"*Sí.*" Her eyes pooled with tears. "He was my lover, and Miguel killed him." She sniffed and turned her rebellious gaze on Fernando. "If you want to know about your precious nephew, *cabron*, you will have to pay me much money."

CHAPTER NINETEEN

Darkness engulfed the compound, but Alberto sat at the table conversing softly in Spanish while Carmen wrapped food in cloths. Lydia had offered to help, but was waved away, so once more she sat on a wicker chair, thinking . . . remembering. It helped to think about home. By now, Sayer would surely be searching for her. She closed her eyes and offered a fervent prayer that he would find the bits of cloth that she left on the trail. Lost in thought, she jumped when she felt a hand on her shoulder.

Alberto put his finger before his mouth to silence her. A moment later, Delora came over with a sack and a stack of clean bandages. "My papa wants you to bring your medicine and come with us," the child whispered, holding up the sack. "But you must be very quiet. Mama will bring hot water."

They made their way silently toward the jail, where Delora's father spoke to the guard. The man looked her way and handed over the keys. Lydia took a calming breath and followed Alberto to a small, single cell in the corner of the room that only contained a chair and a desk.

Delora would have run ahead, but Alberto caught her. "Here," he said in heavily accented English, placing a key in Lydia's hand before he took his daughter outside and waited by the open door.

Miguel rested on this back, lying on the cot in dirty clothes and bandages stained with blood. By the looks of him, he hadn't moved since he was dropped on the filthy mattress. Her hand shook as she slipped the key into the lock. She ran to him and knelt by his side.

"Miguel?" she said, blanching at the sight of a new cut and a dark bruise high on his cheek. "Oh, my darling," she whispered. "I'm so sorry." She put down her sack, retrieved her scissors and cut off the bandage around his head, relieved to find that the bullet had only grazed his scalp.

Carmen came in with a large bowl of hot water and more clean cloths. The two women exchanged glances, but no words were said. Lydia dipped a cloth in the bowl and began to bathe away the blood on Miguel's face. Slowly he opened his eyes, blinking as if trying to focus.

"*Bonita?*"

When she smiled, tears ran down her cheeks. "Yes, my love." He shifted his weight, catching his breath. She gently cupped his cheek. "You mustn't move, my darling."

"*Que paso?* Where am I?" he asked.

"In Rio Salado's jail."

"*Agua,*" he murmured. Carmen hurried away and returned with a glass of water.

"Here," Lydia urged as she braced his weight. He drank as if he were dying of thirst. When he finished, she eased him back down. Once more she took the cloth and dabbed at his head wounds, acutely aware of the heat that radiated from his skin.

"Did they . . . did they harm you?" he asked with a faint tremor in his voice.

"No. I'm well." She dug in the sack and pulled out a little brown bottle—one she had kept hidden until now. "Delora's family is helping us." She picked up the glass and poured a little laudanum into it, then encouraged him to drink.

"You must leave. Go with them," he said hoarsely. "Listen to me. Go with them." He tried to keep his eyes open, but she knew the medicine would soon take hold. *"Bonita . . ."*

"Yes," she whispered, removing the bandage over his shoulder. Her stomach knotted when she realized the bullet was still in his chest, just under his collarbone.

"I beg you . . . save yourself."

"I will save both of us," she said firmly, relieved when his breathing steadied and he fell asleep. Lydia turned to Carmen. "Does your husband have a sharp knife?"

"Sí. I will get it for you."

By the time Carmen returned, Lydia had a needle threaded and had started to sew the gash over Miguel's temple. She finished quickly and cleaned the blood away before applying a fresh bandage. The two women worked together to remove his shirt, then Carmen handed Lydia the knife.

"Thank you," Lydia murmured. She steeled herself to concentrate on her work, not on the man who had taken her heart. Luckily the bullet hadn't broken any bones, and after a few minutes she removed it. Satisfied that the wound was thoroughly cleansed, she applied a thick pad, and with Carmen's help secured the bandage around his back.

"Señorita?" Delora called, and Lydia realized the child had been watching. She cautiously came forward to gaze at Miguel. "He is shivering, but it is a hot night. Is he sick?"

Lydia nodded. "Yes, Delora. He is very sick, but now he will get better."

Delora exchanged a worried glance with her mother. "Papa has a wagon outside. He has filled it with straw and blankets."

Carmen gathered up their supplies at the same time two men came in with Alberto and lifted Miguel off the cot.

"Please, be gentle," Lydia pleaded, following them outside. They placed Miguel in the wagon on a clean Navajo blanket, then Carmen covered him with another.

"How will we get through the gate?" Lydia asked.

Carmen gave her an understanding smile. "The men will think that we are going for supplies. We will cover you with the . . . the—"

"Canvas." Delora gave a bright smile. "They will not see you, I promise."

Lydia gathered up her medical sack and climbed in the back of the wagon, settling down next to Miguel.

"Lie down, *señorita.*"

Lydia obeyed, fighting the fear that dried her throat and moistened her palms as Alberto covered them with a canvas tarp. A few moments later the wagon lurched into motion. Cold with fear, Lydia snuggled closer to Miguel, gleaning the heat from his body.

She tried not to worry, but it was futile, especially when the wagon stopped and she heard Alberto conversing with the guards. Only when they began to roll, did she finally relax and rest her head on Miguel's shoulder, lulled to sleep by the steady swaying motion of the wagon.

CHAPTER TWENTY

"Well," Juan grumbled, wincing when he moved his arm. "Have you found them?"

"I have searched everyone's house. They are not here," Raul replied furiously. "I should have killed him when I had the chance."

Juan swore under his breath, pushed a glass toward Raul, and filled it with tequila before refilling his own.

"Listen to me," he said angrily. "Without Antonio, we have no way to collect the ransom even if we find them." Juan took a sip of his drink. "I do not care who kills Miguel or the woman. All I know is that they both must die. None of us are safe as long as they live."

"Why is that?" Raul asked before he tossed his drink down his throat.

"Because they know how to find Rio Salado, *idiota*. You led them here, remember?" Juan's brows came together. "Miguel was wounded too badly to travel by himself, even with the woman's help. Someone here has helped them, and when you find out who it is, kill them as well."

Juan gave Raul a dirty look as he consoled himself with another drink. "I will have Salena pack us some food and we will try and find their tracks."

"Salena is gone," Raul said, blanching at Juan's expression. "Pablo said she took Miguel's stallion last night and rode away."

"Is there no one here I can trust?" Juan demanded, slamming

his fist down on the table, nearly upsetting his glass. "When?"

Raul shrugged his shoulders. "No one knows."

Juan gave an angry growl. "Then go and get Carmen."

"Carmen and Alberto left early this morning."

Juan glared at Raul. "Who saw them leave?"

"The guard said they went to your sister's to get some fruit and vegetables."

"Did anyone search the wagon?" Juan demanded, his fury apparent in his scowl.

Raul shrugged his shoulders. "I didn't think to ask."

"No, you never think, and that is the problem," Juan grumbled. Juan dragged his hands down his face. "I do not like this at all."

"What do you mean?" Raul asked.

"The fact that Carmen is gone and so is Miguel and the woman." He stood, wincing as he cradled his arm. "Go and get our horses."

"Where are we going?"

"To my sister's house. We will see if Carmen spoke the truth or if she helped them escape. Now go and hurry. We must not fail, *hombre*," Juan warned, "or we may all pay with our lives."

"I will tell you everything, but first I want a thousand American dollars, *comprende?*" Salena hissed, turning away from Fernando's dark expression.

Sayer heaved an impatient sigh and walked to where Fernando stood. "I've got about a hundred dollars. How much did you bring?"

"I brought several thousand—"

"Damn, why so much?" Sayer asked.

Fernando motioned for Sayer to keep his voice down. "I expected to pay for information, but I did not expect to pay it to a woman like her."

"Well, if she knows were Lydia and Miguel are, then isn't it worth it?" Sayer glanced over his shoulder and shook his head. "Let me talk to her a little longer." When he stood before Salena, she smiled up at him.

"Well? Do you have the money?"

Sayer shook his head again and heaved a long sigh. "I'm sorry, miss, but it's just not that easy. You were right." Sayer nodded toward Don Fernando. "That man over there—he's not Don Fernando, but he's a mean *hombre* hired by Fernando to find his nephew. None of us have much money, and there's no time to send for Don Fernando." He took his gloves out from where they were looped over his belt, tugged them on and touched the brim of his hat. "If you'll excuse me, I've got to tend to my horse."

"Where are you going?" she asked, her smile fading.

"Me?" He shrugged his shoulders. "Oh, I'm leaving. You see, it's like I said, we just don't have that much money, and my friend . . ." He glanced at Fernando. ". . . says he can make you talk without it." Sayer grimaced. "I'm not one who condones beating a woman, so—"

"You can't leave me with him," she cried. "He . . . he will kill me."

"Maybe if you give us some information that we could use, I could talk him out of it."

Salena shook her head. "This is a trick. You are trying to frighten me."

"No, I'm trying to save your life, but . . ." Sayer shrugged his shoulders and took a step toward the door. ". . . I think I've done all I can do."

"No. Wait *uno momento.*" She hesitated, looking at Fernando for only a moment before turning her attention back to Sayer. "How much money do you have?"

Sayer pushed his hat off his forehead. "About a hundred dollars." The young woman muttered something he couldn't understand under her breath and squeezed her eyes tightly closed. Finally she opened them and glared at Sayer.

"Miguel killed Antonio," she said impatiently.

"We already knew that," said Sayer.

"Yes, but you don't know where he is, do you?" she snapped.

Sayer heaved another impatient sigh. "Go on."

"Antonio found out about Miguel and the woman—"

"An English woman with red hair?"

"*Sí*, but after Miguel was shot, the woman escaped."

Fernando came closer. "He was shot?"

"*S-sí*."

"Where is Miguel?" Fernando ground out.

"R-Rio Salado."

"And the woman he was with? Where is she?" Fernando demanded.

Salena licked her dry lips. "No one knows."

By the time Alberto stopped to water the horses, Miguel had grown restless, muttering in Spanish, with only a phrase or two that Lydia could understand. She soaked a cloth and bathed his face, trying to answer his questions as best she could.

He asked more than once where he was and how he came to be there. She gave the same answer each time, patiently tending to him as he dangled between reality and illusion. Once more the wagon swayed into motion, causing him to swear as he pressed his fingertips to his head. She found the laudanum and forced the last of it between his clenched teeth, relieved when after a short time he quieted and slept more peacefully.

Lydia didn't know how long she had dozed by his side, only that when she awoke, his clothing felt damp with sweat. "Alberto," she called. "I need more water."

Carmen glanced at Miguel before she spoke with her

husband. "Here," she said as she gave Lydia their canteen. "We could not stay by the river, but there is a spring a little farther. Take what you need."

"If Juan learns that I have helped you, my life will be worth nothing," Salena said, pouting when Sayer lifted her up and onto the back of Jorge's old mare. "When he sees you, his men will shoot you dead."

"And why is that?" Sayer asked as he gathered up his reins and swung up on his stallion. Rounder danced around for a moment before he settled down. Fergus was already on his big roan, Jorge close by on Fernando's horse.

"Rio Salado is an outlaws' hideaway," Fernando said, mounting Diablo. I have heard that it is heavily guarded. Only *banditos,* and unscrupulous women, know where it is, and only very bad *hombres* are allowed inside."

"Juan and Raul, they will be very angry. They will want revenge. Miguel might already be dead." She yelped when Fernando reached over and grabbed her arm none-too-gently.

"You'd better pray he is not, *bruja.*" Fernando released her, then motioned for her to go. "You had also better think of a way to get us inside Rio Salado, or I will slit that pretty little throat of yours."

Salena glared at Fernando for a moment before pressing her heels against the old mare's sides. "Even if you save him," she said, turning and giving him an evil smile, "and you will not, Juan will never let you leave alive, and if you do manage to escape, you will always have to watch your backs."

"How can you be so sure?" Fernando asked.

Her laughter sounded pompous. "Because, *cabron,* you will know the way to Rio Salado, no?"

"Yes, but why should that matter," Sayer countered.

"Because, you know, Juan's secrets will no longer be safe . . .

at least as long as you are alive."

The significance of what she said fell heavily on Sayer's shoulders. "Then perhaps I should give you the same advice."

Her smile faded and she pulled the mare to a stop. "What do you mean?"

"Juan's sure to find out that you led us to Rio Salado. If I were you, I'd also watch my back."

She shrugged her shoulders. "So, you will all be dead soon. It doesn't matter."

"I reckon you could say that, but he might start thinking." Sayer gave her a doubtful smile.

"What do you mean, he might start thinking?"

"Well, if you lead us to his camp, you could as easily lead the law back."

"I would never," she hissed.

"Then if you think Juan believes that, you've nothing to worry about, do you?"

She turned her full attention to Sayer. "You must protect me, *señor*," she cried. "They will try to kill me."

Sayer glanced over at her frightened expression. "Then you'd better convince the guards that we're real bad *hombres.*"

Lydia stayed in the wagon with Miguel while Alberto and his daughter filled the canteens and watered the horses at the spring.

"Is he still asleep?" Delora asked as she gave Lydia one of the canteens, climbed into the seat between her parents, and looked at Miguel over the back of the seat.

"Yes," Lydia said. "But when he awakes, the water will help him get better."

"Someday I will be a nurse just like you," Delora said with a firm nod.

"You will be a good one, too. I just know it." Lydia dampened a cloth to bathe Miguel's face, surprised when his eyes fluttered open.

"*Bonita.*" His voice was barely over a whisper, hoarse and raspy. "*Agua, por favor.*"

She gave him a drink, her stomach knotting when he shifted his weight and groaned.

"Where are we?" he asked. He lifted his hand and carefully touched the bandage around his head, closing his eyes. "*No puedo recordar . . .* I cannot remember."

"Is he feeling better?" Delora asked as she turned around and looked over the seat again.

"Yes, I think he's feeling a little better."

"More water, *por favor.*"

Lydia slipped her arm under his shoulders and, as best she could, lifted him, holding the canteen to his mouth. He drank, but afterwards he seemed even more agitated. She bunched some straw under his back, making a pillow out of her serape.

"Miguel," she said firmly, "you must try to rest."

His hand brushed his thigh and though she didn't realize what he was doing at first, he tried to rise. "*Donde esta mi pistola?*"

"Miguel, you mustn't move," she warned, but even though she tried to calm him, he wouldn't listen.

"*Donde esta mi pistola?*" he said more forcibly.

"He wants his gun," the child answered, watching intently.

Alberto reached under the buckboard's seat and pulled out a gunbelt, tossing it in the straw by Lydia's side. She grabbed it and placed it in Miguel's right hand. He held it tightly on his chest, muttering in Spanish.

"He says he can protect you now," Delora offered. "See? He is better now that he has a gun, no?"

Lydia bathed the sweat from his face. "Yes. Although I do not understand it, he seems to be."

The miles went by slowly, and when next they stopped to fix a broken strap on the old worn harness, Lydia got out of the wagon and stretched her legs. When she returned, Miguel appeared to be more lucid than he had been since they left Rio Salado. She climbed in and sat next to him.

"*Hola,*" she said with a smile. She caressed his cheek, relieved to find his skin cool to the touch.

He gave her a weak smile and picked up her hand. "Tell me, *bonita,* why are we in a wagon. The last thing I remember is being in a jail."

"We are on our way to Las Cruces. Delora's parents helped us escape."

Delora jumped up on the seat, her eyes dancing. "Papa says he helped to repay you for helping him."

Miguel closed his eyes, but Lydia knew he wasn't asleep by the way his fingers closed over hers. "How did you accomplish the impossible?"

"The impossible?" she repeated when he looked at her.

"*Si,* how did you get away from Juan?"

"After you were shot, a stray bullet hit the man who held me. I took his hat, grabbed a serape and ran out the back door as fast as I could. Luckily I found Poco and followed them back to Rio Salado."

His smile faded as he lifted his hand and caressed her cheek. "You are very brave. I owe you my life."

She placed her hand over his, turning to kiss his palm before she leaned closer. "Forgive me for not trusting you. I—"

His smile was tender when he brushed away a tear. "I am here, *vida mia,* and you are here. That is all that matters, no?"

"Yes," was all she could say past the lump in her throat.

"It is just like my story, no?"

She gave him a skeptical glance, but knew exactly where he was leading her. "What is?"

"Us . . . you and me. The way you saved my life, the way the boy pretended to be a *bandito.*" His eyes drifted closed, but his smile never wavered. "We have overcome many obstacles, but in the end we are victorious." Slowly, his eyes opened. "Together, we have accomplished the impossible."

He motioned her closer to accept his kiss, ignoring Delora's giggles.

Lydia was never so glad to see the outline of a house on the horizon. Alberto stopped the wagon in front of the hitching post and stepped down, catching Delora in his arms as the child jumped. She landed with joyous giggles.

"This is my aunt's house," the little girl cried excitedly. "She is *muy bonita* and grows very good vegetables and she has strawberries, and even fruit trees."

An attractive young woman stepped outside with an equally appealing man behind her. Both broke into smiles as Delora ran up to them while her father helped her mother out of the wagon.

"Can you hear what they are saying?" Lydia asked as she helped Miguel sit up.

He nodded, and closed his eyes as if that small movement caused him a great deal of pain. "Alberto is explaining what happened, telling them that he must load the wagon with supplies. He says that he must leave us here, and take Carmen and Delora back to Rio Salado or Juan will be suspicious."

"But they can't leave us."

"Shush, *bonita,*" Miguel said with a tender smile. "His plan is wise. We are three days away from Las Cruces." He held up his hand and listened. "We can sleep in the barn tonight . . ." He paused, then began again. "In the morning, they will lend us two horses. Carlos has a friend in Las Cruces who will return them later."

"But you're in no condition to ride."

Miguel gave her hand a little squeeze. "Listen to me. I am much better. Once we are in Las Cruces, we will send word to our families. You will see, *vida mia,* everything will work out for the best."

Chapter Twenty-One

Morning came too quickly. Lydia splashed some cold water on her face to try and wake up, but she was exhausted and nothing seemed to help the ache in her temples. She thought of Miguel and knew her pain was simply a minor discomfort compared to his. Although he pretended to be fine, she could tell by his lusterless gaze that he still suffered from the effects of his gunshot wounds and the fever. All during the night, he'd felt hot one moment and cold the next, but not once did he complain.

Alberto had brought Miguel a clean shirt and helped him put it on. He strapped the gunbelt around Miguel's hips, insisting he keep it. Even now, as Miguel conversed with Alberto, he leaned against the railing, cradling his left arm in his right.

While Delora's uncle saddled their horses, Carmen came into the barn with her sister, who carried a small sack. "Maria made some tortillas. She wishes it could be more, but—"

"Tell her we are very grateful," Lydia hurried to say.

While Carmen repeated what Lydia said, Miguel came over with the horses, took the sack and tied it to his saddle. Before he could help her mount, she stepped into the stirrup and settled herself on the gelding's back.

"Shall we?" she asked, trying to hide her concern with a smile. She watched Miguel slowly climb on to his horse, closing his eyes for several seconds before he offered his thanks in Spanish.

A cool morning breeze helped the miles to pass as they kept to a steady pace, Lydia believed, in a southeasterly direction. In the distance she could see rocky-faced mountains cavorting in the heat radiating from the sand. They kept close to the Rio Grande as well as they could, but there were scattered farms in the area, and Miguel felt it best that they avoid them. With every hour that passed, she tried not to worry, but it was impossible.

The sun beat down on them, and without her hat, the dry air parched her throat. She wondered how the wide, muddy river could be so close, yet the surrounding land could be so desolate. She was weary, and without Miguel to lead her across the seemingly endless desert, she'd be hopelessly lost. Each time she glanced at him, he forced a smile or said a few words of encouragement, contradicted by the pale color of his skin and the tiny tic of the muscle above the tight set of his jaw.

To pass the time, she told him about her days in England and how she had even attended a ball at Buckingham Palace. "In England, it always rains," she said glancing at the cloudless sky. "Here, it seems to rain only in August. Of course, once in a great while, we'll have a bit in May."

One story led to another and soon she remembered the joyous times shared at Sunday dinners at her sister's ranch, and the wonderful roasts Teresa always prepared. Much to her mortification, when she fell silent, her stomach rumbled loudly.

She smiled at Miguel's soft laughter. "Ah, my poor *bonita* is starving, no?"

"Yes, I am, but surely you're hungry too?"

"*Si,* but I try not to think about it." He pulled his horse to a halt, lifted the canteen and offered it to her, drinking only when she finished. Next he took out one of the tortillas and tore it in half.

"Here, this will help. If my memory serves, there is a place not too far from here. It was once an old pueblo. The people who lived there were scared away by soldiers many years ago. There are trees and shade."

"Sayer fought in the Indian Wars." She began telling Miguel all about Rebeccah's and Sayer's courtship. Somehow, sharing things with him made their situation seem less grim, especially when he asked questions and seemed intent on hearing all the details.

"I remember his young stallion," Miguel said with a smile. "He is a powerful animal. As handsome as my Diablo. When I saw him, he seemed high strung, jumping at things only he could see."

Lydia nodded. "He still does that from time to time, but Sayer is very patient with him, and I'm told he's doing much better. However, as long as I live, I shall never forget how Sayer rode up beside the train—"

"On his stallion?"

"Yes. I saw it all, and I must say, I thought Rounder would kill him before Sayer brought him under control. But, Sayer's very good with horses, and when he got close enough, my sister fell into his arms." Lydia gave a soft sigh. "It was the most romantic thing I have ever seen."

"Sounds a little frightening to me," Miguel said, frowning at her dreamy look. "So, in England it is romantic to jump from a train?"

She laughed at his expression. "Well, not really. Rather, it pulled the heart strings to know that Sayer wanted my sister so badly, he risked his life to have her."

Miguel shrugged his shoulders, wincing a little. "It seems to me that it was your sister who risked her life, jumping from the train."

"It wasn't like that," Lydia retorted, her dreamy smile turning into a frown. "It was . . . well, it was . . . oh, never mind. I suppose you had to be there to understand."

"So what happened to your sister's fiancé, Eduardo?"

"He went back to England. However, before you feel too badly about his situation, my grandmother, ever worried about propriety, gave him a hefty sum to break the betrothal and soothe his ruffled feelings." She fell silent, wondering what her grandmother would think about her elder granddaughter's adventure. Jumping off a train was one thing. Surviving in the wilds of the New Mexican desert, alone with a handsome man night after night, was quite another.

Raul listened while Juan spoke with Carmen and Alberto. Furious, Juan tossed the canvas cover aside exposing several bushels of fruits and vegetables.

"Why is there so much straw in this wagon?" Juan demanded.

"It is for me, *Tio*," Delora replied blinking up at him. "Papa knows I like to take a nap sometimes."

Juan stared down at his niece. Her innocent smile made him feel bad for yelling at her parents. "Very well, but next time you leave, you should tell me." He lifted Delora into the wagon.

"*Adios, Tio.*" Delora cheerfully waved good-bye.

Only Raul waved back. "Now what?"

"We go to my sister's house south of here. We will spend the night and get some supplies."

"That is the best news you have said all day. If I remember correctly, your sister's a very good cook."

Sayer pushed his hat back off his forehead and rested his forearms on the saddle horn. "What did they say?" he asked.

Fernando shoved Salena back on her horse. "She was very convincing. They said we are welcome to stay if we give up our weapons. However, Juan left yesterday in search of Don Miguel." Fernando heaved an impatient sigh. "It seems that someone helped Miguel escape. Juan and a man named Raul Martinez are searching for them." Fernando gave a slight shake of his head. "They have not seen Lydia. They assume she went with Miguel."

"What are you going to do with me?" Salena cried, blanching when Fernando glared at her.

"I have very little use for you now, *bruja.*"

"I am not a witch," she hissed.

"Trust me when I say it is less than what I think you are," he said contemptuously. He pulled out five one-hundred-dollar bills and held them out to her. Her eyes grew round before she glared at Sayer.

"Salena, meet Don Fernando Gutierrez."

Her gasp was audible. "You lied to me."

Sayer shrugged his shoulders. "I reckon I did."

Fernando grabbed her hand and slapped the bills against her palm, speaking so that only she could hear. "If anyone follows us . . . even a small boy, I will blame you, *comprende?*"

She nodded and tried to pull away, but he kept tight hold of her hand. "Listen well, *bruja.* There will be no place for you to hide that I cannot find you if you deceive me. I know you have much money. Miguel told me before he left Mexico that his wallet was full, and when I looked, none of it was left. So, now you have even more—enough to make you happy for a long time. So, I warn you one last time. Do not betray me."

Salena pulled her hand free and turned her old horse. She shouted at the guards, and when the gate opened, she galloped down the path without looking back.

"How can you be sure she'll keep her word?" Sayer asked as

they rode away.

"Fear, *amigo*. She is afraid, and that alone will keep her mouth shut." Fernando cued Diablo into a ground-covering trot. "Come, we may be able to find some tracks."

At noon, Lydia and Miguel stopped to rest at the Indian ruins. Miguel apologized for the pace, saying that they would be able to travel faster tomorrow. This time she insisted that she could take care of the horses, that all he needed to do was watch and make sure she did it correctly. When she finished, she spread their blankets on the sand under some trees and helped him lie down.

"Only for a little while," he said, clenching his teeth as he stretched out on the blanket. "It is better to rest while it is hot and travel more when it is cooler."

When she offered him some food, he refused, and fell asleep the next moment. She tore a little piece of the cloth off that had been wrapped around the tortilla, dampened it and bathed the perspiration from his forehead. After she ate a small portion of the tortilla, she rested beside him and tried to sleep.

It sounded like several women were screaming, and Lydia came awake with a start, sitting straight up. In the distance, the sound came again, and it took her several moments to realize it was a pack of coyotes. Nevertheless, she was wide awake and shivering, listening and watching to make sure the beasts didn't come too close.

"They are hunting," came Miguel's soft voice. He rolled to his back, and in the moonlight she could see his gentle smile as he sat up, took the blanket she had placed over him, and draped it over her shoulders. "They will not bother us."

"How are you feeling?" she asked, touching his forehead. "Your fever seems to come and go."

He caught her hand and gave it a gentle squeeze. "I am fine, but by the faint light on the horizon, we have rested longer than I intended."

At first she deliberated telling him that he needed to rest, but then thought better of it. "I know, and I'm sorry, but I was exhausted. When I saw that you were still asleep, I decided to sleep a little longer."

"So it wasn't for me, but you?" he asked, skeptically.

"Yes," she confirmed as she helped him to rise. "I think I am beyond saddle sore."

Lydia silently swore that if they ever got to Las Cruces, she would never get on another horse. This time when she asked Miguel if they could rest, her bottom truly hurt. He praised her fortitude, stating that by the positions of their shadows on the sandy ground, it was nearly noon.

Together they unsaddled the horse, and by the way he moved, she knew he felt a little better. After he spread their blankets under some scrub cedars, he told her to wait for him while he shared some water from their canteen between the horses.

"Are you hungry?"

When she looked up, Miguel held the knife that he kept hidden in his boot. "And what would you suggest we dine on?"

"There is a feast in the desert if one knows where to find it."

"I'd rather not see you kill a rabbit," she protested, "and I refuse to eat snake."

He feigned a shiver. "As do I."

"And certainly no lizards," she confirmed.

"Do they eat such things in England?" His horrified expression caused her to laugh both at his humor and with relief that he was definitely feeling better.

"No, however we do have wonderful things like blood pudding and—"

He held up his hand and grimaced. "Enough. I am not so

hungry anymore."

She followed him over the rise, catching sight of the vast landscape. It seemed to stretch on endlessly toward more of the rocky, barefaced mountains. The only green vegetation appeared to be several miles away, winding down the valley along the river.

He stopped, pointing a few yards away. "There. What do you see?"

"Cactus. Lots of cactus."

"I will teach you as my grandfather taught me that things are not always as we perceive." His smile eased her trepidation as he leaned over and plucked what looked like a dark-pink, oblong plum growing on the top. He took his knife and carefully peeled it. "Here, take it. It is *higo,* fruit from the cactus. Taste it."

"But won't it prick me?"

"No. I have removed all the spines. It is safe, see?"

He took a bite before he held it out to her. She took the juicy fruit from his fingers and nibbled it. He was right. It tasted sweet and tangy, not at all what she expected, and the ominous-looking cactus was covered in them. He peeled one for himself and ate it, tossing aside the seeds.

"How did you know about these?" she asked as she accepted a second one.

"My grandfather was a very wise man. He was poor as a child. His family lived in the desert. His mother took the children with her when she went to gather food. Though many look at the *chumbera* . . . the prickly pear cactus as menacing, the *higo* . . ." Miguel stabbed another fruit and peeled it. ". . . my great-grandmother saw it as food. After the flower falls, the fruit ripens. When it is dark and soft like this, it is ready to eat. She would gather these and cook them with honey to make a sweet syrup for corn cakes and tortillas."

"Did your grandfather tell you about them?" she asked, bending to pick one for herself.

Miguel smiled sadly as he ate another one. "He did better than that. He took me out into the desert when I was a boy. Instead of the fancy clothes and leather boots my father provided for me, my grandfather made me wear a pair of white, homespun pants and a loose-fitting, white shirt. He gave me a straw sombrero and a pair of sandals, which he had made with his own hands. We took nothing with us except a gun and a knife. We walked for many miles. I was hot and tired. I worried that we would starve, or worse, die of thirst. A headstrong child, I told my grandfather that he was cruel and that I hated him for making me suffer. But soon he showed me many amazing things."

Miguel peeled another fruit for her. "At the time, I was too proud to say I was sorry, but I hope he knew that truly I admired him." He heaved a sigh, then smiled. "That is the curse of being born very rich."

"I've never really thought having money was a curse."

He gave a soft laugh at her doubting expression. "Back when my grandfather took me to the desert, I didn't think it was important to learn how to live without all the comforts my father provided."

He glanced around and heaved a sigh. "But now? Now I wish my grandfather still lived, so he could see the man I have become, but more importantly, so I could thank him."

Lydia almost felt like crying at Miguel's expression. In all the time she had spent in his company, she had never seen remorse flicker in his vibrant eyes. She accepted another fruit and ate it, licking the juice from her fingers.

"I would like to think that those we love understand us better than we understand ourselves." She smiled when he looked up at her. "My mother made me promise that I would come to New Mexico and live near my father for one year, and that I earn my own living so as not to be dependant on the family's fortune. She died shortly after I left England. I never got to say goodbye, or tell her how much she meant to me, but, I think she knew. She was also very wise."

Miguel took her hand and led her back to the short, stubby trees. "Come, we should take advantage of the shade while the sun is high."

"Did you know," Lydia said, "when I thought that you were an outlaw and we were on the way to Rio Salado, I left bits of my clothing tied on bushes whenever I could."

"I was aware of that," Miguel interrupted.

"You were?"

"*Si*. That is why I dropped the bow from your hat on the ground. Like you, I had hoped that your brother-in-law would follow."

She reclined next to Miguel, resting her head on his uninjured shoulder, content to be in his arms. He looked exhausted, and while she thought about Sayer and her family, he fell asleep. She lifted her head and watched him for several moments, admiring his strength before she snuggled closer and closed her eyes.

Chapter Twenty-Two

Lydia awoke and blinked several times to adjust her eyes to the glare of the brilliant white-orange sunrise peeking at them on the horizon. Miguel stood on the rise looking out over the landscape. He had removed the bandage from around his head. The cut on his cheek was barely visible, and the bruises were nearly gone.

He smiled when he saw her, and motioned her closer, bidding her to watch as the sun turned the scattered clouds a brilliant pink with yellow and orange streaks.

"It's breathtaking," she said, turning to examine the healing wound above his temple. "When we get to Las Cruces, I'll take those stitches out."

She continued with her inspection, checking the bandage at his shoulder, pressing gently on his ribs. He sucked in his breath.

"Did that hurt?" she asked, frowning.

He shook his head. "No."

She gave him a skeptical glance, and touched him again. "That hurt, didn't it? And do not lie to me. I know they beat you."

"*Solo un poquito.*"

"Miguel," she scolded.

"All right, just a little," he confessed. "But, not enough for you to worry about. The sun is getting high. Come, we must get the horses and leave."

Together they got the horses saddled. This time they traveled down a path that slowly became a road. They shared a tortilla while Miguel told her stories of his childhood and about his desire to raise horses, drawing her with him into his dreams for their future.

And she grew content to listen and imagined having his children—all twenty, if that's what he really wanted. When finally the heat became unbearable, he rode toward the river and stopped the horses under the shade of a giant cottonwood tree. After he dismounted, he reached up for her, holding her longer than usual and whispering how much he loved her. He loosened the ribbon at her nape, sinking his fingers into her hair so he could spread it over her shoulders.

"I will never tire of the feel of your hair or of looking at the beautiful color," he murmured, bending his head to kiss her fully on the mouth.

She would have said something, but he turned and went to the horses, speaking in hushed tones in his native tongue as he led them to the sandy bank where they drank their fill of water. She watched, admiring Miguel's subtle strength, his endless patience as he scolded one horse when it tried to nudge the other out of the way.

When they wouldn't take any more water, Miguel unsaddled them, and applied the hobbles so they could move around and forage in the lush grass by the river's edge. Miguel dragged the saddles under the brace of trees, out of the sun, spreading the blankets in the shade. He turned and took the last tortilla from the sack and tore it into two pieces.

"Here. Eat," he encouraged. "We will rest while the sun is high. If we ride all night, we will be in Las Cruces early tomorrow morning."

"I suppose by now, Juan knows that Carmen and Alberto helped us escape. Do you think he will hurt them?"

Miguel heaved a tired sigh. "I do not believe he would hurt

233

his own sister. I am sure he will be very angry, but Alberto will not allow anything to happen to his family. In the short time I knew him, I realized that he is an honorable man."

Miguel finished his food, then took a sip of water, offering the canteen to Lydia when he finished.

She drank and capped it before setting it aside. He took her hand and placed a kiss in the palm. When his gaze fused with hers, everything seemed as uncomplicated as their surroundings. He loved her, and she loved him. It showed in his eyes, in the way his thumb caressed the back of her fingers.

"I remember seeing you washing clothes in the river," he said, his gaze bright, his smile brighter. He pulled her toward the river. "Do you swim?"

"Yes, but—" She never had time to finish before he picked her up and tossed her into the slow moving water. The cooler temperature took her breath and it seemed much deeper than the Rio Salado, but when she regained her balance the water only came to her waist. Laughing, Miguel waded in to be with her. She shoved wet hair back from her face and pretended to choke. He was nearly to her, his smile changing to a frown, when she suddenly charged, knocking him over. But he caught her wrist and pulled her down with him.

Laughing, they played in the water, cooling down and at the same time washing away the trail dust.

"You're sure I didn't hurt you?" she asked as they shed most of their wet clothes and hung them on some tree limbs to dry.

"Absolutely. Look," he held out his arms. "Do I not look better?"

"I'll put on a dry bandage and you'll not only look better, you'll feel better."

Wearing only his trousers, Miguel reclined against his saddle and stretched his long legs out on the blanket. "Have I told you

I like it when you wear less clothing?"

She giggled at his implication, and glanced down at her damp chemise. "No. However, if I wear any less, I'll be naked."

"Precisely," he said with a devilish grin as he motioned for her to join him. She brought some clean cloths, knelt down and replaced the bandage over his shoulder wound. "There, that should do it."

A breeze ruffled her hair, blowing several curly strands across her face. Before she could brush it aside, Miguel tucked the wayward stands behind her ear at the same time he pulled her close and kissed her fully on the mouth. Suddenly she couldn't get enough of him. She entwined her arms around his neck, kissing him back, parting her lips to toy with his persistent tongue. He pulled her onto his lap, slipping the thin straps of her chemise off her shoulders.

He rolled, pressing her down on the blanket, grazing the taut nipples of her breasts with the pads of his thumbs before he circled them with his tongue. She moaned, splaying her fingers across the hard muscles of his chest, treating him to what she had just experienced, yet mindful of his healing shoulder.

Slowly, he slid her garment off her hips, taking his time, caressing every inch of her until she felt as if she would scream with the want of him. When he stood, she watched him shed his damp trousers—reveled in the masculine power of his body a moment before he joined her.

He braced his weight on his elbows, taking her face between his palms, his eyes smoky with desire as he gazed down at her. No words were needed, yet there was an urgency in his love-making that frightened her—made her shameless to please him as she implored him to roll over so she could straddle his hips.

She rose slightly before she slid down his full length over and over again. He closed his eyes almost as if he were in pain, but she knew it wasn't pain he felt when his strong hands held her still as he drew in a long calming breath. He pulled her down to receive his kiss, positioning himself over her, tucking her under himself as his hand slipped between their bodies.

At first she wondered what he was up to, then he began to stroke her, at the same time he slowly moved inside her. The sensations he induced grew and expanded until all she could feel were their bodies joined, all she heard was his harsh breathing in rhythm with her own, and all she tasted was his ravenous mouth on hers. She arched against him in pure primal pleasure as he lifted her out of the darkness into the light, where she hovered for several blissful moments. He folded her into his arms, burying his face in the crook of her neck as his body shuddered inside of her, then stilled.

When finally she opened her eyes, he was above her, his forehead damp with sweat, but a look so tender in his eyes, she could have drowned in them and died happy. He rolled to his side, taking her with him before he brushed her hair from her damp cheek, drawing his finger down to trace the slight smile on her lips.

This time his usually lively gaze seemed cloudy with weariness. "Go to sleep," he urged, kissing the tip of her nose. "We have a long ride ahead of us."

By evening, Lydia opened her eyes. In the distance, she heard Miguel's boots crunch on the gravel, getting louder as he approached. She rolled and stretched before standing. After he helped her dress, he gave her a quick kiss and unfolded the sack, emptying out *higo* fruit on the blanket next to her.

"Here," he said softly, handing her the knife. His smile appeared warm and reassuring, but his eyes were dark, almost brooding. "You pretended to sleep, but you have been awake for a long time, no?"

"I slept a little." She knelt on the blanket and began to peel the fruit.

He led the horses to their small camp. After tying them to a nearby tree, he sat down beside her to eat. "I tried to leave quietly."

"You did. I woke later, after you had left."

He gave her a sad smile. "If you were asleep, how did you know I left?"

"Very well, I wasn't asleep."

"It is difficult to sleep when you're hungry, no?"

"Yes, it is," she confessed. "But these are good. They will do for now." She wiped her hands on her skirt, brushing against her pocket, remembering the money she took from his wallet several days ago. She pulled out several bills. "Look," she said, smiling. She quickly counted it. "Forty-five dollars."

"We are rich," Miguel teased. "If only there was a cantina nearby, I would buy you a thick steak."

"Mock me if you must, but nevertheless, this is more than I make a month. It will certainly get us a room for a few days, food, and even hay for the horses."

"*Si, vida mia.* You have done well. When we reach Las Cruces, I will send a telegram to my father. This money will last until he sends more, and after that, *bonita mia,* I will buy you a new gown and all the food you can eat."

He stood and offered her his hand. "Come, it is time to leave."

"We should have left your sister's house sooner," Raul complained as he kicked at some tracks in the sand. "There's no telling who camped here or how long ago."

Juan tossed the discarded bandage at Raul. "Does this tell you anything, *amigo?*"

Raul looked at it and shook his head. "What is it?"

Juan rolled his eyes. "Eee, your eyes are bad. I know it's dark, but can you not see the bandage and dried blood?"

Raul grimaced and tossed it aside, wiping his hand on his shirt. "*Sí*, it must be Miguel's, but why would he have been so careless to leave it behind?"

"Who knows and who cares? We will catch up to him soon enough." Juan untied his canteen, took a mouthful, swished it around his mouth before he took another long drink. "I think they will follow the river until they come to the road, then take it into Las Cruces."

Raul lifted his own canteen and drank, wiping his hand across his mouth. "I did not think they would be so smart at first and now be so careless."

Juan shook his head, looping the strap of his canteen over the saddle horn. "Think, *hombre*. This is a man who pretended to be an outlaw, fooled all of us. He is a man who takes chances. Come," Juan ordered. "Mount up."

"But this is a good place to make camp," Raul protested. "It's too dark to follow their tracks."

"We have no need to follow their tracks. We are going to Las Cruces."

"But I'm tired."

"Stop complaining. If they leave town before we arrive, we may never get the chance to avenge our *amigos*. Now get on your horse. You can sleep *mañana* in a bed instead of on the ground."

Raul heaved a tired sigh. "Maybe he and Don Fernando have joined forces."

Juan ran his hand down the stock of the rifle he carried in his saddle socket. "Do not fret, *amigo*. I have a plan."

"The last plan we had failed," Raul grumbled.

"I am thinking that once we get to Las Cruces, we go and find the marshal."

Raul's mouth dropped open. "Why don't we just go to his

jail and lock ourselves up too, no?" He shook his head. "I think you are *muy loco*. I am not like you. There is a price on my head."

Juan gave Raul a disgusted grunt. "Antonio had a price on his head also. If we cannot have the ransom, perhaps we can collect the reward."

"But Antonio is dead and buried. Who will believe us?"

"Not Antonio, *idiota*, Miguel. Try to use your head once in a while," Juan growled. "Miguel and Antonio look alike, remember?"

Raul nodded. "Oh, now I understand. But, if they see—"

"That is why you must stay in the hotel when we get there. I will inform the marshal about Miguel and once the reward is in our hands, you and I will return to Rio Salado."

Juan gave a sinister laugh. "Who knows? Perhaps Miguel will hang before he can convince them they have the wrong man. Now, do you want to stay here with the lizards, or ride the night through so that we are in Las Cruces before the cock crows?"

Dawn broke on the horizon as Miguel and Lydia rode into the town of Las Cruces. A few people were up and about, paying no attention to them as they rode down the street toward the large false-fronted hotel.

"Thank heavens," Lydia muttered as she eased down off her horse. "I can hardly wait to bathe, but first I want a large glass of water—clear water, without the mud."

Miguel agreed. "Go and get us a room. I will take the horses to the livery."

When he returned, he asked the lady at the counter which room Lydia was in, then slowly climbed the stairs. The room looked nice, and the bed was larger than most. When he entered, Lydia turned, holding a half-full glass of water. She immediately filled it from the pitcher on the bureau and held it out to him.

"After I see how your shoulder is doing, I suggest we find the bath house, and . . ." She cupped his cheek, and was pleased when he placed a kiss in her palm. ". . . and you can get your hair cut and a shave."

"First I must wire my father. How much money do you have left?"

"Thirty-eight dollars. How much will the livery cost to board the horses?"

"They will wait until after my father sends some money." He took another drink and put the glass down. "We have enough money left to buy a good meal and some clean clothes, no?"

She glanced down at her rumpled skirt and travel-stained blouse. "If we're conservative."

He took her hand and led her to the door. "Only until my father responds, then, *vida mia*, the sky will be the limit."

An hour later, Lydia soaked in a brass tub filled with hot, fragrant water. The proprietor had taken a liking to her and even provided rose-scented soap for her hair at no extra charge. With it wrapped in a thick towel, Lydia leaned back and enjoyed feeling clean.

She thought about Miguel, hoping a few days of rest would ease his fatigue. The wound on his shoulder had closed, but he needed lots of rest and good food to rebuild his strength. She warned him to be very careful while he bathed, not to move his arm very much, and told him that he still needed a bandage for a few more days. If everything went as planned, Miguel's father would answer his telegram and tomorrow all their financial worries would be over. In the meantime, she had a new sunflower-yellow dress waiting, new shoes and a bonnet to match. They would meet outside, and together, find a restaurant.

Chapter Twenty-Three

Sayer reclined back against the straw where he had placed his bedroll. Though it was a far cry from a bed, it beat sleeping on the ground as they had for more nights than he cared to count. Fernando wasn't too far away, using his serape as a pillow and looking quite comfortable.

They had followed some wagon tracks to a small farm. The young Mexican couple there had allowed them the use of their barn, only after Fernando had slipped them a generous amount of money.

"Well, it was awfully nice of Mrs. Gonzalez tae make us some supper," Fergus said as he bunched some straw under his blanket as he sat down and took off his boots. "I would have eaten just about anything."

"I do not think, since I saw you last, *mi amigo,* that you have missed many meals."

"I thought you were sleepin'," Fergus countered.

"How can I sleep, hey?" Fernando asked. "You whisper louder than most men talk in normal voices. If what *Señora* Gonzalez said is true, we should find Miguel and *Señorita* Lydia in Las Cruces in two days."

"Providing they stay there that long." Sayer rested against his overturned saddled, his hat down over his eyes.

"If they are as tired as we are," Fernando said over a yawn, "they will take a few days to recover, and I am sure Miguel will send word to his father, and possibly even Doctor Randolph."

"We should get some sleep," Sayer added, rolling over on his side.

"Aye," Fergus agreed, giving a long, loud yawn. "The sooner we sleep, the sooner we'll be awakened by the smell of another home-cooked meal. We mustn't forget that Mrs. Gonzalez promised us breakfast."

"I had no fear of that with you along," Fernando chided.

Lydia couldn't sleep. Even when she snuggled close to Miguel, her thoughts drifted back to the last few days, to Alberto and Carmen, then, reluctantly, to Raul and Juan. Surely they would try to follow them. Even though Miguel assured her they were safe, Juan wouldn't give up so easily. His fear of having Rio Salado discovered outweighed the man's power to reason.

She gave a soft sigh and tried to think about how happy her father sounded in his telegram, promising to meet her at the stage depot in Santa Fe in four days. As she thought of her family, of several different ways she would tell them about Miguel, she didn't realize that her fingers toyed with the scant hairs on Miguel's chest until he caught her hand and turned to give her a kiss.

"You are restless, hey?" His soft voice flowed over her like the warm breezed from the opened window. He put his knuckle under her chin and kissed her again. "Tell me what troubles you."

"I have this sinking feeling that something is going to go wrong," she said a little desperately. "What if Juan or Raul follows us?"

"Shush, *vida mia*," he whispered, stroking her hair, cupping her face. "Do not torture yourself like this. Everything will work out. You will see. Raul is a wanted man. He will not come here, and Juan is a coward."

"You're probably right," she reluctantly agreed. "There is the little matter of the wanted poster. What if the same thing that happened in Santa Fe happens here?" She turned to him, feeling suddenly desperate. "Maybe we should pack a few things and leave . . . or go to the marshal's office and show him the poster before he discovers it himself."

"The marshal is out of town, and the man he left in charge did not know when he would return. So you see, you must stop worrying," he murmured. "Besides, your family deserves to see you, and I am sure that you told me you wanted to see your little niece. We have a good plan. You will take two weeks and visit your father and sister, while I take care of business here and help the people in Rio Salado. Afterwards, I will come for you and meet your grandmother and we will be married." He pulled her closer, placing a kiss in her hair.

Although she still couldn't shake an uneasy feeling that something might go wrong, she had to admit Miguel was right. For now she wouldn't think about it. For now she would simply enjoy the feeling of being in his arms. There would be time for tears and concern tomorrow when she left him. She moved closer, brushing her bare thigh against his. "I'm not tired," she whispered, nibbling his ear. "Are you?"

"I was, but no more. There is only one thing I can do, *vida mia*," he responded with a voice so sensually soft she shivered. "I think I know a way to take your mind off your troubles, hey?"

She loved the way he ended his remarks with a question. In fact, as he caught her hands, held them prisoner above her head while he nuzzled her neck, she loved everything about him. He kissed her mouth, teasing and toying, and then he raised his head and looked lovingly into her eyes. Slowly, he released her wrists and left a trail of hot wet kisses down her neck, between her breasts. His warm mouth moved over her, catching a rosy peak between his teeth, drawing gently until she writhed in blissful agony. He tasted every inch of her, circling her navel with his tongue.

"Miguel," she moaned, as he spread her legs, nipping at the inside of her thighs as his hands caressed the smooth plain of her belly. Her fingers sank into his hair, and she nearly cried out in wanton pleasure as he drove her to the brink of sensual delirium. A moment later he was above her, driving full-length inside of her, whispering her name over and over again with each powerful thrust.

She arched her back as she wrapped her legs around his waist, taking him deeper as her body joined his in an instinctive dance—his gaze as torrid as his touch. She cried out and buried her face in the crook of his neck. He clutched her tightly to his chest, all the while whispering sweet words of love as she reached her climax, moving slowly with each sensual contraction. He drove deeper, over and over again until he squeezed his eyes tightly closed. Every muscle in his body grew taut as he uttered her name.

When their breathing drifted back to normal, he opened his eyes and smiled. Slowly, as if letting her go was the hardest thing he had ever had to do, he eased down beside her, unwilling to release her as he placed a kiss on her forehead.

"You make me crazy," he said, raking his hair off his sweat-dampened forehead. "I will never get enough of you, *vida mia*. Never."

"Nor I you," she whispered breathlessly. She rose up on her elbow and gazed down at him. "Let's get married in the morning."

His brows snapped together. "I thought you wanted to wait, to have a big wedding after I speak with your father and grandmother?"

"Not any more," she said urgently. "I don't care what they think. I'm old enough not to need their permission."

He touched her lips with the tip of his finger. "Your stage leaves very early. Though I would gladly accept your proposal, there is no time, nor do I want to face my mother and tell her there will be no wedding."

"You would have married me at Rio Salado."

"*Si,* that is very true, but at Rio Salado my mother knew nothing about you. Now she does. I told her all about you in the telegram I sent my father."

He reached up and kissed her pouting mouth before he got out of the bed, completely at ease with his state of undress. After he lit the lamp, he went to the door where his new jacket hung and pulled out a small box.

"This is for you," he said, slipping back into bed. "A little something to remind you that you belong to me on your trip back to Santa Fe." He placed the small parcel in her hands. "I was going to give it to you *mañana,* but I want you to have it tonight instead."

Lydia held her breath for a moment when she opened his gift. Never in her life had she seen a more beautiful ring. She lifted the sparkling emerald from its velvet cradle and held it up to admire its fire.

"It's exquisite," she said breathlessly.

He took it from her and slipped it on the third finger of her left hand. "This is only a small token of my love, *vida mia.* When I get to Santa Fe, I will replace this ring with a wedding band."

He lifted her hand and kissed it, caught her in his arms and pulled her down with him as he stretched out on the bed. "Now, will you let me get some sleep?"

He grunted when she elbowed him gently in the ribs. They rested quietly for several moments.

"I must never forget," he began. His voice drifted off until she couldn't stand it any longer.

"Miguel?"

"*Si, bonita mia?*"

"Forget what?" she asked.

"That because your hair is the color of fire, your temper is also fiery hot."

"I do not have a temper," she protested, resigned to rest against his shoulder when he gently pushed her head down. "I'm sure you're mistaken."

"You are absolutely correct," he said, yawning. "I must have you confused with another woman."

She lifted her head. "What other woman?"

"The one I found among a bunch of *banditos* weeks ago. If my memory serves, she had red hair like yours, but her disposition wasn't as . . . how should I say it . . ." He grunted again when her elbow found its mark.

"Sweet?"

"Sweet . . . yes, that is the word I was looking for . . . most definitely." He rolled and gave her his best smile. "No other woman could please me as you have, *bonita*, so I beg you, lie down and let us get some sleep."

"Very well," she said, feigning reluctance, as she accepted a kiss. "Of course, you do realize that I'm not the one with the questionable disposition. You are."

He yawned again, and nuzzled her ear. "Whatever you say, *mi amor.*"

Marshal Quade and his men rode into Las Cruces just as the sun peeked over the distant mountains. Their search for Antonio Garcia had been futile and more than a little disappointing. Quade stepped down from his horse and tossed the reins at the stable boy. "Rub him down good, Johnny. I'll be in my office later if anyone comes looking."

He headed down the street, tired and hungry. It already felt warm for so early in the day, and because of it, the door to his office had been left open as he stepped inside. "What's been going on around here, Matt?" the marshal asked of his deputy as he hung his hat on the rack by the door.

"Been pretty quiet. But I can see by your expression you didn't find Garcia."

"Nope. Ran into a couple of men looking for him near Santa Fe. They think he's kidnapped a young woman."

"Son of a buck, is there anything that *hombre* won't do. He deserves to be shot on sight."

"Yeah, well, I'm bushed. You got anybody in the back?"

Matt shook his head. "No, cells are empty."

Marshal Quade opened the door then paused. "I'm going to take a nap. Wake me if you need me."

Miguel hung his new sombrero on the rack and led Lydia to a table. After they ordered breakfast, they started talking about when they first met. "I cannot believe it took me so long to trust you," she said. "But then, you didn't exactly explain everything to me either." She added some cream and sugar to her coffee.

He added some cream to his coffee and took a sip before speaking. "I tried, but you wouldn't listen. Do you remember when I told you my name?"

"Which time?" she questioned with an impish smile. "In Santa Fe when I sewed your arm? On the trail to Rio Salado, or in my room when you seduced me?"

He grinned. "No, when Raul captured you." He reached into an inside pocket and pulled out his wallet, removed a wanted poster and held it out to her.

"Where did you find that?" she asked, glancing around to make sure no one noticed. "Is it wise to have it?"

Miguel shrugged his shoulders. "Tell me, what do you see?"

"I-I see you."

"*Si,* and so did the young man who shot me and also the honorable sheriff of Santa Fe. He arrested me, and after you left, I spent two days in jail while I awaited word from my father to prove my innocence."

"Then what happened?" she asked.

"I left for a prearranged meeting with your brother-in-law. It was hot, and my arm ached. While I rested in the shade of some trees, I saw that you were in trouble."

She smiled. "I remember Raul's expression when he thought you were Antonio."

He nodded. "It is what saved our lives. After Raul told me his plans for you, I could not let them take you to Rio Salado alone."

He took another sip of coffee. "Look closer at the poster, and tell me what it says."

She did as he asked, reading until she came to Antonio's description. Her voice stilled and her head snapped up.

"Well?"

"I-It says his eyes are brown, and . . . and there's a small scar on his cheek."

"And what color are my eyes?"

"Blue . . . dark blue," she confirmed.

"Precisely. And is there a scar on my cheek?"

She shook her head and cupped his cheek. "No, just a small healing cut."

"But no scar yet," he said flatly. "I tried to explain that to the sheriff, but like you, he is as stubborn as a mule."

He took the poster and put it back in his jacket. "That day I had another piece of paper, *bonita,* one that would have chased away all your doubt, but unfortunately, a paper that, if found on my person, could have put us in even more danger." When she looked as if she didn't understand, he felt compelled to continue. "Do you remember the dead man back at the rocks?"

"Yes, but breakfast isn't really the time to speak of him."

"Do you remember when I went back, after I had told you he was dead?"

She nodded.

"I put the telegram my father sent, the paper that proved my identity, on the body. We were very close to the MacLaren ranch, and although I did not know that you were part of his family, I had hoped that *Señor* MacLaren would find the body and when he read the paper, he would see that the dead man was not me." He gave her one of his arrogant smiles. "I am, of course, much better looking."

She put her napkin in her lap as she shook her head. "There's still something bothering me. Explain why you keep talking about Don Fernando as if he's alive."

"I assure you. Fernando is alive. He only pretended to be dead so he could escape with his family to Mexico."

"But, Sayer told me he was gone—"

"*Sí*, gone." He gave her an understanding smile. "But not dead." Miguel put down his cup for the waitress to refill it. "The colonel and my uncle were very good *amigos*, no?"

"Yes, the best of friends," she confirmed, adding more sugar and more cream to her second cup of coffee.

"And you have come to know the colonel very well, *sí?*"

She nodded, lifting the cup to take a sip.

"Then how could you believe he could kill his best friend? You must trust me when I tell you, the colonel helped my uncle escape. He only told you Fernando was dead so no one would follow him to Mexico." Miguel smiled. "Fernando told me about you, but I thought he had to be, how do you say . . . *esta pasando un poco* . . . stretching the truth. No woman could be as beautiful. But now I have seen you, been with you these difficult days, and I know that your beauty goes beyond what I see. I am a very lucky man."

Their food was served, and while they ate, they talked about their future. Nevertheless, by the time they finished, Lydia wasn't very happy.

Miguel paid for their meal. "Do not look so sad," he encouraged as he walked with her toward the depot. "Just keep thinking how nice it will be to see your family and your new niece."

Juan jerked his head back so as not to be seen when Don Miguel and his woman walked past the alley where he hid. Luckily, he had left Raul with the horses at the livery and was on his way to get a room at the local hotel, staying to the side streets and alleys. He had been about to cross Main Street, but nearly ran into Miguel. Had he not felt the need to check the street first, he surely would have been discovered. Licking his dry lips, he smiled at his good fortune. Cautiously, he poked his head out again to see where they were going.

It was easy to spot Miguel. The black sombrero stood out among the other, more conservative hats some of the men wore. And the woman—she looked more beautiful than he remembered, dressed as a fine lady, her hair all piled up in curls under a fancy, feathered bonnet. Shielding his eyes from the sun, Juan watched as they walked down the boardwalk toward the depot. Slowly, it dawned on him that they might leave before he could put his plan into action. Nearly frantic, Juan ran back to the livery.

"You are back quickly," Raul stated as he got up from the hay where he rested.

"Come," Juan ordered, out of breath. *"Pronto."* He grabbed Raul's arm, shoved him out the door and around the back where they wouldn't be seen. "Don Miguel is here. I think they are going to the stage depot. If he gets away, our plan will be ruined." Juan lifted out his pistol and checked the chamber.

"What are you doing?" Raul asked, scratching his head. "We

can't shoot him. All of Las Cruces will hear us."

"You *idiota*, I have no intention of shooting him unless he forces me to do so. Then it will be self-defense." Juan looked hard at Raul, his frown turning into a smile. "Wasn't Antonio wanted dead or alive?"

"I think so."

Juan gave Raul a disgusted glance. "You think so?" he repeated, shaking his head. "You have the mind of a flea." He shoved his pistol back in his holster. "Try to remember. If he was, I could just shoot him and still collect the reward."

Raul shrugged his shoulders. "I can't be sure."

Juan gave a disgusted grunt. "You make your way to the depot, and stay in the alley. Make sure he doesn't leave. I cannot risk killing him. They might not pay the reward."

"So what will we do?" Raul asked.

"You hide in the alley by the depot and watch. I am going to go and get the marshal, and I do not want him to find you, *comprende?*

Juan left the stable with his sombrero pulled nearly over his eyes. Carefully, he made his way toward the jail.

"May I help you?" A young deputy looked up from a pile of paperwork on the desk.

"I would like to see some wanted posters, *por favor.*"

"Are you a bounty hunter?" the deputy asked as he pointed at the posters tacked on the wall.

Juan stared at the posters, cursing under his breath as he read "dead or alive" under Antonio's picture. "Does it matter if I am?" he asked impatiently. "I would still get the reward, no?"

The deputy shrugged his shoulders. "Sure. We don't care how they're caught, just as long as you get the right man."

CHAPTER TWENTY-FOUR

Juan laughed bitterly. He could have gunned down Miguel and still collected the reward, but his disappointment was alleviated a little when he glanced at the amount of money offered for Raul.

"Well, do you know where any of these men are?" the deputy asked impatiently.

"*Sí*, I do." He touched Antonio's poster. "I know where this man is, and . . ." He dragged a dirty finger over to Raul's poster. "I also know where this man is hiding."

The deputy stood and gave him a skeptical glance. "Can you take me to them?"

Juan gave him a wide smile. "*Sí, señor,* but only if you promise that I will get the rewards."

"First things first, pal."

Juan waited by the desk while the deputy left the room. He returned a moment later with another man. "This is Marshal Quade."

"Marshal," Juan acknowledged, pulling a dirty bandana from his pocket and dabbing at the sweat on his forehead.

"This man says he can take us to Antonio Garcia," the deputy mentioned.

"Where is he?" the marshal asked, reaching for his gunbelt and hat.

"Do not be so impatient, *amigo.*" Juan pointed to Raul's picture. "This one is hiding in the alley by the depot." He gave the marshal a superior smile. "And, this *hombre,* he is with a very beautiful woman with red hair and wearing a fancy dress. They are also at the depot. You'd better hurry before he leaves."

"Ain't you coming?" the young deputy asked as he and the marshal stepped out the door.

"Me?" Juan shook his head. "I have no desire to look upon their evil faces again, *amigo.* I will wait here for my reward."

Sayer was the last to leave the Gonzalez farm, shaking Mr. Gonzalez's hand and thanking Mrs. Gonzalez for the food and shelter, pressing several bills into her palm in payment for the food. He swung up on Rounder and touched the brim of his hat. "I'll be sure to give my wife your recipe, ma'am." Sayer led the others out past the barn and toward the southeast.

"Do you think even if *Señora* Rebeccah followed her instructions, she could make biscuits like that?" Fernando teased. "If I remember correctly, she could burn water."

Sayer grinned. "Yup, she still can, but now we have Teresa."

"And who is Teresa?" Fernando asked.

"She's Becky's maid." Sayer grinned. "And one hell of a good cook."

"So," Fernando said, "you are certain your sister-in-law and my nephew will go to Las Cruces?"

"No, it's just a hunch. If I were Miguel, I would go to the nearest town and wire my family. Then I'd put Lydia on a stage and send her home to her family. The only town big enough to have both a stage depot and a telegraph is Las Cruces."

Fernando nodded. "Since we have nothing else to go on, your hunch is as good as any, hey?"

"Yeah, but there could still be a problem."

"What kind of problem?" Fernando asked with a worried frown.

Sayer guided Rounder around a thick patch of cactus. "A

while back, when we first started looking for Lydia, we met a posse from Las Cruces. Seems the marshal had a personal interest in finding his man—he gunned down the marshal's brother."

"So? Antonio is dead. Certainly he wouldn't mistake Miguel . . . *Dios mio,*" Fernando ground out, hastily crossing himself. "Come, we must get to Las Cruces as fast as possible."

Lydia took a long, deep breath and smoothed the skirt of her iris-blue traveling suit. She adjusted the angle of her hat while Miguel spoke with the man at the ticket counter. She tried to tell herself everything would be all right, but she had a nervous feeling in the pit of her stomach, a nagging voice in the back of her mind, telling her to beware.

Cautiously, she glanced around, but saw nothing suspicious. They were safe. Antonio was dead. Both their fathers had been contacted, and now all she had to do was go home and start planning their wedding. Miguel stood next to her, more handsome than ever in his black bolero and concho-studded trousers, a matching black sombrero resting on his back, held there by the black-leather cord. The pearl handle of the new pistol he had purchased contrasted sharply with the new engraved black-leather holster.

The breeze caught a lock of his ebony hair, and when he brushed it back, he looked at her and smiled. Her heart did a little dance and she sighed with relief with the knowledge that he felt completely at ease.

"One for Santa Fe," he affirmed, paying the man. Once his purchase was made, he led her a little ways away from the others buying passage and folded her gloved hand over his arm. "In four days you will be greeted by your father," he said with a very satisfied smile.

"Are you sure this is the best way?" she asked.

"Most definitely, *vida mia.* To have you ride with me all the way would take twice as long, and it would be torture for you."

"For me or you?" she challenged.

His eyes sparkled, but he managed to keep a straight face. "I love the freckles on your nose. They are—"

"Don't change the subject."

"For you, *mi amor*. You are coming along nicely with your riding, but the stagecoach will be much more comfortable and get you home *muy pronto.*"

Lydia gave a small sigh. "I suppose you're correct. However, I cannot shake the feeling that there's something wrong. I'm sure I read something in the newspaper about this place."

"Las Cruces?" He made a sweep with his arm. "What could possibly trouble you? I have been here many times. Did we not enjoy ourselves at the hotel?" His smile became scandalous. "And the food at the restaurant, it was excellent, no?"

Lydia nodded. "It was. In fact, this gown is quite comfortable and very fashionable. Rebeccah will think I bought it in France." She fingered his lapel, pausing to straighten his black silk string tie. "And you look very handsome in your new jacket."

He flicked at an imaginary piece of lint, tugging his cuff over the sleeve of his crisp white shirt. "I am, how you say—"

"Handsome?"

"*Si, apuesto.*"

She laughed at his arrogant expression. "Extremely so, and that's another reason I should stay, to make sure the ladies here know that you belong to me."

He feigned concern. "That is a worry," he said. "But, if I am pursued, I will try to discourage them."

"And so shall I . . . that is, if any of the gentlemen I will be traveling with make ungentlemanly advances."

Miguel shrugged his shoulders. "There is no need for you to worry."

"And why is that?" she challenged.

He picked up her hand and kissed the back. "I have already explained to them that you are mine, *bonita*, and should I learn that they were discourteous—"

"Discourteous?" She gave a soft laugh.

"*Si*, discourteous in any way, I swore that I would find them and settle things as only two gentlemen can do."

"I know I shouldn't ask, but how do two gentlemen settle these things? I shan't condone a fist-fight."

Once more his smile looked cunning. "Oh, no, it is much more civilized than that. Why it is simple. We meet privately, somewhere quiet, always at dawn, and preferably with pistols."

"A duel?" she cried, trying hard not to laugh.

He frowned. "Absolutely."

"Dueling is illegal and terribly unfashionable."

He leaned closer as two ladies walked past. "Need I remind you that that is precisely what you said about kidnapping?" He didn't give her time to respond; instead, he pulled her tightly into his arms.

"Miguel," she scolded. "This isn't proper in public."

"No? But it is effective." He kissed her deeply without restraint until she slipped her arm around his neck and kissed him with all the longing she felt. When finally he pulled back, they were both a little breathless.

She arranged the lace netting of her hat, glancing first at the man waiting for the stage, then at the two attractive ladies standing on the boardwalk, inwardly smiling when they quickly looked away. "I do believe a public display of affection is most effective, even if it is against what I've been taught to be proper etiquette."

"*Si*, and enjoyable too." He pulled her down to sit beside him on the bench in front of the depot, holding her hand. "I will be at the *rancho* in no more than two weeks—"

"Two weeks seems like a very long time," she protested.

"*Si*, in two weeks, to speak with your brother-in-law and," he said with a wink, "to meet your grandmother. If your father is there, I will ask for your hand and his blessing." His smile filled her with unexplainable joy.

"I will make sure he's there," she said, pressing his hand to her cheek. "However, two weeks is a dreadfully long time."

He kissed the tip of her nose. "You did not think so when I asked you to marry me the first time, remember?"

"Never mind," she replied. "I feel bad enough that I didn't believe you. But that was before. I promise I will never doubt you again." She heaved a sad sigh. "I rather think the next two weeks will drag by slowly."

"For me as well, *vida mia*, but there are some matters I must tend to before I leave."

"Things more important than our marriage?"

He put his hand over his heart. "You wound me. Nothing is more important."

She gave him a tentative smile. "I'm teasing. Now tell me, what are you planning to do while I'm pining away at my sister's ranch?"

"I must take the marshal to Rio Salado."

"But what of Alberto and Carmen? What about the other women and children who live there? How will they survive after the authorities learn of their hiding place and take away their husbands?"

Miguel gave her an understanding smile. "I have no intention of destroying their families. However, I want Raul and Juan to pay for what they have done. They are *banditos*, *bonita*, and if they are allowed to stay, Rio Salado will continue to be a refuge for the lawless. But that is not all. Diablo is there. I must go and get him, and I have a proposal for Alberto and Carmen." Miguel patted his pocket. "Along with a little something to thank them for their help."

"I have a feeling it's more than a little something."

He shrugged his shoulders. "Just enough to fix up the hotel and perhaps build a small school. If there is a place for the children to learn, more families will come. I have asked my father to send some of my *vaqueros* with a few head of cattle and a few good horses. With a little help, Alberto could learn how to be a rancher, and Carmen, perhaps she and some of the other women could run the hotel. Her sister will benefit as well, when they receive the seedlings."

"Seedlings?" she asked incredulously.

"*Si,* pecans are very profitable. They live close to the river and have water with which to irrigate. They can sell travelers, as well as the patrons of Rio Salado's hotel, fresh produce."

"When did you figure all this out?" Lydia asked, impressed with everything he said.

"Do you remember when you could not sleep when we were out on the desert? Well, you were not the only one. It occurred to me that Rio Salado is the only town for a very long way that has water, and soon, it could become a very nice place for weary travelers to stay."

Lydia leaned her head on Miguel's shoulder. "You're wonderful," she murmured. "They will be so happy. But, don't forget to make a sign. It is rather secluded, and I know a sign will help."

"I will make it myself."

They watched as some men hitched a fresh team of horses to the stage and called for the passengers to prepare to leave. Lydia blinked back the sting of tears. "Promise you'll come for me soon."

Miguel pulled her into his arms. "I swear it." He brushed a tear away and gave her a tender smile. "*Bonita,* listen to me. We are safe now. The nightmare is over."

"Yes," she agreed with a wobbly smile.

"You will be much more comfortable on the stage than on a horse," he reminded her.

"Yes, yes, of course." She dabbed at her eyes with a lace handkerchief before she accepted another kiss.

"Now, give me a bright smile." His eyes twinkled, and once more her heart twisted with indecision. The driver held open the door, and Miguel was just about to help her inside when he felt the cold steel of a pistol pressed against the back of his head.

"Hold it right there, you son of a bitch."

Miguel slowly raised his arms as he turned, placing himself between the danger and Lydia. He glanced at the revolver now aimed at his heart, noticing the badge on the tall man's chest. He took a calming breath, aware that no matter what he said he would not be believed. "I do not suppose there is the chance you would let me explain?"

"Sure. You can explain everything after you tell me why you had to gun down a fifteen-year-old boy." The marshal's sneer looked as threatening as the deputy's beside him. "He was my kid brother."

Miguel winced with the knowledge that Antonio had been capable of such a deed. "I could never do anything like that. I am not Antonio Garcia, and I did not kill your brother."

"You're a liar." The marshal took a step back and motioned toward the gun strapped around Miguel's hips. "Why don't you reach for that fancy shooter, so I can blow your brains out and save the judge from having to hang you?"

"Dear Lord!" Lydia cried. "Stop, please. I assure you, you're arresting the wrong man."

Miguel watched the marshal intently. "I swear to you, I am not Antonio Garcia. I just look like him. My name is Miguel Estrada."

"Take his gun, Matt," the marshal ground out. "And frisk him."

"Marshal, please," Lydia said, aware that a small crowd had gathered to watch. Now that it was too late, she remembered reading about the marshal's young brother dying at the hands of a notorious bank robber. "I know this man. Listen to him. My name is Lydia Randolph, and I swear to you, this is Don Miguel Estrada."

"*Bonita*," Miguel warned. When she looked at him, he gave a subtle shake of his head. The moment the marshal turned her way, she realized what Miguel had tried to tell her.

"You're his friend?"

"No, she is not," Miguel ground out as his wrists were pulled back and cuffed.

"Shut up and let her speak." The lawman turned back to her. "Well?"

Lydia cast Miguel a desperate glance. "Yes. My name—"

Marshal Quade grabbed her arm. "Let's go." He motioned for Miguel to start walking before he released Lydia and let her walk beside him.

Miguel cast Lydia a brief glance, and spoke so that only she could hear. "You must tell these men that I took you against—"

"I will not," she said softly.

"*Bonita*, do not argue. You must do as I say."

The marshal grabbed Miguel's arm and pulled him roughly around. "If you've got something to say, pal, say it loud enough where I can hear it, *comprende?*"

"*Si*," Miguel said, and looked directly at Lydia. "*No me puedes ayudar si estas en la carcel.*"

The marshal backhanded Miguel. "In English," he growled furiously, shoving Miguel toward the jail.

Lydia clutched her satchel tightly to her breast, trying hard to remember her brief lessons in Spanish. She repeated the phrase over and over so she wouldn't forget it, thinking about it as she stepped through the door of the marshal's office. Only when they began to search Miguel did she realize what he had said. *You cannot help me if you are in jail.*

"Marshal Quade, please. I cannot tell you how relieved I am that you've finally captured this man." She gave the marshal a small smile when he turned toward her. "I am Lydia Randolph. I was kidnapped by this man over three weeks ago outside of Santa Fe. You can send a telegram to my father, Doctor James Randolph to confirm my story."

She took a calming breath, trying not to look at Miguel while the deputy took his hat, jacket and gun-belt, then told his prisoner to hold out his hands as the cuffs were removed, replaced with thick iron manacles.

"Do you know a retired colonel by the name of—"

"Sayer MacLaren," she interrupted with an eager nod, dragging her eyes away from Miguel. "Yes. He is my sister's husband. Is he here?"

Her hopes dwindled when the lawman shook his head. "Nope, but Colonel MacLaren has been searching for you. I saw him on the trail a while ago."

The marshal turned toward his deputy. "Find anything?"

"Nothing," Matt said, stepping back.

"Good. Put him in a cell."

The deputy led Miguel away, closing the door that separated the main office from the cells. Lydia took a shaky breath and was about to suggest that she be allowed to leave when the marshal caught her elbow in a firm but gentle grasp. "Come with me, Miss Randolph. If we hurry, we might be able to catch your stage."

CHAPTER TWENTY-FIVE

"I know I look like a man named Antonio Garcia," Miguel began, trying to reason with the deputy as the man led him to a jail cell. "But you must believe me, I am not. Read the poster on your wall, *por favor.* You will see for yourself."

"I don't need to read any poster. I know who you are, and this time, you're not going to get away so easily. Now, sit down before I knock you down."

Miguel sat on the cot in the cell while Matt shackled his leg irons to the ring in the center of the stone floor.

"Go to the bank and speak with . . ." Miguel shook his head. "I cannot remember his name, but he received a telegram from my father. How do you think I got these clothes, hey? My father sent me the money."

The deputy's expression never changed. Hate flickered in the depths of his eyes. "I doubt that. You probably stole them, just like you probably stole the money that's in your wallet."

"That money, as I have tried to explain, was sent to me from my father. I used some of it to buy these clothes from the store in your town as well as clothing for Miss Randolph—the woman you insulted. Her father is—"

The deputy stood after making sure the chain was secure and stared down at Miguel. "I don't give a damn how many names you toss around, pal. All I know is that the last I heard, Marshal Quade said Don Miguel was dead. I'll admit you look a little different all cleaned up, but you're still the son of a bitch who killed his brother, so shut your mouth before I plant my fist in it."

"Look at me . . . at the color of my eyes," Miguel demanded when the man walked out of the cell. "The man who killed his brother had brown eyes."

"Don't all your kind have brown eyes?" Matt replied sarcastically as he closed the cell-door and locked it.

Miguel grabbed the bar, swearing as the heavy manacles cut into his wrist. "You are making a mistake. All I ask is that you go to the banker and speak with him. He may still have the telegram from my father."

"That won't bring the marshal's brother back."

"No, and for that I am sincerely sorry." Miguel heaved an impatient sigh. "But his brother's killer is dead. I know. I shot the *cabron* myself."

"Well, you can tell your story to the marshal as soon as he gets back," Matt said with a smirk. "But don't count on him paying any attention. He's not the type to listen to a bunch of lies."

"Where did he go?" Miguel asked with a frown.

"He took the lady you kidnapped and put her on the stage," Matt replied before he walked down the hall.

"Listen to me," Miguel shouted. "I can—"

The door separating the cells from the office slammed shut.

Lydia thanked the driver for stopping at the edge of town, slipping him several bills for his trouble. She picked up her satchel, and keeping to the side streets, made her way to the mercantile.

"Say, weren't you in here just the other day with that handsome Mexican fella?" the old woman asked while Lydia looked at the counter containing the handguns. "Ain't much to look at since he took the pearl-handled Colt. And I'll be darned if another Mexican man didn't come in just a little while ago and bought my second best set. I suggest you wait a few days. At least till the drummer comes by."

Lydia took out some more money and held it up. "I need one now, but I'd prefer you didn't tell anyone about it." She pressed a few bills into the woman's hand.

"I won't tell a soul. I'm the kind of woman who thinks ladies ought to carry guns," the proprietress said with a nod. "Now what can I help you with." She lifted a small derringer. "This is nice and would fit in your reticule."

Lydia pointed at a Colt .45. "I'll take that one and that holster."

The woman took down a rather plain, brown-leather holster. "You're gonna need bullets."

Lydia opened the box. "Will you show me how to put these in?"

The old woman never glanced up, just loaded the gun and slipped it in the holster. "Anything else I can help you with?"

"Yes, I need a split skirt, a blouse, and if you have my size, a leather vest and riding boots." She also purchased a wide-brimmed sombrero with a chinstrap and two serapes, asking if she could change in the back room. Before she left, she bought some dried fruit, a couple of cans of potted meat and a tin of crackers, stuffing them and her gown into her satchel, giving the old woman her feathered hat.

"I ain't never had a hat quite like this one," the proprietor said with a wide grin as Lydia shrugged into the serape. "And just in case you've never shot a gun before, it's a whole sight easier if you pull the hammer back first, then squeeze the trigger."

Lydia glanced down at her over-stuffed satchel, and pulled out the gown. She guessed by the woman's small stature that it would probably fit. "Here, you might as well have this to go with your new hat."

The old woman's eyes brightened and as she muttered her thanks, Lydia headed toward the door, glancing out as she tucked her long red hair into the sombrero and pulled it down over her eyes to obscure her features. Carefully scanning the faces of the passersby, she stepped outside and crossed the street on her way to the hotel. She procured a room under a fictitious name and climbed the stairs. Once inside she turned and locked the door.

Lydia sat on the bed for a moment, gathering her thoughts, remembering the proprietress's words. *And I'll be darned if another Mexican man didn't come in just a little while ago and bought my second best set.*

It had to be Juan or Raul, she surmised, tossing her satchel on the chair so she could take off her boots. She yanked off her hat and ran her fingers through her hair, wondering why they would have ventured into town, so close to the law. The knowledge that they might be there tied her stomach into a sick knot.

Bunching the pillows against the headboard, she suddenly started as another name came to mind. Fernando. It could have been Don Fernando. Relief nearly made her shoulders sag. But even if he was here, there was no time to try and find Miguel's uncle. Convinced she could carry out her plan alone, she settled down and made herself comfortable, content to wait until it got dark. If she happened to run into Don Fernando, all her problems would be over. If not, they were just about to begin again.

The marshal sat in his chair, drumming his fingers on his desk as he had for the last hour since Randy and Joe brought in the other prisoner, Raul Martinez. Just as they were told, the Mexican bandit was hiding in the alley by the depot between two barrels. Other than swearing that he would get even with someone named Juan, he hadn't given the deputies any trouble. In fact, except for his smell and rumpled clothing, he seemed to accept his fate.

Bill stared at both Raul's and Antonio's posters, but didn't see them. His mind was on other things as he tried to recall his conversation with Colonel MacLaren when they had met on the trail. *Don Miguel is dead. We think the men we're looking for killed him and kidnapped my sister-in-law. Her name is Lydia Randolph. She's got long red hair, not too tall and pretty as a picture.*

The door to the jail opened and slowly he looked up.

"Bill, are you all right?" His wife's smile filled with compassion. "When you didn't come home, I got worried."

"Yeah. I'm sorry, Susan. I kind of lost track of time."

"Randy told me you caught the man who killed Garret." She put her hand on her husband's shoulder. "It's over now, sweetheart. Come home. You're exhausted. Let someone else guard him."

"Maybe you're right. I could use a hot bath and one of your home-cooked meals."

"Well, Marshal Quade," she said, taking his hat down from the wall. "Come with me. I know just where you can get one."

Juan stepped out of the local bathhouse searching for a place to get a drink. The silver-studded gunbelt strapped around his waist matched the design of the *conchos* on his fancy brown trousers. The ruffled shirt he'd bought felt a little tight, but under his bolero, he didn't think anyone would notice. Later, with the reward money he got for Miguel and Raul, he could order a dozen shirts that fit, if he wanted a dozen.

Right now, he wanted a drink and a thick steak, and after that he would get a room and perhaps even a willing woman. Juan smiled with the knowledge that when he returned to Rio Salado, he would be a rich man. And, after Miguel and Raul were hanged, he would have nothing to worry about.

"Fergus and I are going into town alone, and that's final," Sayer replied, stopping just outside of Las Cruces.

"That is an excellent idea," Fernando stated tersely. "Except I will not allow it."

Sayer glanced at Jorge. "There are some rocks back down the road a ways. It's as good a place as any to make camp."

"And I am sure Jorge will do so," Fernando said with a firm nod.

Sayer turned his gaze to Fernando. "You can help him."

"I will not," Fernando refused. "I am going to town with you."

"The hell you will," Sayer countered drawing his .45. Sayer inwardly winced at Fernando's wounded expression. "Need I remind you that you left New Mexico a wanted man? Now step down."

Fernando obeyed, but his features hardened and his hands curled into fists.

"Jorge, take his horse and head on back to those rocks." When the older man hesitated, Sayer told him not to worry, that it was for Fernando's own good. "You need to listen to me," Sayer continued. "I'm not taking any chances. I'll speak with Marshal Quade."

Fernando frowned. "There is no danger. He does not know me."

"Someone there might, and that's enough reason for you to stay here. If Miguel's there, I'll find him, or he'll find me." Sayer turned to make sure Jorge was a ways down the road before he shoved his Colt back into the holster. "I'll send word as soon as I know something."

The rattling of the key in the lock woke Miguel from his nap.

Since they'd brought him in that morning, there had been little to do but sleep. He grabbed the bars and pulled himself up to a sitting position. "What time is it?" he asked the deputy when he came into the cell and undid the chains.

"Nearly five, pal." Matt motioned for Miguel to stand up. "Thought you might want to take a walk to the outhouse."

"Take me first," Raul muttered, slowly sitting up.

"How long before the judge arrives?" Miguel dragged his hands down his face before he flexed his stiff left shoulder.

"Couple more days."

Miguel took a deep breath. He thought of Lydia as he followed Matt down the hall, relieved that she'd do her best to help him.

"Get going, pal, I haven't got all day, and your friend there says he needs to go."

Squinting against the bright sunlight, Miguel stepped outside. The privy was only a short distance away, but he stumbled because of the chains. The guard jammed the muzzle of a rifle into his back, goading him on.

After he had finished, Miguel glanced toward the road on his way back to the jail. "It is not possible," he muttered in disbelief. He stopped and shielded his eyes against the setting sun as the man on the big red stallion continued on down the road, followed by an older man wearing a faded Army uniform.

"Get moving," the guard growled, nudging Miguel in the back again.

"I know that man. He is Colonel Sayer MacLaren," Miguel said, turning his attention to the guard. "He can tell you who I really am."

"Move," the guard repeated.

Miguel ignored him and glanced at the road, at the red horse disappearing from sight.

"Col—" Pain exploded in his neck and shoulders. He sank to

his knees and tried to keep from passing out.

"I said, get going," the guard warned, raising his rifle to hit him again.

"No," Miguel ground out through clenched teeth. "I will go . . . I will go."

Sayer handed his reins to the boy at the livery while Fergus tied his horse to the hitching post. "Rub him down and give him some extra oats," Sayer said as the boy led the stallion inside. "Well, it'll be dark in an hour. We might as well see if we can get a room for the night."

"That's the best thing I've heard in days," Fergus said, pausing only to tell the boy what he wanted done for his horse. "And, then maybe we could see if'n the restaurant is open. I could use a steak." He held up his hand, his thumb and forefinger about two inches apart. "This thick with all the fixins."

They headed down the boardwalk toward the hotel, glad to see someone lighting a lamp through the window. "Looks like we're in luck," Sayer stated as he pushed the door open.

An old man looked at them over the top of his glasses. "Can I help you boys?"

"Two rooms if you've got them," Sayer asked.

"Yup. Six bits."

Sayer tossed the money on the counter. "Have you seen a young woman with red hair—"

"Yup, stayed here for a couple of days. She was with a real nice Mexican fella."

"Do you know where they are?" Sayer asked as he picked up two keys.

"Nope, checked out two days ago."

"Both of them?"

"Yup, they was together as far as I know." The old man raised a grey brow. "Stayed in the same room."

"Well, thanks for the information." Sayer gave a key to Fergus. "I'm going over to the jail before it gets too late. You go on to the restaurant and order. I'll be back shortly."

It didn't take long to find the marshal's office, but when he tried the door, it was locked. He banged on it with his fist, but no one answered, nor did a light appear in the window. Swearing under his breath, Sayer headed back to the restaurant.

Matt stepped out of the privy, tugging on his suspenders. He picked up the lantern and went back to unlock the jail. He put the lamp on the desk, checked his pocket watch, and picked up the newspaper to finish what he'd been reading. A little while later, and right on time, the marshal came in and hung his hat on the hook by the door.

"How was your supper?" Matt asked as he got up from the marshal's chair.

"Fine. You can't beat Susan's cooking." The marshal sat down and heaved a tired sigh. "Any trouble?"

"Nope. Other than the fat one complaining that the food's no good, not a word."

"Well, what did you find out?" Fergus asked as Sayer took a seat across from him.

"Nothing. The place was locked up, and since it's late, I decided to come back and eat. I'll check with them first thing in the morning. Have you ordered?"

"Aye, two thick beef-steaks."

The meal was worth the extra price they had to pay for keeping the cook later than the usual seven o'clock. While Fergus finished his second piece of blueberry pie, Sayer leaned back in his chair. The woman came out with the coffee pot, but he waved her away. "No thank you, ma'am. I've had my share."

Fergus accepted another cup, adding some cream and sugar.

"You gents aren't from around here, are you?" the plump young woman asked.

"No, ma'am, we're down here looking for my wife's sister and possibly a man she could be with." Sayer leaned closer. "She has red hair, about your size and big green eyes."

"Your sister?" the woman stated doubtfully. "I saw her here just a few days ago."

Sayer cast Fergus a quick glance. "When . . . exactly?"

"Well, let me think. I do believe the last time they were in was the day before yesterday. She always came in with a Mexican gentleman, and they always sat over there."

"Do you know if they're still in town?"

The woman paused to think. "I don't rightly know for sure." She headed toward the kitchen, then turned and gave Sayer a sympathetic smile. "I'd check with the stage depot when it opens in the morning, if I were you. The last time they were here, she was dressed all fancy like, not like the type to be riding off on a horse. Now that I think about it, I do believe I overheard them arguing."

"Arguing?" Sayer repeated. "What about?"

"Something about buying only one fare. If she's your wife's sister, you might like to know that I don't think the man was planning to go with her."

"Do you know what happened to the man?"

"Can't say as I do. He must've left town, 'cause I haven't seen him since. Oh, I almost forgot this." The woman put the bill on the table. "That'll be four dollars."

Sayer took out his wallet. "Is it possible to get some food to take with us?"

She gave them another impatient look. "I suppose so, but it'll be another dollar, and 'bout the only thing we've got left is some cold fried chicken."

"That'll be just fine, ma'am. Thanks." Sayer pushed away from the table. "Well, at least it's a relief to know Lydia's safe. Maybe in the morning, we'll have everything cleared up. Meanwhile, Fergus, my old friend, you can take this chicken to Fernando and Jorge."

Fergus made a face. "I've no desire tae do any more ridin', if'n you know what I mean."

Sayer laughed and handed Fergus the basket. "What's a few miles to an old war horse like you?"

Fergus came around a brace of cedar and found Jorge sitting by a small fire tending to a pot of beans. When Fergus asked where Don Fernando was hiding, Fernando stepped down from a rocky ledge, carrying his rifle.

"We cannot be too careful," Fernando stated.

"I brought you somethin'." Fergus gave Fernando a cloth-covered basket. "It'll be a wee bit better than those beans you've got cookin' on the fire."

Fernando tore it open, and grinned. "Fried chicken. At least you were thinking of us, hey?" He took a large bite from a leg, closing his eyes as he passed the basket to his companion. "Heavenly."

"Aye, the food there is almost as good as Miss Bonnie's back in Santa Fe."

"Now, *mi amigo,* what did you learn about Miguel?"

Fergus shook his head. "Nothin' for sure yet. We willna be able tae get any answers till mornin'. The jail's locked up tighter than a drum. However, the lass that brought our food said she saw Miss Lydia with a Mexican man."

"Miguel?" Fernando asked.

"I'm fairly sure it was, but she said Lydia took the stage. If'n it was Miguel, and I'm not sayin' it was, he stayed in Las Cruces."

"So why the frown?" Fernando asked tossing the chicken bone into the fire.

"Well, the colonel and I was hopin' tae see him, either at the hotel or at the restaurant where we got that chicken. There isn't another place tae eat. Since the town seems to close up a wee bit early, the colonel's thinking Miguel might have already gone tae his room for the night."

Fernando nodded. "It is a relief to know that *Señorita* Lydia is on her way back to Santa Fe, but, like you, I am still worried about Miguel."

Fernando took another piece out of the box and took a bite, chewing for several moments before he spoke. "So I assume you are returning to Las Cruces tonight?"

Fergus grinned. "Aye, you bet I am. I paid for a room with a feather bed and I intend on usin' it. Tomorrow I'll do some more checkin', startin' with the bank—"

"The bank?"

"Aye. The colonel thinks Miguel would have wired his father for some money. Says they had tae have it tae pay for Miss Lydia's passage. If'n that's so, the banker's sure tae know about it."

Raul sulked in his cell, muttering threats each time Miguel made a move. Finally, when Miguel could stand it no longer, he motioned for Raul to come closer with the pretense of having something very important to tell him. When Raul leaned over, Miguel caught him by the throat and mashed his face against the bars. "I will tell you this only one time, *hombre*," Miguel ground out. "Say nothing more to me, or next time I will not be so gentle."

He shoved the gasping man back, sickened by the way he sank down on the floor in fear and cried for the guards.

"What the hell is going on in here?" the marshal demanded

as he came down the hall with the lantern.

Raul pointed a dirty finger at Miguel. "He tried to kill me." He pulled down his shirt and showed him the marks Miguel's fingers had made on his neck, and touched his face where it was still red. "See, I am not safe even in your jail."

The Marshal stared at Miguel through the bars of his cell. "I warned you about causing trouble." He left for a moment, returning with Matt. The deputy carried the same rifle he had earlier that day. "Keep that on him, Matt."

"Sure thing, marshal. If he even blinks wrong, I'll blow his head off."

The marshal stepped into Miguel's cell, unlocked his wrist and ankles. He took a step back and pulled out his revolver, using it to motion him to stand. "Get up real slow."

"Ha, they are going to take you out back and shoot you, like the mad dog you are," Raul goaded.

"Shut up," the marshal ordered. He turned back to Miguel. "Walk."

Miguel's gaze never wavered, nor did he feel the need to question the two men as he walked down the hall. He had seen the hate in the marshal's eyes before, and already knew what Matt was capable of. Although his mind raced and his fingers curled into fists, he managed to remain calm. He was directed to open the door, to step outside and walk around to the back.

"Kneel down," the marshal ordered.

Miguel turned to confront them. "So, this is how you will rid yourself of your mistake?" Miguel asked flatly. "I hope you can live with yourself once you learn the truth."

"What mistake?" Matt jeered. "We're just taking care of a problem a little early, ain't that right, marshal."

"That's right, Matt." The marshal motioned to Miguel. "Now, do as I say. Turn around and kneel down."

CHAPTER TWENTY-SIX

Lydia pressed back against the outside wall of the marshal's office and peeked around the corner. Her heart hammered into her chest. Miguel stood with the marshal and his deputy, and in the moonlight she could see that the shackles had been removed and that they both had weapons aimed at him.

"If you're going to kill me," Miguel began with a calmness that caused her stomach to knot as she realized why he'd been released. "Allow me the dignity to face my executioner."

"There will be no execution tonight, gentlemen," Lydia said with an air of authority.

Miguel almost didn't believe his eyes. Lydia stood there, holding a large caliber revolver. Her features were mostly obscured by a large sombrero and a black and grey serape. Her feet were spread and her hand looked steady, but he knew if they forced her to fire, he was in as much danger of getting shot as they were. He quickly pulled the hidden knife from his boot and came up behind the deputy, pressing the knife against his throat. The marshal spun, first glancing at Miguel and his deputy, then back at Lydia.

"Do as my *amigo* says, Marshal Quade. Put your weapon on the ground and kick it toward my friend . . . very slowly."

"You son of a bitch." The marshal hesitated for a moment, as if he were weighing the odds, looking at Miguel and then over at Lydia, but finally he did as he was told, and took a step back with his arms raised. "Let him go."

Lydia holstered her Colt. She quickly picked up the marshal's gun, turning it on the lawman. Miguel relieved Matt of his rifle, handing it over to Lydia before taking the deputy's revolver. "Now, let us go back inside, and I suggest you walk very slowly and do not make any sudden moves."

The marshal hesitated. "If you're who you say you are, you won't shoot us. And if you did, the sound of the gunshot would bring the whole town down on you."

Miguel nodded. "That is true." He held the knife so the blade twinkled in the moonlight. "However, there are other, more silent, ways to kill, no? Are you willing to risk the life of your deputy? For I swear to you, I have nothing to lose."

"All right, I'm going, but you better get a long way away from here, 'cause I'll make you a little promise too. This ain't over. I'll hunt you down to the ends of the earth, if that's what it takes."

Miguel motioned for Lydia to follow, as the marshal led the way back to the jail. The moment they came down the hall, Raul clung to the bars, begging to be freed.

"It is the woman," Raul gasped once Lydia stood in the doorway. "*Señorita, por favor,* forgive me. Tell Miguel to let me go and I will swear that he is not Antonio."

Miguel ignored his rambling, motioning for the marshal and his deputy to go into his old cell. When the door was locked, he put the knife back in his boot.

"I thought you searched him," the marshal growled at Matt.

"I did, but who would think to look in his boots?"

Miguel shoved the gun into his belt. "I will tell you once more that I am not Antonio, but I know that you still refuse to believe me, even though you are both alive. Look closely at me, *señor,* and remember my face as the face of Don Miguel Estrada. My father is Don Enrico Dominguez Mendoza Estrada. As I tried to explain, he wired permission to your banker to give me five thousand dollars, most of which is still in your bank under my name. Tomorrow, when one of your men finds you and lets you go, all I ask is that you confirm what I say. It will save you a very long ride through a very hot and dusty desert."

Matt flashed a worried glance at his boss. "What's he talking about?"

Lydia stepped closer and took off the sombrero. "He is trying to tell you, had you only given him the opportunity, that he could have proved who he was."

"Come, *vida mia*," Miguel said, escorting her into the front office. He strapped on his gunbelt, put on his sombrero and shrugged into his bolero. A quick search of the marshal's desk produced his wallet and new pocket watch. Antonio's poster caught his attention. He picked it up, walked back and shoved it through the bars. "Perhaps now you will have the time to read this a little more carefully, hey? But no matter. The man on that poster, as I told you, is dead."

Miguel grasped Lydia's arm and stepped cautiously out of the jail, drinking in a long deep breath of fresh air. Blending in with the shadows, he led them carefully toward the stables, pausing only to make sure the young man who cared for the horses still slept.

A horse he recognized as the colonel's nickered a greeting, and with a sly smile, Miguel headed toward the stallion's stall.

"That's Sayer's stallion," Lydia gasped, turning wide eyes toward Miguel. "He must be here!" She went to another stall and pointed at a large roan. "And this is the sergeant's gelding. I'd know him anywhere."

"Good, we will take them both."

"Take them both?" she repeated with a perplexed frown. "Why? We can go to the hotel and—"

Miguel pulled her closer and smiled down at her. "For a moment I had considered finding the colonel, but it is very late,

277

and I will not take the chance of being captured again. Especially now that you are an accomplice." He kissed her quick. "Who would rescue me if we were both in jail?"

"But—"

"Trust me, *bonita*. El Paso is only half a day's ride south. We will go there and send another telegram, only this time we will send it here, to Colonel MacLaren. If we are followed, Mexico is just across the border, and we can stay there until we can clear our names."

He quickly saddled the roan gelding and gave her the reins. He grabbed the bridle hanging on the gate of the stallion's stall. "Rounder is a not a suitable name for a prize such as yourself," Miguel whispered, leading the stallion out of the stall and tossing a saddle on his back. He turned to Lydia, finding her already on the animal's back, adjusting the strap of her hat under her chin.

"Tonight we must ride quickly through town, *comprendes?*"

She gave him a reluctant nod.

"Hold on to the horn, *vida mia,* and lean slightly forward. Your horse will follow mine." Miguel turned and scratched the stallion's neck, and gracefully swung up on his back. "Come, *mi amigo,*" he whispered to the horse, "show me what you can do."

Miguel pressed his heels in the animal's sides. They bolted out the door, the gelding close behind. Scared to death, Lydia clung to the horn and leaned over the galloping horse's neck as Miguel had advised her to do.

With the wind stinging their faces, Miguel gave the stallion his head, urging him onward until the lamplights of Las Cruces were no longer visible. Sure they weren't being followed, Miguel slowed the stallion, and as she knew he would, the gelding followed suit. There was no need for words as they walked the animals while the lather of sweat on their coats dried.

"*Parese alli mismo,*" a voice in the darkness ordered. The sound of a rifle being cocked gave Miguel reason to obey. He cued the stallion to move a step ahead, in front of Lydia. Slowly he raised his hands.

"What did they say?" she asked in a frantic whisper.

"Just stay behind me," Miguel ordered.

The ghostly forms of two men wearing serapes stepped from behind some brush, their boots crunching loudly on the sand as they approached. The stallion snorted, took a step back and bolted sideways in fear of the approaching men. A gunshot shattered the silence, and Lydia screamed, trying desperately to control her own skittish mount. The stallion reared. Miguel hit the ground hard, knocking the breath from his lungs. He tried to get up, staggered to his feet, but, still recovering from his wounds, his knees buckled. Somewhere in the distance he heard a man swear. He tried to move, but collapsed.

"*Dios mio,*" Fernando cried. "I have killed my own nephew."

Sayer stepped down from the boardwalk, checking his watch. Eight o'clock. He tried the handle at the jail, and was pleased to find it unlocked. The office was vacant, but that didn't stop him from checking the cells. If Miguel was there, he was determined to find him.

He opened the door, not at all surprised to see three men in cells, all asleep, all snoring. One was clearly of Mexican descent, lying on his back, his snores the loudest. The other two were fair headed, the taller of the two on the cot with his back to Sayer. The other man slept on the floor, using his hat and vest as a pillow. "Hey," Sayer called cautiously. "Hey, pal, wake up."

The man on the cot woke with a start, nearly tripping over the man on the floor as he jumped to his feet. There was a badge pinned to his chest.

"Colonel?" the marshal muttered.

"Marshal Quade? What in blazes are you doing in here?"

The marshal raked his fingers through his hair. "I'll tell you over some coffee. For now, just grab those keys over there and get us the hell outta here."

Miguel slowly opened his eyes, wincing when he found himself on a blanket in the shade of a large rock formation. He was thirsty and his leg hurt. He rose, groaning in despair as he inspected a neat bandage on his thigh just above his knee. "Blessed Mother," he muttered angrily. "What more can possibly happen?"

Fear stabbed into his chest as he realized Lydia wasn't there. He painfully got to his feet, bracing his back against the rock when he heard approaching footfalls. He glanced down, surprised to find his pistol still in its holster. Drawing his gun, he swallowed to ease the dryness in this throat.

"If he does not wake soon, I am taking him into town to see a doctor. I do not care what the colonel said, I will—"

Miguel could hardly believe his eyes. *"Tio?"*

Fernando broke into a wide grin, rushed up to Miguel and embraced him, ignoring his nephew's painful groan. "Miguel, forgive me, *sobrino.* I did not know it was you."

Miguel tried to speak, but Fernando's grip was too restrictive. Finally, when he couldn't draw a proper breath, he shoved Fernando back, yet held on to him for support, relieved to see Lydia. "*Tio*, I have never been so happy to see anyone in my entire life."

Fernando pulled him back into his arms. "Forgive me, forgive me."

"T—" Again the air was chased from his lungs when his uncle hugged him.

"I swear to the Virgin, I did not know it was you," Fernando repeated, crossing himself.

"Tio!" Miguel shouted, shoving away and nearly falling when

his leg wouldn't bear his weight. Fernando caught him and helped him over to a rock ledge where he could sit down. "I am all right. Please, calm yourself."

Lydia rushed to his side and checked the neat bandage. "It's just a flesh wound," she said with a sympathetic smile. "But on the brighter side, Diablo is here."

"Thank God I found you," Fernando said. He went to Lydia and hugged her. "And you, *señorita*. Thank God for both of you."

His uncle's expression looked so pitiful, Miguel felt bad for yelling at him.

Fernando swiped at his eyes. "I have been so worried and then . . . then I almost—"

"*Tío*," Miguel warned. "Look at me. I am fine. We are fine. Everyone is fine." When Fernando nodded and sniffed, Miguel took pity on him and held out his arms. "Come here and give your nephew a hug."

"Your man's not here," the marshal stated as he leaned back in his chair and stared at the paper in his hand. "And, I suppose it's a good thing he got away." Sayer saw the man's remorse when he raised his eyes and they locked with his. "Last night, I wasn't thinking too clear. You see, it was . . . well it would have been Garret's . . . my brother's birthday." The marshal swiped his hand down his face and heaved a sorrowful sigh. "According to this telegram, I could have killed an innocent man."

"I don't condone what you did, but I understand why you did it." Sayer picked up his hat and stood. "I reckon you'll verify that telegram from my father-in-law, and my story when you talk to the banker?"

"Yeah, just as soon as the bank opens. Oh, and colonel, your sister-in-law—at least I think she was your sister-in-law—well I put her on the stage, but I reckon she found a way to get off.

She helped Miguel last night."

Sayer frowned. "You saw Lydia?"

"Mostly I saw the Colt .45 she had pointed at my heart. She was dressed differently, but I think I recognized her voice. I hope you find them."

"Thanks. I'd best be heading out. Maybe I can catch up to them before they do something desperate." Sayer put on his hat and stepped outside. Fergus stood there with two horses.

"Where's Rounder?" Sayer asked.

Fergus pushed his hat up to rest on the back of his head while he scratched his ear. "I'm hopin' Don Miguel took him, as well as my gelding."

"What? Both are missing?"

"Aye, Rounder's gone. Stolen along with my gelding some time last night."

"Son of a buck," Sayer ground out, stepping into the saddle on the big grey mare Fergus had bought. "Well, don't just stand there. Let's go send a telegram to James and Rebeccah. We've got to tell them that Lydia missed the stage, and then we've got to tell Fernando what happened. After that, I'm going to track down Miguel and get my damned horse back."

An hour later, Sayer rode into Fernando's camp, not too surprised to see Miguel and Lydia sitting in the shade conversing with Fernando, who carved on a limb obviously intended to be used as a crutch. When Sayer got off his horse, Lydia ran into his arms and he spun her around.

"If you aren't a sight for sore eyes," he said, pushing his hat off his forehead. He turned to Miguel, noticing the bandage around his leg as he offered his hand. "Don Miguel, it's good to see you in one piece."

"*Señor* MacLaren," Miguel began, but was instantly asked to use Sayer's first name. "It has been a while, but like you, I am very glad to see someone who knows who I am."

"Sayer, have you heard from Papa or Becky?" Lydia asked. "I wired them that I was coming, and then—"

Sayer held up his hand. "I sent them a telegram just a little while ago after the marshal said you missed your stage, but more importantly, I want to know how you broke this *hombre* out of jail."

Lydia gave a disbelieving sigh as she put her arms around Miguel and leaned closer. "At the time, I had no idea. I just made up my mind that he wasn't going to hang for something he didn't do."

Sayer matched her smile. "I want to hear every detail."

Lydia had no sooner finished her story than Jorge came down from the rocks, announcing that a single rider approached. Miguel limped to where he could see, shaking his head. "Quick, *Tío*, come here. I want you to do something for me."

Juan jerked his horse to a halt when Fernando stepped out from behind some rocks carrying a rifle. *"Buenos dias, amigo,"* Fernando said, cradling the weapon in the crook of his arm as he pushed his sombrero off his forehead. "It is very hot for so early in the morning, no?"

Juan stared at Fernando. "I think you have mistaken me for someone else. I do not know who you are, or why you are in my way. If you intend to rob me, all I have is what you see, and a man cannot survive in the desert without his horse."

Fernando laughed. "I don't want your horse, *amigo*. All I want is a little information. Someone told me you might know a man by the name of Don Miguel?"

Juan shrugged his shoulders. "I did. It is a terrible shame, *señor*. Don Miguel is dead. Killed by Antonio Garcia almost a week ago."

"Antonio Garcia?" Fernando watched his prey closely. "I heard differently. I heard that Don Miguel pretended to be

Antonio to fool his cousin. Perhaps you know him . . . Antonio's cousin . . . his name is Raul. Raul Martinez?"

Again Juan shrugged his shoulders and shook his head. "I do not recall."

"Perhaps I can refresh your memory, *amigo*. You see, Don Miguel is alive. Of this I am sure. And Antonio, he is dead, killed by Miguel in a gunfight, as you said, a week ago."

"Someone told you a lie." Juan tried to guide his horse past, but Fernando caught the animal's reins.

"Now I am really confused. I think we need to get this straightened out. Don't you agree?"

Juan shook his head. "There is no reason to do so. It is as I say, *señor*. Don Miguel is dead. I saw him killed with my own eyes."

Fernando scratched the back of his neck. "Then what happened to Antonio?"

"He is waiting to hang back in Las Cruces."

"No . . . he is? How did you know that?" Fernando said with a skeptical frown.

"Because, I turned him and his cousin in to the marshal myself."

"And you collected the reward?"

Juan visibly swallowed as he shifted nervously.

"Let me see," Fernando began. "I am not a smart man, but if there was one thousand dollars offered for Raul, and somewhere I remember seeing five thousand dollars offered—"

"T-two . . . it was only two," Juan stammered.

"*Si, si, muchas gracias.* Now, where was I? Oh, I remember. There was a two thousand dollar reward for Antonio, dead or alive . . ." Fernando paused to count on his fingers. "That would make you a very rich man, no?"

"N-no," Juan stammered. The next instant, he planted his foot on Fernando's chest and shoved him back. At the same time he drew his gun only to have four men step out from behind the rocks, each with a weapon pointed at him. His finger froze on the trigger, but he threw the weapon down as if it burned his hand.

"Do not kill me." Juan's hands shook as he pulled out his wallet. "Take this if you must, but I beg you, do not kill me."

Fernando got up, brushed the dirt from his clothing and took the wallet, checking to see if the money was inside. "Eee, this will do nicely, no?" he asked, turning to the others. Fernando knew Juan watched him and didn't notice as one of the others stepped forward, limping slightly and using a makeshift crutch.

"*Hola*, Juan."

The last of the color drained from Juan's already pale features. "Don Miguel," he rasped.

Miguel accepted the wallet. Like Fernando, he took a moment to look inside. "What do you think will happen when word gets out that you turned your *amigos* in for the rewards?" He didn't give Juan time to answer. "Where are my manners? I have not yet introduced you. Juan, this is my uncle, Don Fernando Gutierrez. I believe you have heard the name before, no?"

Fernando stepped forward and gave a little bow.

"S-*si*," Juan answered.

Miguel limped a little closer and motioned for Juan to lean closer. "I believe you remember what I told you, that he has a very bad reputation for revenge. He has been known to cut out a man's heart and feed it to the wolves."

Juan's hands flew to his chest. "S-*si*."

Miguel gave a soft laugh. "But, as long as you stay in Mexico, and as long as we never lay eyes on you again, there is nothing for you to worry about. Agreed?"

"A-agreed, *Señor* Estrada. I swear you will never see me again."

Miguel frowned. "Then why am I looking at you now?"

Juan gathered up his reins and spun his horse around, whipping at the animal's rump with his hat.

"That was almost mean," Sayer said as he came up alongside Miguel, followed by Lydia. "Why, he was shaking like a leaf in the wind."

Miguel put his arm around Lydia and they all walked back to their camp. "Believe me," Lydia said with firm conviction, "he deserved every moment of it."

"He did, indeed," Miguel agreed. "It was the only way I could be sure the innocent people back at Rio Salado would be safe."

"So you're still planning on going back?" Sayer asked.

"*Si,* but first I must return to Las Cruces and get the rest of the money my father sent. Most of it is still in the bank."

"This time, we will go with you," Fernando said firmly.

"Not if I have anything to do with it," Sayer corrected. Fernando muttered something in Spanish, causing Miguel to laugh. "What did he say?" Sayer asked.

Miguel shrugged his shoulders. "He said you are his very best friend and that he will do anything you say if it makes you happy."

When Lydia giggled, Sayer gave a skeptical snort. "Yeah, I'll bet."

Miguel gathered up Diablo's reins, wincing a little as he mounted the big black. "Someday soon we must make time to talk about breeding some mares to your stallion." Miguel glanced over at Rounder. "He is a good horse, even if he is a coward." He grinned at Sayer before he pushed his sombrero down firmly on his head.

"Sergeant Carmichael, will you ride with *Señorita* Randolph?" Miguel asked.

"Miguel, what are you thinking?" Lydia chided. His wink was answer enough.

Miguel turned back to Sayer. "Perhaps you would like to test your cowardly stallion against Diablo?" His grin left Sayer no room to refuse.

Sayer swung up on Rounder's back and nudged him over, beside Diablo. "You're sure your leg is up to it?"

"It is my horse who will be running, not I," Miguel said with a grin. "Care to make a small wager?"

"How much?" Sayer replied.

Miguel glanced down at his uncle. "How much, *Tio?*"

Fernando gave a disgusted grunt. "The man was a colonel in the Army. He has no money, except that of his wife. But, no matter, I will cover his bet on one condition." Fernando put his arm around Lydia and gave her an arrogant smile.

"And that is?" Sayer asked.

"That I may attend my nephew's wedding at my . . . your *rancho.*"

Sayer cast a quick glance at Miguel, shaking Fernando's hand. "Very well, I'll wager one thousand dollars that Rounder can outrun Diablo." Both men gathered up their reins.

"Wait, wait," Fernando cried. "One thousand dollars?" He shook his head. "But Diablo is much older and—"

"Do not listen to him," Miguel complained. "Come, *amigo.* May the best horse win," he shouted, digging his heels into his stallion's sides.

"Eee," Fernando cried, standing next to Fergus. "Who is ahead?"

Fergus pulled out his wallet. "I've got fifty dollar on the colonel."

Fernando nodded. "Very well, fifty it is." Fernando's worried frown turned into a sly smile. "I cannot think of an easier way to double my money."

CHAPTER TWENTY-SEVEN

Lydia sat in a rocker on the veranda with her sister and grandmother, rocking Rebeccah's baby in her arms. Kaiser dozed in the shade, next to Rebeccah's feet. While Becky and her grandmother chatted about the weather and when the men would return from Santa Fe with much-needed supplies, she silently condemned herself for the thousandth time for letting Miguel talk her into coming ahead on the stage while he went back to Rio Salado.

She heaved a sigh, smiling down at the baby, remembering the time she and Miguel had talked about having children. *Vamos a tener muchos bebes hermosos—we will have many beautiful babies. Mostly chicos. Boys.* Lydia's smile widened. *How many children do you want?* she remembered asking, recalling how he had shrugged his shoulders before replying, *If we are married very soon and we stay married for twenty years . . . I would think we could have fifteen . . . maybe twenty little ones, no?* She stared down at her infant niece, offering a little prayer for his safety and immediate return.

"Lydia?" Rebeccah repeated.

Lydia glanced at her sister. "I'm sorry, did you say something?"

"Yes. Why don't I take the baby while you go inside and take a nap."

Lydia almost laughed. Ever since she got home, her little sister had done nothing but coddle her. On the other hand, her grandmother had done nothing but complain about her choice of a husband.

"I'm not at all tired. I'm fine." She gazed out over the long, fenced path to the main road, hoping with all her heart she would catch a glimpse of a large black stallion. She pictured how he would look when he finally arrived—he on his beautiful black horse, prancing up the drive, ever the gentleman to impress her grandmother. She turned for another look, disappointed to see the long path empty; just the heat waves dancing on the ground, distorting the horizon.

"Do you remember Lieutenant Williams?" her grandmother asked.

"Yes," Lydia responded, groaning inside. She offered another prayer that she could somehow muzzle the old dowager. "He was under Sayer's command last year. I danced with him at Rebeccah's wedding. He was very charming."

"He has always had an eye for you," Katherine said. "And he's rather handsome in his uniform."

"Yes, he was," Lydia added without enthusiasm. "Miguel is very handsome too."

"Well, while you were away, the Lieutenant paid a little social call," Katherine began. "I daresay, he seemed most concerned for your welfare, and he and I had a delightful chat. He is such a nice young man. Did you know his father and mother are English? His father is in Parliament. He expressed a desire to visit them, offering to act as my escort should I ever decide to return home."

"Really?" Lydia said with a bright smile. "When are you leaving?"

Her grandmother frowned and cleared her throat. "I haven't given it much thought. He's a captain now."

"A captain," Rebeccah said. "My, how time flies."

"I was just thinking that very thing," Lydia added, cooing at the baby. "Just wait until Uncle Miguel sees you; he's going to say Katie, *que nina tan hermosa.*"

Rebeccah's mouth dropped open. "You know how to speak Spanish?"

Lydia returned her sister's smile. "Just a little. A darling little girl named Delora taught me, and so did Miguel. When he arrives, I'll ask him to teach you, too."

The old woman gave a skeptical laugh. "*If* he arrives. How do you know for sure he's even coming? He could have changed his mind. I should think the least he could do is send you a telegram to let you know of his whereabouts."

"There's no need," Lydia said patiently. "I know where he went. He had many things to do, and if I recall, there wasn't a telegraph office in Rio Salado."

"The telegraph is a wonderful invention, don't you agree, Grandmama?" Rebeccah asked, trying to draw the dame's attention. She frowned when she was completely ignored.

"There is always a way to send word if it is important enough," the old woman retorted.

"I can imagine that someday soon we'll be talking with each other over wires like they are doing back east. Won't that be exciting? Rebeccah inquired.

Katherine heaved a very bored sigh. "Men who are late are usually irresponsible and are topics for gossips who advocate scandal. In short, my dear, they are often scoundrels who cheat on their wives." Katherine smoothed her skirt. "Didn't you say he should have been here before now?"

"Yes," Lydia managed to say, irritated by her grandmother's insult. "He's obviously been delayed."

"Just a little," Rebeccah added with a cheerful smile. "But I'm sure he'll be along any day now."

"Well, while we're waiting for his arrival," her grandmother said with a superior sniff, "I took the liberty and asked Captain

Williams to come for supper next Thursday."

Lydia gave her grandmother a cool smile. "How nice. I'm sure he will enjoy meeting Miguel. Perhaps later we'll start planning your trip to England?"

Katherine raised her chin ever so slightly. "I-I'm not sure I want—"

"If you leave in a month, you'd be there three weeks later. Let me see," Lydia said, hesitating for effect. "Why, you could be home for the holidays."

"Holidays?" Katherine repeated, sitting a little straighter. "How in God's name did we get started on my return to England? We were discussing that irresponsible Mexican fellow."

"My goodness," Rebeccah said, shielding her eyes with her hand. "Who could be riding that fast to cause such a trail of dust. Has he no concern for his horse in this heat?"

Lydia cast a quick glance in the direction her sister looked— not on the path, but farther out past the fence, a good distance down the road. A horse and rider were racing at a breakneck pace. Her heart slammed against her breast as she slowly got to her feet.

"Becky, take Katie." Lydia handed her sister the baby and shielded her eyes once more to be sure. "It's Miguel," she murmured. She turned to Becky and cried, "It's him!" She gathered up a handful of skirt. "It's Miguel," she said a little breathlessly.

"You should remain seated," Katherine said in a superior tone. "Proper young women do not rush ahead to receive gentlemen callers." Katherine flicked a ladybug off her skirt. "Lydia? Lydia, where are you going?"

Lydia didn't answer; she caught up even more of her skirts, exposing a scandalous amount of pantaloons as she began to run down the stone walk toward the fence that surrounded the house.

"Oh, dear," Rebeccah muttered, standing to watch her sister throw open the gate. I'm not sure, Grandmama, but I don't think she's overly concerned with what's proper at the moment. Here, hold Katherine Louise. I'd best close the gate before Kaiser gets out."

Lydia never saw her Grandmother's disapproving frown or the satisfied smile on her sister's face. She only saw the man on his big black horse, galloping toward her.

"I don't believe he sees her," Katherine stated, standing to get a better look. "Why, I believe that horse out of control! Rebeccah, call her back. She could be trampled."

"Don't worry, Grandmama. He's stopping," Rebeccah assured her.

The man pulled his horse to a grinding halt. The animal reared, not once but twice, and both Katherine and Rebeccah couldn't suppress their little gasps of fear. The man swung down the next instant, without a care for the horse that trotted with a flagging tail toward the mares and foals grazing on the other side of the fence.

"My goodness," Katherine gasped again as the man, after taking two long strides, caught Lydia in his arms and spun her around. To her horror, her granddaughter wrapped her legs around his waist and they kissed for a very long time.

"Well," Rebeccah said with a dreamy smile. "I think she missed him. Don't you agree?"

Rebeccah turned to her grandmother whose mouth had fallen open. "Come, Grandmama, perhaps we should give them a little privacy and go inside until we are properly introduced." She caught the old woman's hand, but practically had to drag her away.

"Good heavens. Look at them," Katherine cried in dismay.

"Her behavior is beyond scandalous. Why . . . why, no respectable man would allow it."

Rebeccah cast one last glance at the pair still kissing on the path. "Don't fret so much, Grandmama. I do believe Miguel likes her just as she is."

"I-I thought you weren't coming," Lydia said, gazing up into Miguel's dancing blue eyes the moment her feet touched the ground. She adored the way he covered his heart with his hand.

"You wound me," he said with his roguish grin. "An army of ten thousand men could not keep me away."

"Then what took you so long?" she cried, accepting another hug and several more kisses.

When finally he held her at arm's length, his smile widened. "Among other things, my mother. Look and see for yourself." He turned her and pointed at the entourage in the distance. "That, *vida mia,* is my father, my mother, my aunt, my grandmother and fourteen other family members. They have come to see if your family is good enough to be united with mine, and if my grandmother likes your grandmother, there will be a very big wedding." He held up two fingers. "Possibly two."

Lydia's smile turned to one of shock. "Your family?" she repeated. "Our wedding? Possibly two?" she cried in joyous disbelief, then broke out into laughter. "And did I hear you say they want to see if my family is good enough?"

"Forgive them, they are how do you say . . ."

"Snobs?" she finished, almost unable to control her giggles. "I believe they and my grandmother will get along famously." She kissed him again, then pulled back and frowned. "Two weddings?"

"*Si,* one here for your family and one in Mexico for the rest of mine."

"There's more? Family, I mean?"

"*Si,* there is much more. Did I not tell you that I have seven sisters, all of whom are married with children? To leave them out of such a monumental occasion would be scandalous."

"Seven sisters . . . oh dear," Lydia stammered. "Your mother . . . your grandmother, but, I-I . . . my hair isn't done . . . and this dress, I can't possibly greet them in this dress."

"Shush, *bonita mia,*" Miguel whispered as he nuzzled her ear. "They are still a very long way away and they move torturously slowly."

He caught his horse, lifted her up into the saddle, and settled in behind her, wrapping his arm tightly around her waist. "Say the word and we will run away. I can pretend to be a *bandito* and—"

Lydia turned, put her fingertips against Miguel's lips, looking deeply into his eyes. "I love you, and if your family wants to see me to make sure I'm good enough, then I shall simply have to comply with their wishes."

He gave an exaggerated sigh. "Are you sure? You realize that they will keep us apart until the vows are spoken. We could find a quiet little church somewhere far away, wake the priest and be married tonight."

Lydia cast a look over her shoulder at the small wagon train that slowly approached. "It is tempting," she murmured, frowning for effect. "However . . ." she gave him a teasing smile. "I simply have to change my dress. You, on the other hand, will have much more to do than change your clothing to prove to my grandmother that you are good enough for me, especially after the spectacle you just made of yourself."

"You think?" Miguel said with a feigned frown. "I can be very charming when I want to be."

She gave him another smile. "I'm certain of it."

★ ★ ★ ★ ★

Lydia glanced in the mirror at her reflection. Her conservative chignon looked neat and orderly, her usual style, suited to her profession as a nurse and her status as future Duchess of Wiltshire.

It was the same with her gown. The ivory lace accents at her throat dipped and curved, exposing a modest amount of flesh, but her mother's diamond and emerald pendant distracted the eye from the swell of her breasts, as did the subtle shimmer of the mint-green satin gown.

Tiny silk flowers were gathered on her left shoulder matching the bouquet at her waist on the right. A lacy ruffle added to the short, pleated-puffed sleeves. Lace-trimmed satin swept the floor, flowing in smooth folds where more flowers crowned the lace-adorned, pleated bustle.

Satisfied that her gown appeared to be the epitome of good taste, she put on her diamond and emerald earrings, scrutinizing her hair. As she stared at her reflection she decided it looked just a little too severe.

She tugged a few sun-streaked strands of curly red hair loose to frame her face, a few more to caress her nape, plucking curls here and there until there was nothing left of her original hair style. Smiling, she pinned several small silk flowers into the curls to accent the upsweep of her once neat and orderly chignon.

"Well, you certainly look like the highborn lady I raised you to be," Katherine stated proudly as she stepped inside. "However, after witnessing your audacious performance this afternoon, I must admit I'm a little disappointed that you have cast your gentility aside in favor of that brash foreigner."

"Foreigner?" Lydia smiled at her grandmother. "I believe you could be categorized as a foreigner yourself."

"Women of our status are expected to comply with certain

amenities, Lydia. You've only known Miguel for a short time. I had always thought it fitting that you marry an Englishman."

Lydia turned away from the mirror and faced her grandmother. "I have learned that life is too precious to let propriety deem what is and what is not fitting." She kissed her grandmother's wrinkled cheek. "Do you remember when we were leaving for England? When Sayer begged Rebeccah to stay?"

"Of course, I do," Katherine stated with an indignant sniff. "I was mortified when she leapt into his arms while he galloped alongside like some . . . some hooligan."

Again Lydia smiled, taking her grandmother's hand and patting the back. "But Sayer isn't a hooligan, nor is he anything but kind and loving and the perfect man for Rebeccah, don't you agree?"

Katherine raised her chin defiantly, a trait she had often used to intimidate her own daughter as well as both her granddaughters. "Sayer is the exception, I'm sure."

Her stately barb made Lydia shake her head and take a patient breath. "Miguel is the exception also, Grandmama. When you get to know him, you will see that he is kind and loving and the perfect man for me."

"He cannot even speak English properly, Lydia. And have you seen the . . . the *multitude* that came with him?" The dowager gave another noble snort. "I'm surprised they didn't bring some chickens and a cow as well. It will cost a fortune to feed them all."

Lydia gave a soft laugh at her grandmother's indignant expression. "I shall pay for it from my own estate. Now." Lydia straightened the cameo at her grandmother's throat. "You must put on your very best smile this evening. I shan't have Miguel's parents believing that we're stuffy."

"Stuffy?" Katherine repeated indignantly.

"Yes, Grandmama. Good manners are one thing, snobbery is

quite another. Now I think it would be wise if you helped Becky with refreshments."

Katherine tottered off to see if the servants had followed her instructions about seating arrangements. She was about to go into the kitchen when she noted a tall Mexican man had followed Sayer inside. The man wore dusty boots, a travel-stained serape and sombrero. He seemed to pause once he stepped down into the living room, then glanced around as if he approved.

"You there," Katherine called, raising one grey eyebrow. "You and the other drivers may wait outside."

Fernando flashed a quick glance at Sayer, who was in the process of pouring him a brandy. When their eyes met, Sayer's were dancing with devilish delight.

"I will wait here," Fernando said, matching the dame's dauntless stare. "This was once my home, and your granddaughters are my friends . . . and one of them is soon to be family."

"Really? Perhaps if you tell me your name, I will allow you to stay, *after* you remove your hat and . . . whatever that is you're wearing, and wipe the dust from your boots."

Sayer choked on his brandy.

"Forgive my manners." Fernando took off his hat and gave a gentlemanly bow. "I, *Señora* Stone, am Don Fernando Gutierrez. You may not have heard very much about me, but I assure you, I have heard some very interesting things about you."

Fernando ignored the old woman's gasp. "I have only just arrived after a very long and tiring ride. Perhaps we can get better acquainted later, at the celebration of my nephew's betrothal to *Señorita* Lydia. However, first I am going to have a brandy with my old friend." Fernando motioned to Sayer. "He and I have much to talk about. You see, I am interested in buying some of your horses. He tells me you are a, how do you say it—"

"Expert," Sayer concluded quickly.

"*Si*, you are an expert equestrian."

Katherine's features softened. "Why, thank you, Don Gutier-rez."

Fernando went to the table, poured a generous sherry and handed it to her with one of his best smiles. "Call me Fernando, *Señora*. All my friends do."

Rebeccah had done wonders with the tiled patio on such short notice, Lydia thought as she found a few moments to be alone. In preparation for the lavish dinner planned for tonight, a dozen vases filled with fragrant flowers sweetly scented the warm evening air, reminding Lydia of the grand party Don Fernando had given when he owned the ranch.

On each post hung an ornamental wrought-iron sconce, cradling a thick white candle. They illuminated the courtyard and the white wrought-iron chairs and benches. Tables had been set up close to the house, and it seemed to Lydia that every young woman Teresa could find helped to set them with sparkling silver and delicate China.

Lydia plucked a flower, enjoying its sweet scent as she strolled slowly around, catching her breath when a strong arm came around her waist and she felt herself pulled back against a very hard, very familiar chest.

"*Buenas noches, vida mia*," Miguel whispered as he nuzzled the sensitive spot below her ear. "Hmm, have I ever told you that you are a very beautiful woman?"

"Yes, I believe you have," she murmured, tilting her head so he could more easily kiss her neck.

"And your hair . . . *bonita*, have I ever told you how soft and silky it is?"

"Why, I do believe you have."

"Well, then," he said, his breath warm against her skin. "That is *bueno*, because a woman should hear . . ." He gave her a little squeeze, splaying his fingers across her ribs. ". . . as well as feel how much her man loves her."

Slowly she turned in his arms. He wore a midnight-blue bolero and trousers trimmed in tiny black braid and adorned with elegant, silver *conchos*. His crisp white shirt was edged in the finest Spanish lace. Instead of the studded gunbelt she had grown accustomed to, a maroon sash was knotted around his waist.

"Have I ever told you how handsome you are?" she asked, sliding her hand up his lapel to straighten his black tie.

He caught her hand, kissed her palm and shook his head, frowning as if he were trying to remember. "No, I do not believe you have ever said that."

She cupped his cheek and trailed one finger down around his moustache, pausing on his lips a moment while he kissed her fingertip. "And have I ever told you how distinctive your eyes are, or how utterly sinful your smile is?"

A slight smile tugged at the corner of his mouth. "No, I do not believe you have," he whispered, his gaze fixing upon hers, filled with the promise of a lifetime of love.

"Well, they are," she murmured. "Everything about you is totally, completely irresistible." She pressed intimately closer, slipping her arms around his waist. "And a woman should let her man know how much she loves him, don't you agree?"

"Completely, *vida mia*," he whispered a moment before he captured her mouth in a long, intoxicating kiss. "She should most certainly let him know such things."

ABOUT THE AUTHOR

Donna MacQuigg is a second-generation native of New Mexico and has enjoyed many years of raising and training Arabian horses with her husband and two children. Donna has spent hours in the saddle, riding trails in the beautiful Sandia and Sangre de Cristo Mountains. She enjoys hand gunning, archery, knife throwing, and a little gardening on the side. Having taught young students horsemanship and riding skills, her experience with horses adds to the authentic flavor of her books. Donna has published six historical romances. This is her third western set in the Southwest and the sequel to *The Doctor's Daughter*, May 2007. She looks forward to receiving your comments at donnamacquigg@yahoo.com or visit her Web site at www.donnamacquigg.com.